TELL
ME
NO
LIES

AF123609

ALSO BY ALEX SINCLAIR

The Last Thing I Saw
The Day I Lost You

ALEX SINCLAIR

TELL ME NO LIES

bookouture

Published by Bookouture in 2018

An imprint of StoryFire Ltd.
Carmelite House
50 Victoria Embankment
London EC4Y 0DZ

www.bookouture.com

Copyright © Alex Sinclair, 2018

Alex Sinclair has asserted his right to be identified
as the author of this work.

All rights reserved. No part of this publication may be reproduced,
stored in any retrieval system, or transmitted, in any form or by
any means, electronic, mechanical, photocopying, recording or
otherwise, without the prior written permission of the publishers.

ISBN: 978-1-78681-438-8
eBook ISBN: 978-1-78681-439-5

This book is a work of fiction. Names, characters, businesses,
organizations, places and events other than those clearly in the
public domain, are either the product of the author's imagination
or are used fictitiously. Any resemblance to actual persons, living or
dead, events or locales is entirely coincidental.

To my supportive wife and inspirational daughter

PROLOGUE

I smiled at my husband in the light of the half-moon, returning a heartfelt grin he gave me, not knowing in that fleeting moment that our lives were about to change forever. The item stirring around in my coat pocket could be the very object that would either make or break our relationship in the next few minutes. I glanced away, wondering how such a tiny thing could generate the most powerful of reactions.

"Cappuccino for Grace," shouted a man from the coffee truck we were standing by.

John accepted the hot beverage on my behalf and handed it over to me a moment later. I welcomed the warmth of the cardboard and wrapped both hands firmly around the cup, taking a much-needed sip.

"How is it?" John asked me as we stepped out of the way of the other night owls who were out lurking about in the streets of our small town on a Saturday night.

"Perfect, thank you," I said with a smile. I realized he had only ordered a cappuccino for me. "Why didn't you order one for yourself?" I asked.

"I'm full from dinner," he said.

It was unlike him to skip getting a coffee when we went out for dinner. We always stopped by at Trevor's coffee truck after a meal. And this particular night out wasn't just an excuse to hit the town and spend some money; we were celebrating our five-year wedding anniversary.

"We should probably get going," he said. "It's getting late."

"Are you sure? We could head over to one of the bars and grab a drink if you'd like?" I was trying my best to delay what I was desperate yet scared to talk to him about: the final anniversary present I had for John in my coat pocket.

John ran a hand over his chin for a moment in thought. "No, it's okay. I'd rather get you home and to bed—if you catch my drift." He raised his brows at me and leaned in to kiss me on the cheek.

I playfully nudged him sideways as we walked along the street. "Is that right?" I asked him before I took another sip of coffee.

"Yeah," he said with a boyish grin.

"And what makes you think you're getting lucky again, huh?"

John's arms outstretched wide. "Come on. It's our wedding anniversary. Twice in one day is pretty much guaranteed."

"We'll see," I said as I drummed my fingers on my coffee cup while staring into John's eyes with a coy grin. I'd missed this side of him so much. We continued to stroll down toward his car. The powder-blue street lights above guided our way along the sidewalk. A planted tree took up a portion of the path every hundred feet or so along the cozy street.

My evening bag hung from my wrist with a gift inside that John had given me. He'd decided to ignore the traditional wood gift that was customary for celebrating five years of marriage. Instead, he got me a gold watch with a light gray leather band he'd knew I'd like. The time had frozen on the clock at ten past ten, so I didn't bother to put it on just yet. John promised to get it fixed for me the next day.

It wasn't the kind of gift I was expecting, but I loved it all the same. Besides, I was more concerned about what I was giving him than anything else. It was all I could focus on.

Our night wasn't exactly going perfect—a long week of draining work had made us argue over nothing, as per usual—but we'd pushed through and managed to make it into something of a good time overall. The last few months we'd drifted somewhat apart with our busy lives, but everything was back on track. It had to be. Now was the perfect moment to ask him the very question that was dying to come out of me. I looked up into the clearing sky to the stars above and drew in some air, letting it out again a moment later.

We came to a stop in the street level with our car. It was parked across the road. Once we crossed over, we'd be back in John's sedan and headed for home. I was running out of time to ask him my question. I should have done it back in the restaurant but something kept interrupting me enough so I'd lose my nerve.

John took a step out into the street. "John, wait," I said, almost in a panic.

He turned around and headed back to me. "Yeah, what is it?" He stared down at me, his breath visible in the cool night air.

I tried to speak as I returned his gaze, but my mouth just opened and closed with no words coming out. Not now.

"What is it?"

I grabbed the small box in my pocket. I tried to pull it out and use it as a way to communicate exactly what it was I was trying to ask him, but something made me freeze. Why couldn't I ask him? I already knew what his answer would be. Was I more nervous about how I felt about this than anything else? My brain chose the worst times to stop working.

"I forgot what I was going to say, sorry," I said. It was all I could blurt out.

He flashed me a smile. "That's okay. I do that all the time. I'm sure it'll come to you."

"Yeah, hopefully." I lowered my head away from his eyes. I couldn't hide my embarrassment.

"Come on. We better get moving," he said with an outstretched hand.

Half crippled and unable to maintain a conversation, I reached out to grab hold when John's cell chirped out loud. His hand withdrew and reached into his pocket as his phone continued to ring. I frowned at him for not having his cell on silent during our anniversary dinner.

"Sorry, honey. I just need to take this. I'll be one second."

I stood there on my own, frustrated as hell, as John said hello and wandered off while he spoke to the person on the other end. Who would be calling him at this hour? It wasn't terribly late in the night, but it was well after business hours. Was the world against me today?

John walked almost a car length away from me as he spoke on the phone. He was mostly saying yes and nodding to the person on the other end of the line. The call didn't sound personal in the slightest, more as if he were talking to his boss. He glanced back at me for a moment and then looked away.

I turned from him and placed my coffee cup down on the arm of a bench seat that sat along the sidewalk. I pulled out the final gift I had for John from my pocket. I stared down at the bagged present, knowing it held a felt box big enough to house an engagement ring. I slid it out of the bag and opened its lid. There inside sat a wooden pacifier I'd had custom made to ask John the one question I'd been dying to say to him all day and now all evening: will you start a family with me?

I ran my finger over the smooth grain surface and wondered if it was the right time to ask him such a question. We were both so busy with our careers at the hospital. John especially. A baby had the potential to throw everything out of balance and upset our relationship. But we'd spoken at length about having kids one day. John more so than me. This wouldn't be a shock at all for him to hear. In fact, he'd be over the moon. I was the one dragging my feet a little on the subject. But we'd been married for five years and were in our mid-thirties. Now was the time to do this. If not, when?

I closed the lid and returned the gift to its bag and my pocket. I drew in a lungful of the cool night breeze and let it flow back out again as I closed my eyes and generated the courage needed to ask John the question the moment he got off his cell. I had to stop messing around and finally do this.

I turned around and saw him walking across the street toward his car, still on the call. Was he about to get in the car? My moment was slipping away. I wanted to do this while we were out to dinner and not at home. Things would get awkward if I had to ask him to come back over to me. I dashed out into the empty street and went to call his name, but he stopped suddenly before I got the chance.

"What the hell?" I muttered as confusion set in. What was he doing? A bright glow suddenly bathed the side of his gray coat and drew my eyes toward the source of a loud disturbance. John turned his head toward the light and sound. My brain took a moment to fathom what it was I was seeing when a light-blue pickup truck slammed into my husband and rolled right over the top of his body in one blinding moment. The driver screeched his brakes hard and came to a sliding stop more than a few hundred feet away. I stared at the truck, frozen on the spot like an icicle, as the driver hit the gas and sped off into the night.

My body went slack. I felt my knees lose all of their strength and I stumbled. I dropped the gift and heard it clatter onto the sidewalk. John lay in the street a good distance from where I had just been speaking to him. Terror gripped me from all sides. What was I supposed to do? I couldn't think straight until I saw a few people rush over to his side. They had come racing out from the nearby restaurants.

I closed my open mouth and charged toward my husband, remembering how my legs worked. "John," I shouted, louder than I ever thought was possible. I dropped to my knees next to him and reached out both of my hands toward his bleeding face.

"John?" He responded to my movement and tracked my eyes. He would get through this. He just had to keep fighting.

He stared up at me, his breath gasping through blood-stained teeth. "Grace, I have to tell you—" He coughed and choked as his neck strained to hold his head up.

"Tell me what?" I asked as I grabbed hold of the back of his head.

John's skull fell back to the ground with a thud, squashing my fingers a little. His eyes glazed over and stared out into space without blinking. His chest no longer rose and fell. I was witnessing him giving up.

"No," I muttered. "Come on, John. Not now. Not like this." I swiveled his head toward me as a crowd gathered around us. I prayed and begged for him to respond to me, to blink, to breathe, but he didn't move. The light in his eyes faded out before me.

It was our five-year wedding anniversary, and I had just witnessed my husband die.

CHAPTER 1

Now

It's been six weeks since John died. Six long weeks of pain, denial, and guilt since my life changed forever. Had someone told me when I was younger that I would be burying my husband of five years at the age of thirty-five, I would have thought they were insane. But here I am, precisely forty-two days after witnessing the love of my life's gruesome death at the hands of a hit-and-run driver, about to bury him six feet under the soil of our quiet town of Sherbrook, Oregon.

This technically wasn't John's first funeral. The closest people in his life had already paid their respects by throwing an informal funeral mere days after an aging light-blue pickup slammed into him only a short distance in front of me and shattered his body into an unrecognizable, broken mess. As anyone could imagine, I was in no shape to attend the funeral let alone emerge from the dark void I'd fallen into when the arrangements were made, so the proceedings moved embarrassingly forward without me.

Now, I am standing in an early spring rain that refuses to ease up, staring down at John's grave wondering how this all came to be.

I read his tombstone over and over.

Beloved by family. Cherished by friends.
John Dalton
1982—2018

I didn't pick the words. That task, among many that I was beyond capable of achieving, fell to his friends. It seems awkward to me to say that John was "Beloved by family." Apart from me, he had none. He came from a series of group homes in Portland and knew nothing about his mother or father. He had no idea if he even had any relatives at all out there. I was the closest thing he had to family. But John had many friends, friends that did what they could to put together an informal funeral his wife should have taken care of. It's a failure on my part that I can never undo and am forced to live with for the rest of my days.

The pouring rain is set in for the day. I feel every drop against my skin as it penetrates my black trench coat and soaks through to my long black skirt suit. In my hands, I hold a closed umbrella that I refuse to open. It doesn't seem right that I get to be the one to stay dry and comfortable when my husband's body lies in a wooden box about to be lowered into the wet earth.

"Mrs. Dalton?" a voice says to my right. It sounds distant, but I know it's right there. "Mrs. Dalton? Grace?"

"Yes?" I ask as I snap out of my trance to glimpse over to the pastor. It's just the two of us out in the cold, lowering John down to his final resting place. I don't want a single person out here other than myself and the pastor John requested to bury him. I have to face this day on my own despite the numerous offers I've had for people to accompany me.

My closest friend, Jennifer, was the first to put up her hand the way she always did to join me, but I had to decline. I should have been strong enough to bury John when he was killed and not have hidden away in a dark bedroom in my home for all this time like a coward. I would have stayed in that room forever if it wasn't for Jennifer. During my attempt to hide from the world, I received an unmarked package at my front door. I assumed it was yet another care package from Jennifer. I almost didn't bother to open it, but when I did, I found a box of chocolates with a message written in cursive that read, "*It's time to move on.*" I was angry at first at the blunt message, but the words got through to me and made me take action.

I couldn't help hiding away for six weeks, though. I was there when John died—almost as close as the pastor stands near me now when my husband's life was snuffed out. I watched the light extinguish from his eyes. People didn't understand what that kind of experience did to a person's soul.

"Are you ready to proceed?" the pastor asks.

I turn my head away and lower my stare to the casket. It's not a question you want to ever have to answer. I never thought I'd see this day until I was at least eighty years old. Instead, I am a widow at thirty-five. How does this kind of hell come to be?

"Grace?" the pastor urges again. His schedule is overloaded, and I am taking up too much of his time. I never realized how precious a commodity time was until now.

"Yes. I'm ready," I say. I'm not, though. How could I ever be?

"Very well." He clears his throat as he probably had a thousand times before this day to say the words that were meant to comfort people in their time of need. "We are gathered here today to show our love and respect, and to say our goodbyes to our brother, a man of God, John Dalton."

I try not to shake my head as the pastor mentions God. John was barely religious. He never went to church or so much as said a prayer when it came down to it. His only connection to God was via one of the Catholic group homes he grew up in. John rarely spoke of the place or showed any belief in the religion, yet still, he told me countless times to make sure he was buried by a Catholic pastor. Maybe, deep down, he did believe, but he didn't want to tell me so.

I attempt to avoid hearing the next string of words out of the pastor's mouth as he continues on to deliver more religious lines to me like I'm ripe for converting. I don't have the heart to tell him it won't work. Ever. Not after seeing my husband struck down for no real reason. Not after losing everything.

"John was a beloved husband to his wife, Grace Dalton. For five wonderful years, John supported, loved, and cherished his wife until his life was cut tragically short."

Five years. It isn't a rough length of time we'd been married; it's the exact amount of time we'd been married. Why did John have to be killed on our anniversary? It seemed like an additional punctuation mark on top of the pain his death generated. The cruelty of that night never ceases to amaze me.

The pastor begins to quote scripture at me again, trying to relate the old words to my situation. I try to understand where he is coming from, but I can't absorb the dogma he is so desperate for me to ingest. Not after that night. Not ever.

The night, as I call it, comes to me in waves, slowly building up until the point of no return to crash hard into the forefront of my mind with an unstoppable force. I wish I could forget, but I see that moment, over and over, that brief second when time slowed down, and I saw that faint recognition in John's body language when he knew he was going to die. I often laid awake at night wondering what his last conscious thought was before the pickup struck him down in the quiet street. Did he think about past regrets or the future he would never see? Did he think about us?

"But this will not be the end of John's existence, because he will forever live on in our hearts until we meet him again."

I wipe away the flow of tears that have merged with the rain and try not to imagine how bad my makeup must be. I did what I could to look my very best for John, not that it seems to matter. It's silly to think that I spent extra time this morning making sure I wore something he would have liked and styled my dark brown hair the way he loved it. I never have to worry about that again, do I? The dead can't be impressed.

The thought sends a stab down into my chest, one I can never stop until my body no longer feels pain. It's a day I look forward to—one I know is a long way from coming. If at all.

The pastor begins to wrap up and subtly takes a peek at his watch. He has another funeral to attend to today with more than just a single grieving widow. My one-on-one session isn't holding his attention the way a burial with fifty or more sad people could. Did he feed on grief?

"You can go," I say to the man, wanting him gone.

"Oh, no, I don't mean to be rude, Grace, it's just we are already ten minutes past the allotted time I could spare today."

"It's fine," I say as I turn and face him. "I would like to be alone for what I have to say to John next, anyway. Thank you for your time today."

The pastor nods at me with a forced smile and slinks away in the rain. I ignore his hastened footsteps in the mud and refocus on John's casket. When I am ready, I will push a lever and watch as he is lowered down into the ground one inch at a time into the cold damp soil. I don't want anyone but me to do this task for John. I owe him that much. The company I hired to handle John's intimate funeral will then fill the grave in.

"John," I say. My eyes look left and right. It feels strange to be talking to a wooden box that holds my dead husband. "I love you, and I know I always will. You are the one and only man I ever want or will want in my life. That will never change, no matter what."

I let a slow breath fall out of me as I close my eyes and try to stop myself from shaking as I prepare for the next words I have to say. I can't believe I'm even going to speak them. I know I won't get an answer in return, but I have to get them out of my system.

"I have to know something about that night. Something you said just before that pickup hit you and changed our lives forever."

My eyes begin to sting with tears. I can't feel the rain anymore. I can't sense anything.

I huff out a sharp lungful of air. "What were you trying to tell me?"

CHAPTER 2

Six weeks ago

I woke up the way I always did on the morning of our anniversary: overly excited. But this wasn't just any wedding anniversary; it was our fifth, marking five years as husband and wife. Plus, there was something even more amazing about it. Something I felt was the perfect time to finally act upon.

As I rolled out of bed and stretched, I thought about the traditional five-year wedding anniversary gift that I'd gotten John. My options were limited to items made from wood, so I went with the best idea I could think of: a custom wooden etching with our names and the date of our wedding. I doubted John would really like or appreciate the gift, but it wasn't the only present I'd be giving him today. Gifts aside, the milestone was something to be proud of in my mind.

Five years. I shook my head. It was a long time to be married to a person in today's time of quick divorces. We'd had our share of ups and downs and testing moments the way any couple did, but we'd gotten through them together. Particularly, the last few months we'd fallen into a rut with our rigorous work schedules. John also had to study many hours each night and attend seminars for his residency at the hospital, which only served to drive a wedge between us.

But despite the tests and hardships we'd reached a checkpoint that would only propel us along to the next one.

I turned to John's side of the bed knowing that he would already be up and ready to leave for his shift at the hospital. By chance alone, I had the day off, but I wasn't going to sleep in. Not today.

We both worked at Bellflower General Hospital in Portland. We'd met at the facility six years ago and were married only one year later in a whirlwind romance. I'd never fallen in love with someone as quickly as I had John. I couldn't help myself.

At the time, John was just starting out as an intern, and I worked part-time as an orderly while studying to earn my Bachelor's degree to become a registered nurse. We were both on our own professional pathways, each with their own difficulties.

It wasn't the most relaxed life concerning spare time, and our relationship wasn't always easy, but I loved that we shared the same workplace as well as our home. The hospital demanded attention twenty-four hours a day, seven days a week, and it always came first. The patients never stopped flowing in and out of the building, no matter how tired or desperate we were for a break from the endless grind.

But we got to where we wanted to be. I worked now as a registered nurse while John was a resident on his way to becoming an attending physician in a large team that worked in the ICU. Both roles had their stresses and difficulties, but we both toiled away with pride nonetheless.

I currently worked in the recovery room and dealt with patients post-op. I went from loving my job to hating it several times per week. Usually, it depended upon what kind of patients I had to deal with, and I'd seen them all. The range was extreme, from your sweet old grandma who was in because she'd had a fall and needed a hip replacement, to your dotty dementia patients who didn't mind taking a swing at you when they woke up from their anesthetic thinking you were an enemy from the past. Entitled princesses would come in alongside caring mothers. Businessmen who threatened to sue every member of staff they came across co-existed with dying teenagers who were undergoing one last op to try and beat their disease peacefully.

The hospital was a beast, but it was the type of wild animal John and I both loved, and we faced it together. Now, after all of this time, after the years of trudging the halls of Bellflower General while navigating the sometimes choppy waters of marriage, we had made it to the five-year milestone.

I threw on my dressing gown and checked myself in the mirror. My tired face and dark brown hair stared back at me. I attempted to adjust my ponytail into something presentable before I moved downstairs. John would be preparing to leave for the thirty-minute commute we had both gotten so used to taking to the hospital. Either one of us could drive to work with a blindfold on.

It might have seemed a robotic life to spend long twelve-plus hour shifts in the same building, walking up and down the same halls, talking to the same people who were practically built into the foundation of the facility, but I couldn't see myself doing anything else for a living. I loved the industry and was fascinated by every aspect of it.

John felt the same. At least I assumed he did. He never complained about being a resident who worked in an ICU. He seemed to love it. He could have left in the past few years to take a different pathway and become a General Practitioner for a private clinic with set hours and decent pay, but I doubted he could abandon the rush of a hospital. At least not yet. Not while he still had the energy his thirty-six-year-old body afforded him.

I walked out of our bedroom past John's study and strolled through to the kitchen-living area of our open-plan home, thinking John would be there drinking his coffee. His routine had been somewhat different lately. More sporadic than normal. Work was demanding the world from him, making him stay back for longer and longer than what seemed safe. This was on top of sending him away on professional development seminars.

"John. You still here, honey?" I called out, ever hopeful.

He didn't answer, so I figured it was the perfect time to head to the garage and fish out his gifts from the hiding place I used for all of the presents I bought for him. I often wondered if he knew about the secret spot and pretended it didn't exist or if he was like most men who couldn't find things around the home unless their wives showed them. The thought made me smile.

I opened the creaking door to where our two sedans were parked off the side of the kitchen. John's car was still home meaning he was still around. I had time to safely pull out his gifts and present them to him before he left me all alone for twelve or thirteen hours.

I flicked on the light and realized one of the two bulbs had burnt out, making it harder to see the back wall of the garage where I had hidden John's surprises. I crept along in my slippers to the dusty corner of the room and shifted around some golf clubs he never had and probably never would have time to play with. The bag revealed an old cardboard box we still had from when we moved into the house one year ago.

It was the first home we bought together, one that pushed our budget to its absolute limit. We purchased the house thinking it would be enough to last us for a good ten years. There were several things we inevitably got wrong, of course. It seemed so simple to buy such a thing on paper as you stood over floor plans and decided how you would furnish each room and what purpose it would hold. But until you truly lived in a home and breathed in its walls, walked up and down its corridors, you could never understand how your life should have been laid out.

I pulled out two presents. One was wrapped while the other sat in a small gift bag. The first gift—the custom wooden artwork—was a pain to package, but the second gift took no time at all, being a small box that fit in the palm of my hand. The second gift was the one I was most excited to give to John.

It made the first present almost pointless. I didn't even care if he had forgotten to get me something. His positive reaction to my gift would be more than enough to make me happy. I couldn't wait to see his face light up.

As I walked back through the garage with my two surprises in hand, I noticed something strange about John's car. His dark blue Nissan Altima had wet tires and had left track marks leading out of the garage as if John had just come back from somewhere quite recently. It made no sense, as we'd slept in the same bed all night.

I smiled when I realized he may have only remembered what day it was today and rushed off to one of those twenty-four-hour malls to get me something last minute. I shook my head with a coy smile and reminded myself to grill him on the issue later.

I didn't care that badly if he had forgotten. I really didn't. We both had busy lives. His was more hectic than mine, in general, being a doctor in training. We both had to continually keep up to date with the latest in medicine, but John's job demanded more of his spare time even though we managed to keep up a reasonable social life. We'd had an argument on occasion about who did more work and who had it worse in the hospital, but ultimately, his job held higher responsibilities than mine and always would.

I didn't care. I had no ambitions to spend all that time to become a doctor. It wasn't like I didn't feel smart enough or have the confidence to pull off that kind of career move; I just enjoyed being more hands-on with the patients than the quick in and out mentality some doctors had. Plus, I didn't need the debt John was slowly accumulating in his education.

When I walked back into the kitchen, I spotted John standing by the counter dressed in his casual wear that he would later change out of when his shift started. I had no idea where he'd come from. It didn't matter. I was too excited to see him.

"Hi, honey," I said as I shoved the bigger gift behind my back. I put the smaller one into my dressing gown pocket. I felt a sting of nerves wash over me all of a sudden.

He turned around, partially surprised to see me coming from the garage. "What are you doing?" he asked with a furrowed brow.

"None of your business," I said guiltily. His short, yet wavy brown hair was pushed to the side and seemed to be standing on its ends. He was wearing his thick-rimmed glasses while our coffee machine brewed away quietly in the background.

It took a moment, but John returned my smile once his mind worked out what I had been up to. "Is that so?" he asked as I slowly crept up to him, barely hiding the main gift behind my back.

"Yeah," I said as I closed the gap between us as he faced me with his body. I squished up closer and kissed him on the lips. "I definitely don't have anything hidden behind my back." I could barely contain the grin on my face.

"Clearly," John said. He tried to grab at the present playfully. Towering over me with his slender frame, I dodged back to avoid his half-serious attempt to seize his gift.

"Do you have anything hidden behind your back?" he asked.

"Depends."

"Depends? On what?"

"Whether you got me something decent or not." I placed the wooden frame in one hand so I could slap him lightly against the chest. "Come here, you jackass." I set the gift down and pulled him in for a proper kiss. He wrapped his arms around me. I felt his powerful arms grip me tighter than usual as his tongue found its way into my mouth. Even after five years he still sent butterflies to my stomach when we kissed in such a way.

It had been a few weeks since we'd kissed with any passion. With our demanding jobs and spare days or nights often spent seeing close friends, we didn't reserve enough time for each other. It was beyond frustrating and something I decided then and there that we needed to work on. I had to make more time for us. I didn't want to imagine what would happen otherwise.

"So, what is it? What have you got for me?" John asked like a giddy kid at Christmas.

"You'll see," I said twisting away.

He groaned. "What is it?"

I shut him up by handing over the custom wooden artwork. He ripped it open in a hurry, possibly because he had to leave sooner than later to avoid the early-morning traffic.

"Wow, that looks amazing," he said. "How did you even do this?" he asked as he ran his finger over the etching.

"Internet."

"Of course," he replied with one hand outstretched. He placed the artwork on the counter and glanced down at me. He grabbed my face with two gentle hands that had comforted countless patients over the years and kissed me again. "Thank you, baby. And a happy five-year anniversary."

"Happy anniversary, honey," I said in return. I felt like we were newlyweds in that brief moment, that we were ready to take on the world. Was this all that had been missing between us lately?

"I still can't believe it," he said. "Five years. That's a long time. Seems like yesterday we were walking down the aisle in front of everyone. Makes you think."

"I know. It goes by in a flash. Way too quick." My eyes flicked away from his as I thought about that five years. There had been the occasional day when I thought being married was the hardest thing in the world, when an argument would last for days and days, but everything always worked out for the better in the end. And this next moment would cement our future and start the next phase of our lives. It had to.

"I haven't got you anything yet," he said. "Well, I have, but you won't see it until later tonight."

I doubted he actually had anything for me, and I didn't care. I felt the small item in my pocket, dying to come out. But something held me back from giving it to him just then. Maybe I could wait until we went out for dinner? It would be the perfect moment. One where I wasn't wearing a dressing gown and slippers.

"Well, I better get a move on. I've got a hell of a day ahead of me."

"Call in sick," I said, only half joking as I wrapped my arms around him again.

"I can't," he said. "It's just one of those days you can't avoid." He gently released my arms and slid them away from his body. "I'll see you tonight, honey. I'll be back in time before we head out to dinner."

"I know," I said understanding. The hospital always came first, before us. I slumped down a little as the fantasy of us spending the day in bed together faded before me.

"I'll be back as soon as possible. Enjoy your day off."

"I'll try." I watched as John gathered his things from the island bench in our kitchen and went through the side door to the garage. He closed it with a thud. A few moments later, I heard the rumble of his car's engine and the rattle of the garage door opening.

I reached into my pocket as a pang of regret hit me. I pulled out John's second gift and realized I would have to spend the entire day wondering if he would be ready to receive what I had in mind for him.

I slid out a felt box from a gift bag, and rotated its hinged lid open as delicately as possible. Sitting inside was a tiny wooden pacifier that gave me a glimpse of the future we were about to embark upon the second John accepted my idea to start a family. I knew he would say yes. He'd been hinting the idea at me for the last year. I hadn't been ready to consider the thought back then, but I was prepared for it now. At least I thought I was.

I took in a deep breath and focused all of my courage. As soon as we'd finished our meal in town, I was going to ask John if he wanted to start a family.

If only I had known what was coming. If only I had given him that damn box before he left for work, maybe John wouldn't have taken that call, maybe John wouldn't have been distracted on the road. Things would have been different.

CHAPTER 3

Now

After I've lowered John six feet down, I leave his grave on two shaky legs that trudge down a hill through wet grass and mud, bringing with me the dirt and grime of the cemetery. I don't care about the mess. Nothing could make my life more of a mess. The rain overhead thickens and pounds down through my black layers harder than before. I should have worn something waterproof, but I couldn't think straight when I was getting ready this morning.

Jennifer is waiting for me in her car. She climbs out the second she sees me coming. Despite telling her that I needed to bury John on my own, I couldn't keep her from driving me to the cemetery and waiting in the parking lot for the funeral to finish. She insisted on being there for me and didn't want me driving around at such an emotional time. I didn't argue with the idea, not wanting to have to face the rest of the day with a million painful thoughts running through my head.

"How are you?" Jennifer asks as she opens the passenger door for me. An open umbrella sits above my head in her hand as if she's my limo driver.

I shrug at her, not wanting to answer. We haven't spoken much over the past six weeks considering we usually chatted on the phone every other day at a minimum. I climb into her Toyota sedan and reach out to close the door myself. I don't need Jennifer to give me the full chauffeur experience. She's already done more than enough for me by driving me here. I pull the door closed before she has a chance.

Staring out of the windshield through the rain, I feel like I'm trapped in a muddled fog. I can't seem to focus or think straight as my mind only sees John's casket lowering into the earth, inch by inch, where it will remain for the rest of time. His life is over while I have to continue on. It isn't fair in the slightest.

For the last six weeks, I asked myself over and over why I got to continue living. It hardly seemed just. If I had been walking by his side at the time of the accident like I was supposed to, we both would have died. There would be no one left behind to deal with the pain. I know it does me zero good to think about that night in such a way, but I replay it in my head countless times per day and wonder if I would have been better off to have died alongside my husband.

I can't fall victim to that kind of logic, though. I know it's a slippery slope to go down that can be hard to recover from. Naturally, regret takes the place of anything dark the second I manage to push it from my mind.

What if I had called out his name when he was walking across the street? Would any of this have happened? My therapist calls it survivor's guilt. I think that's just a friendly way to package up the misery I go through every time I wake up in the morning and remember who I am.

The driver's door opens and slams shut again. Jennifer swivels in her seat into a comfortable position, spraying rainwater in all directions. She takes a moment to rub her hands together to warm herself over one of the a/c vents. I didn't even realize, but she had left the car running with the heat on.

"Ready?" she asks me.

I nod. Words are still too much effort for me at the moment. They may be for a long time to come.

"Do you have the address of the lawyer's office?" she asks me.

I close my eyes for a moment and sigh. I'd all but managed to forget the other task that needed completing today. After weeks of missed phone calls and ignored emails, I had no choice but to see John's lawyer about his estate. There was some delicate thing the lawyer wanted to discuss that was apparently too sensitive for the phone and had to be dealt with in person only. It's the last thing I want to talk about, but I foolishly decided I would handle John's funeral and his legal matters all on the same day.

"I have a card in my bag," I mutter. I lift up my handbag from the floor of the sedan and rummage through it until I find a half-crumpled business card for the lawyer's office in Portland. I'd tried to throw the thing away a few times after receiving it in the mail, not wanting to face the reality that John was dead and his estate needed to be dealt with. It almost seemed like acknowledging John's lawyer made his death seem real. The box of chocolates and its message somehow got me past that thought.

"Here," I say to Jennifer without looking at her. One glance into her eyes will make me burst into tears again. She takes it from my weak grip and keys the address into her cell so she can locate the building. A moment later, we are on the road heading toward the next task I've been avoiding.

I don't know what's worse: burying John or handling the aftermath of his death. As husband and wife, we had arranged everything to go to one another in the tragic event that one of us was to die while the other survived, not that we had much money or assets to our name. If anything, his death has left me with a mortgage I now can't afford. I wasn't capable of suing anyone for a wrongful death as the driver of the light-blue pickup that killed John had never been found. A friend of John's suggested going after the state for compensation, but I didn't want to spend the next few years battling away in a courtroom only to lose the case and wind up with more debt in the form of legal fees. Nothing would bring John back, either, so I just wanted to move on if I ever could.

I had no idea why our lawyer needed to speak with me considering everything should have been straightforward. Once I'd managed to crawl my way out of the dark void I'd spent the last six weeks in, thanks to the chocolates, the urgency in his voice on every message he left finally got me to call him back. I knew I had to deal with it eventually, so I arranged a time to meet with him.

"Should be there in about thirty minutes," Jennifer says.

I nod my understanding and don't say a word. We drive in silence for the next twenty minutes. Jennifer and I would typically be chatting away the entire time, but there is nothing ordinary about this day. There's nothing I want to discuss.

"What did you want to do after?" she asks.

After? There was no after. At least not for me. I don't answer.

"We could go out for a bite to eat. You look like you could use a good meal."

"Do I?" I reply. I'd lost a bit of weight since John died, but I wasn't wasting away or anything.

"Yes. I think you need a decent feed, Grace. You don't need to starve yourself as some sort of penance. You need to face the facts and accept that what happened to John was not your fault."

I turn to Jennifer with wide eyes that begin to well up. "It *was* my fault, though. I made him lose his concentration and not see the pickup coming. John died because of me."

Jennifer pulls the car over in a hurry and parks in a side street that is nowhere near the lawyer's office. She shuts the engine off and lets out a heavy sigh. "I get that you're feeling guilty right now. I really do. But you need to stop blaming yourself and face the reality of the situation. John died in an accident you had nothing to do with. You didn't speed through the streets and run him down in a pickup. You didn't drive off after. It's not your fault."

I stare at the glove box in front of me, studying the pattern on the surface that flows down from the dashboard. I have no answers for Jennifer or anyone else who tells me the same thing. There's no point arguing or getting upset. It doesn't change anything. It doesn't make my problems go away. It doesn't bring John back from the dead. It never will.

I turn to Jennifer in the confined space of her car. "I'm sorry," I say. It's the best I can offer her. I know she'd continue to listen to me whether I apologized or not, but I have to make sure I don't push her too far away. If I lose Jennifer, I don't know what I'd do. I know I'm going to need her moving forward more than anyone else.

"That's okay. Let's just get to this meeting and get you back home again. Sound good?"

"Yeah," I mutter. The thought of home is a mixed one at best. On the one hand, I can't stand to leave it. When I stepped out the front door this morning, I wanted to run back inside like a person crippled with agoraphobia. But if I'd gone back inside, I would have had to face the fact that I possess a house that is intended for a small family. We couldn't afford much, but I still remember convincing John to get a home with a second bedroom so we could one day have children. Now, that empty room will never be filled.

We are already back on the road by the time I realize the conversation with Jennifer is over. Life moves on whether I want it to or not. I keep my eye out for the lawyer's office in the city. I can't help but wonder why John chose a firm for us in Portland and not one closer to home to deal with such a grim matter. Maybe he never thought the day would come that one of us would have to bury the other. I know I never pictured this.

The idea makes me think of his last moment of life in this world. I have no clue who had called him before he died or what he was discussing. His phone was destroyed in the accident along with his body. I had previously gone through the five stages of grief on that subject alone. At first, I tried to tell myself it was someone from work, but no one had come forward to tell me so. Anger soon took over that I'd never know who had spoken to him last or what had been so important that it could interrupt our anniversary celebrations. Then, like a cliché, came the inevitable bargaining. I told myself I'd forgive the person who called John if they merely came forward. That failed like a lead balloon when no one did, sending me spiraling down even further than I had previously fallen. I eventually came to accept that I would never know who John had spoken to only moments before he met his end.

"We're here," Jennifer says as we pull into a parking space. It's late Saturday morning, so there are only a dozen or so people in the street of this rougher industrial part of the city. It's not where I'd expect to find a lawyer's office. My eyes snap up to a sign embossed in brass on a black façade that reads Law Offices of Thomas Hart. I let out a long sigh as the reality of this meeting hits me hard. I know I've been in denial for the last six weeks about my financial status. It's no secret that the mortgage will eventually ruin me.

"Come on," Jennifer says as she lightly prods me on the arm. "You can do this."

"Okay," I say to her as I wrap my fingers around the door handle. I close my eyes for a moment as if this is nothing but a bad dream I can't seem to wake from. When I open my eyes back up the world is still the same. John is dead, and I am left to deal with that fact.

CHAPTER 4

I sit with Jennifer in the waiting room of the Law Offices of Thomas Hart, battling a wave of nerves. The office is a small operation with a tiny space big enough to house a reception desk, four uncomfortable visitors' chairs, and a single coffee table laden with outdated magazines.

The aging receptionist leans over the counter of her desk and smiles. "He won't be too much longer. His meeting is running a little over."

"That's fine," I say, returning her smile with a flash. I'm not in the mood to comply with any social standards, so I snap my eyes away from hers before she tries to strike up a conversation. I wouldn't know what to say to her anyway. I've been cooped up for six weeks like a shut-in.

It feels odd to be on this side of a waiting room. For a few years, I assisted one of the senior nurses at the hospital with triage in the emergency department. Just thinking about it sends a shudder down my spine. It was the hardest job I've ever had in the hospital. I never once enjoyed trying to work out who was a priority case needing medical attention first and who had just come in with a minor complaint that a twenty-four-hour clinic could handle. I received more abuse in that role than any other in my life. People would yell in my face, spit at me, threaten to come through the locked security door, and all different kinds of vulgarities I've pushed down to the depths of my memory.

In the end, it wasn't the ill-treatment a triage nurse received on an hourly basis that made me request to be put anywhere else in the hospital. It was the impact it had on me as a nurse. I started to see the patients as numbers and not names. I became jaded and lost all empathy and care I felt for the individuals. I'd begun seeing the emergency room as a pen that held herds of cattle that needed processing. That was not the nurse I ever wanted to be.

"How are you coping?" Jennifer whispers to me, leaning in. Her question pulls me from my distracting thoughts.

Her inquiry is a loaded one at best that I can't fully answer without the constant reminder that my husband is gone. "Fine," I say with the shake of my head. "I just want to get this all over with, you know?"

"Yeah, I get it. I can't even begin to comprehend what you've gone through these last six weeks, but you know you can always talk to me about anything. No matter how big or small it might be."

"Thank you," I reply to the same words I've heard from my friend over and over. I lower my eyes to the carpet, studying the subtle stains that the average person possibly wouldn't notice. I don't deserve such a caring friend as Jennifer. Especially when I sit here and feel annoyed by her desire to comfort me through this difficult time. But, it's not her that I'm upset with; it's myself.

I turn to Jennifer and give her a smile and say no more. Ever since John died, she has been trying to get me to open up and confide in her, but I keep turning her visits away, and I don't know why. I can see clear as day that she only wants to help me.

We've been close friends for over five years, but after that night I have only communicated with my therapist and no one else. Even Doctor Sylvain only gets half the story. We converse over the phone and not in person. I couldn't stand the thought of traveling to a doctor's office every week to chat about my pathetic life.

"You can go in now," the receptionist says.

I glance up at her eager face and snap back to Jennifer's. "Thanks for waiting with me. This might take a while, sorry."

"That's okay. I'll head out and grab a coffee down the street. Just text me when you're done." She gives me a quick hug and stands up.

I force myself to my feet with a huff once she starts walking toward the exit. I slowly make my way in the opposite direction, dragging my feet to the meeting I've spent weeks trying to avoid. It's not that I'm afraid of John's lawyer or anything so strange; I merely have used every excuse not to face reality and accept John's death. Settling my husband's estate seems like closing the final chapter on his life. Once this meeting is over, there will be no more John.

"Second door on your left," the receptionist calls out to me. I mutter my thanks to her as my heart skips a beat. This is it. The meeting is about to begin.

As I walk along a narrow corridor I wonder why Thomas Hart can't get off his butt and greet me like a professional himself.

"Come in," he calls out with a grunt as I arrive at his door.

I walk into his office, seeing the nameplate he has on the thick timber door that reads "Thomas Hart, Esq." The man doesn't seem to fit the distinguished title when I finally lay eyes upon him. A bushy mustache and a balding head sit atop a bulky frame that barely squeezes in behind the desk in his small messy workspace. Thomas is busy scribbling something down on paper and doesn't look up when he tells me to take a seat.

I pick the left chair of two that sit opposite him, noticing almost immediately the scratches and discolorations they possess. I settle into place on a squeaky chair and wait for him to finish whatever it is he is doing.

I study the lawyer and try to hide my surprise when I see just how sloppy the man's handwriting is. He continues to scratch out words on paper that don't at all seem to be related to John or me. I need to speak before I scream. "I thought you were in a meeting?" I ask him, realizing no one exited the room before me.

He looks up from his work with narrowed eyes directed at me. "Video chat," he says, pointing at his computer with his pen. The laptop is shoved off to the side of his desk.

I give him a weak smile and bite my lip as he returns to writing his notes down. I didn't mean to be rude. I'm nervous and concerned as to why I'm even here. It's not the first time I've said something awkward and stupid, and it won't be the last.

"Okay," Thomas says. "John Dalton." He grabs a folder to the side of his desk and plonks it down in front of him, confirming he was spending time from my meeting working on someone else's file. I ignore what I can't control and focus on John's paperwork. I'm amazed to see that things are still done on paper. In our ever increasingly electronic world, I still manage to find people that like to do things the old way.

"So, Mrs. Dalton. Firstly, let me reiterate my condolences. It's truly a tragedy what happened to your husband."

Thomas had said something similar in every voice message he left me. The same lack of sincerity exists in his voice as ever while I fight through the scratching pain in my throat that is attempting to choke me up with tears again. "Thank you," I mutter out of politeness.

"I can't even imagine what you are going through, Mrs. Dalton."

"Please," I say raising a palm. "Call me Grace." I can't handle hearing my surname at the moment. It's ultimately John's name.

"Sorry, Grace. The reason I've been trying to contact you for the past month or so is to discuss John's estate in person. I would have sent you a letter, but there are some things in here that are far too sensitive to risk falling into the wrong hands." He stabs at the manila folder with his index finger, forcing me to lean forward with wonder. I feel my breath quicken as Thomas clears his throat. What in the hell is he going to tell me?

"It's unfortunate that John has unintentionally left you in a bit of a financial bind."

My head jerks back slightly at this lawyer's bluntness. I scratch the back of my neck and admit the truth. "Yes. The mortgage is more than I can handle on my own. Every day I'm getting closer to losing the house." It was another reason I had managed to pry myself from the darkness of my bedroom and arrange this meeting. If I let the problem continue, I'd be forced out of my home.

"Okay. Well, you may or may not know that any debt John personally had gets paid out of his estate. His student loan is not your problem. Unfortunately, though, the mortgage falls to you because you both shared the repayments and were married."

Were married. I hate hearing those two words. It makes me think we got a divorce or something. As far as I'm concerned, John and I are still married. He just happens to be dead, is all.

I silently curse myself that we never took out any insurance on the bank loan in case one of us died. I remember we both laughed at the idea and thought it was a waste of money. I guess when you are still relatively young you think you are invincible. Neither one of us ever expected such an event to occur in our lifetime. With both of us working hard at the hospital, we seemed to be able to get by financially.

"There's no way in hell I'll be able to afford to pay the mortgage repayments for much longer. I'm going to have to think of some other means to survive like renting out a room or downsizing entirely."

I close my eyes. The thought of renting out the spare bedroom that we had reserved for a child that would never come to exist brings me close to tears. Selling up seems just as overwhelming. John and I bought that house together. We picked the colors to repaint the walls. We argued over the best way to arrange our furniture. We put ourselves into every room. I gulp down the pain and face Thomas. "Is there anything else you can suggest I do to avoid losing the house?"

"That's what I was about to get to. The reason I got you in here today was to discuss something I'm beginning to suspect John had failed to ever tell you about."

I feel my chest tighten as I clutch at my elbows and lean forward. "What is it?"

Thomas crosses his arms and tilts his head to his chest. "The million-dollar life insurance policy John took out for you both a few months before he died."

CHAPTER 5

My head begins to spin as I try to understand what Thomas Hart has just said to me. The lawyer stares at my gaping mouth with a frown as he stays leaning forward. I can't seem to say anything. I'm stuck.

"Is everything okay, Grace?"

"Uh, yeah," I say, exhaling, "but I don't think I heard you right. Did you just say that John took out a one-million-dollar life insurance policy before he died?"

Thomas smiles out of the corner of his mouth as he rolls back in his oversized leather office chair. "Yes, he did. For both of you. It's a bit of a shock, I take it."

"Yes. Yes, it is. I don't even know what to say to that."

"There's little to say. John felt the need to protect both of your futures in the event one of you died. You see, he took out a first-to-die, joint life insurance policy with a payout of one million dollars. Basically if one of you were to die, the surviving spouse got the money."

I shake my head as my mouth tries to form words. This can't be real. "A joint life insurance policy worth a million dollars? That must have cost a lot of money to have."

"They're not the cheapest policies around," Thomas says with a shrug.

I try to understand how John managed to pay for this without me knowing. We got by okay, but things were tight from week to week. I can feel my eyes dart around in my head as I try to work this out. "This is crazy. How did he pay for this?"

Thomas riffled through some notes and quickly read them to himself. "According to this the payments all came from John's account."

"John's account?" I asked. "Do you mean our joint account?"

"Uh, no, sorry. His account. It's empty now. I take it you didn't know he had another account, did you?"

I shake my head and turn away. I kept a close eye on our money. Every transaction I knew about. The only things separate we had were two credit cards with very low spend limits on them. John's was all paid up at the time of his death.

"Why would he keep this from me?"

Thomas purses his lips and glances away from me for a moment. "Why he didn't tell you about any of this is none of my business. But let me tell you something between the two of us: he's not the first client of mine to keep secrets from his partner, and he won't be the last."

I fail to see how Thomas's words are supposed to comfort me as I give the man a frown in return. I can only be so polite and hold back the overwhelming amount of thoughts running through my head for a short time longer. "I just don't..." I can't even finish my sentence. If I do, I might explode. I don't know how I'm supposed to feel right now. Angry? Betrayed?

Thomas holds up both hands with squinted eyes. "None of my concern right now, Grace. All I need from you is your understanding of how things proceed from here."

"What do you mean?"

The lawyer narrows his brows at me. "The money, of course. I just told you John's estate has a pending one-million-dollar payout coming its way. Do you understand what that potentially means for you?"

I glance around the poorly decorated room for answers that aren't there. My eyes settle back on Thomas again as I give him a shrug. What else is this man going to tell me?

"Didn't think my words had sunk in properly. I'm saying that once this payout goes through, it will be used to inject John's estate with much-needed funds. Once John's medical school loans are paid for, you will be left with around $900,000, minus my modest fee. Enough to start over, enough to keep your house, and almost enough to retire if you manage the funds correctly."

I stare at Thomas as if he just told me the room is about to be set on fire. With that much money, I could pay off the three-hundred-thousand-dollars-plus mortgage that is sitting over my head and still have plenty of money left over. My troubles would be gone. But it all seems too perfect to be true. "Are you serious? Just like that my financial problems go away?"

"In a manner of speaking yes, but with a few things that need to be sorted out first."

"What things?" I ask growing tired of this overwhelming conversation. I'm about ready to up and leave, but I keep myself grounded to the chair.

"Well, one thing mainly. There will be a full investigation into John's death before a single cent of the money will be released. The insurance company is within their rights to do so considering John only held the policy for two months before that unfortunate night."

"What exactly do you mean by 'full investigation'?"

Thomas lets out a huff. "Simple, really. The insurance company will conduct an investigation of their own to rule out anything untoward that could see the policy canceled."

"Untoward? Like what?"

Thomas places both hands on his desk and leans in with a tilt of his head. "Like, hypothetically, if there were anything to suggest a conspiracy to murder John for the money."

My mouth falls open as I back away from Thomas one inch at a time. My heart feels like it is about to explode. "Murder? I didn't even know this policy existed. What are you getting at exactly?"

"Whoa, calm down. I'm not saying that's what happened. Not at all. But you'd be surprised what people are willing to do these days for a bit of cash. Just a hypothetical to prepare you for that unlikely scenario. I'm sure there's nothing that will give them cause to deny you the funds."

"It could be denied?" I try to contain my rage as Thomas doles out one frustrating piece of news at a time. I'm close to walking away from this supposed professional right now.

"Hey, just a warning, is all. These insurance companies can be meticulous. They will think up any number of scenarios to get out of paying. You'll be fine, though."

I can feel my nostrils flaring up as my breathing begins to calm down. I lower my head and shake away the anger. I have to calm myself. "Is that all?" I ask without making eye contact. I'm afraid if I lock eyes with this lawyer again I'll say something I'll regret.

"That's all, Grace. You're free to leave once you look at John's estate forms and sign here." Thomas slides a letter across the desk at me that is multiple pages in length. "Once the investigation concludes, I'll contact you regarding the final amount John's estate is worth minus my fees. Provided the insurance company finds no cause to deny, you should see a once-in-a-lifetime payment come into your account fairly quickly." Thomas places a pen down by the form.

I pick up the pen and try to read the letter in front of me. Without my glasses on, I can't read it well, so I pull them out of my handbag and put them on. I can barely understand what I'm reading, but the section about the investigation is crystal clear. My wrist freezes in place. Signing this document is the final piece of John's life I have left to tie up. Once I finish scrawling my signature on the dotted line, there will be nothing else left to do but to move on. It doesn't feel right. He doesn't deserve to have his life looked into in such a way. I glance up at Thomas. "Do I have to sign this right now?"

"No," Thomas says as he carefully takes the letter and places it with a pile of papers in John's folder. "Take the paperwork home with you and read it over. Just sign and send it back to me when you are ready. But don't sit on this for too long. The sooner we get the ball rolling, the sooner you will receive the payout that is potentially coming your way."

"Okay," I mutter to show my understanding. My mind swims with too many thoughts at once. I realize I need to get moving. "Thank you for your time today."

"Not a problem. There's no charge for our little chat, of course. Everything will be deducted from John's estate."

"Great," I say with a forced smile. I want, more than anything, to unload all of my pain and confusion upon Thomas, but I know it won't help in the slightest. My therapist's words won't let me get into that frame of mind without feeling guilty.

Thomas loads the small pile of paperwork into the folder for me to read over and sign. "Just mail your signed copy to this address or drop it in. Either is fine."

I collect the folder, take off my glasses, and shove both items into my handbag, still reeling from what I've been told by Portland's most relaxed lawyer. Why did John trust this clown to handle something as delicate as his estate?

"Have a good day, Mrs. Dalton," Thomas says. "Oh, and if you have any questions, give my cell a call. The number's on this business card."

I don't respond as he makes a show of placing his business card—the same card I already have—in the folder. I walk out of his office on autopilot, without saying another word. The receptionist tries to engage me, but her voice sounds muffled in my head. I push open the door to exit the building and feel the weight of the city hit me head on the second my feet touch the pavement. I instinctively cross my arms over my chest to stay warm.

What have I just been told? Was any of that meeting real?

A rush of turmoil hits my body all at once. I bite my lips and close my eyes as I wander down the empty street. I should be contacting Jennifer right now and calling her for support, but I can't find the strength to pull out my cell and dial. I just keep walking, unsure where I'm headed.

I feel my wedding ring press against my arm and drop my hands down to spin it around my finger the way I have for the last six weeks. The habit seems to be the only thing that stops me from falling into a panic attack as I feel my breath ease down.

The documents in my bag feel more cumbersome than they should. I should have signed them then and there and gotten this awful process out of the way, but I can't let John go. Not yet. I need time to think. I need time to take this all in.

Thomas's terrible approach of telling me aside, I know the insurance company will be sending someone out to investigate John's death the second I sign. After today, I have no idea what they may or may not uncover. Maybe I don't ever want to know.

I thought I knew my husband. I thought we were best friends who shared everything with one another. To find out John had a secret bank account to fund a secret policy covering either of our lives to the value of one million dollars makes me question our marriage. What did he think was going to happen that would see one of us dead this early on?

I reach the end of the block, not knowing where I am or where I'm going. Jennifer's worried face enters my mind. I know she'll be upset with me for walking off like this, but I need some time to myself to clear my head. I should never have organized this meeting on the same day I buried John. So stupid.

As I mutter thoughts aloud to myself, I reach the end of the block and need to look up at the traffic. I see a man on the other side of the wide street staring at me as people on the sidewalk pass him by. He is wearing a black hooded sweatshirt with the hood up and dark sunglasses despite there barely being any sun in the sky. I don't have my glasses on, but the man looks familiar.

I rummage through my handbag past the thick document and find my black-rimmed glasses. I place them on my face and adjust the frame to get a better look at this stranger who feels the need to stare at a defeated woman coming out of a lawyer's office. Just as I am about to yell out what's his problem, he turns and walks away.

Deciding that this is the person I want to unleash my pain upon, I follow him for a few steps until I realize how stupid I am being. The man could be anyone. I come to my senses and reach into my bag to find my cell. I need Jennifer to collect me before I do something foolish.

The man comes to a stop on the next corner and glances back at me through his heavy shades. A realization hits my brain as I see his face as clear as day now that I have my glasses on. It can't be. I have to be seeing things, but I swear I'm staring back at John.

The man gives me a coy smile from the side of his mouth the way John used to and turns away. He walks off into a crowd of people in a hurry and rounds the corner before I get a chance to yell out to him.

The blaring horn of a taxi almost blows me off my feet as I narrowly miss getting run over.

"Grace!" Jennifer yells. "What the hell are you doing?"

I turn back and face her, still out on the road. She rushes to me and grabs hold of my elbow. I am guided back onto the footpath as the taxi driver hurls abuse at us out of his open window.

"Sorry," I mutter. "I don't know what came over me. I thought I saw..." I can't finish my sentence. Not without sounding insane. I shake my head and slouch down and away from my friend. "I'm sorry. Can we go?"

"Okay, but you need to be careful," Jennifer says with a furrowed brow.

I know she wants to say more and grill me as to why I almost suffered the same fate as John, but she's too good a friend to push me.

We walk back to her car in silence. Once we settle into her sedan, Jennifer hands over a coffee she's bought me. I take the hot beverage but place it immediately into a cup holder. I know after what I just witnessed I won't be able to drink so much as a sip without spilling it.

CHAPTER 6

Then

After John left for work, I decided not to re-bag his gift. I wanted to keep it out to help me to rustle up the courage I'd need to show him the wooden pacifier at dinner. It felt like I would be proposing to him in a strange sort of way. When you got down to it all, I kind of was suggesting something far more demanding than marriage to him. Our lives would never be the same once we introduced a little person into our world.

Agreeing to start a family was a huge commitment. The idea took me a good while to come around to and accept as the best way forward. I knew it wouldn't be easy. It couldn't be. I had no delusions about it. Motherhood would be one of the most challenging parts of my existence. I'd seen enough young mothers come through the hospital when I visited a few co-workers in the maternity ward to understand it was not an easy journey to take. I wondered if the mothers knew what was ahead and how they'd handle it. Too many of them didn't realize that once you'd gotten through the hell that was childbirth you then had to care for this tiny human.

I had put off the entire idea of having a baby in my twenties. There was no way I could make the sacrifice then. When I turned thirty, my body didn't suddenly demand that I fall pregnant the way some women's did. In fact, I said I was more focused on my career to become a registered nurse whenever someone asked me when I was planning on having children. It was my way of rebelling.

People were so forward with the whole idea as if that was all I was good for. I was asked by my parents outright when I was going to give them grandchildren long before John and I ever met. When we got married, my parents were so convinced we'd have kids straight away that they began buying us all of the essentials we'd need to properly care for a newborn. They stored it all at their home on the other side of Portland despite never being asked to buy the items in the first place. When we told them it wasn't going to happen for at least a few years, they didn't keep their disappointment to themselves.

With time, they came to accept that they would have to wait until we were ready. And here we were, finally willing to take the plunge. I hadn't told my parents anything yet. I figured it would be a surprise they could wait for once I'd actually fallen pregnant.

I knew John would say yes in a flash to the idea. He had ultimately been waiting for me to be ready the past few years. He knew not to put pressure on me about the topic and had been as patient as a person could be. It wasn't until I turned thirty-five that I started to realize I was getting older and that my age might reduce our chances of us falling pregnant.

Forgetting the past for a moment, I got dressed for the day, did my hair, and put on some makeup on in the space of twenty minutes. I had the process down to a fine art.

I sat down to eat some breakfast at the island bench of our kitchen while aimlessly browsing Facebook on my cell. Being up so early to catch John before he left for work meant I had to wait until a reasonable time for Jennifer to wake up and send me a text to know she was ready for me to come around. We had made plans to go shopping together, in Portland of all places. I didn't love heading in that direction on my days off, but there was little else I could do to convince Jennifer to shop somewhere local. She worked in town for an accountant and needed to escape the limited confines of Sherbrook. As much as we both loved the area, it was not the kind of town to be stuck in.

Nine o'clock eventually came by. I knew my friend would have already been awake for at least half an hour getting ready for me to come over.

My phone buzzed in my hand with a text from Jennifer a few minutes later. Gathering up my keys, I drove over to her home across town, where I parked out the front of her house and tooted the horn. She emerged from the front door a moment later looking all too keen for our shopping trip. As she approached my car, I debated whether or not I should tell her about my plan to ask John about starting a family. I knew she would be honored to be in on the knowledge, but I was having enough trouble focusing on the task to have someone else in my head knowing about it.

"Hey," Jennifer said when she opened the passenger door and climbed on into my aging Subaru Forester. She settled into her seat and let out her breath.

"How are you? You seem a bit flustered?" I asked.

"Don't mind me. Just got a text from my damn boss. He wants me to come in this afternoon, so we better make this shopping trip one to remember."

I smiled out the corner of my mouth as I pulled out into the road knowing there was one way I could make this morning a memorable one for us both. I thought of the perfect way to tell Jennifer about my intentions as I drove.

She continued to complain about her boss and talked about quitting. She was always talking about leaving to me as if I had a say in the decision. I told her to do whatever makes her the happiest the way I always did. I knew she just needed to vent and would most likely keep the job. I had my own hard days to contend with that drove me to the edge. I thought about what impact having a baby would have on my career. Would my time away make people take me less seriously as a professional? Was I risking losing everything I'd worked so hard for? Once John became a physician, he'd be earning enough money to support our household. I might never go back to the job that I loved out of a sense of loyalty to my future child to stay home with them until they were old enough to go to school.

"So what do you think?" Jennifer asked me.

I turned to her with wide eyes and blurted out the first thing that popped into my head. "About what?"

"About what I was just talking about. Were you even listening?"

"Sorry, I was. Tell me again." I didn't mean to block her out and think about myself. It was hard not to given the drastic lifestyle change I was about to propose to John.

"No, it was nothing special," Jennifer said, waving me off with no offense in her voice. "Tell me, though, what's got a hold of your brain so much that you can willingly block me out, huh?"

I turned and smiled at her. "Nothing."

"Nothing? That face doesn't look like nothing? What's going on? Tell me now."

"Not yet. When we get to the shops."

"Oh, you're such a pain in the butt. I hate when people do that."

"It'll be worth the wait, I promise."

"Better be," Jennifer chuckled.

We arrived at Floyd Center in Portland and parked. The three floors of the old shopping mall sat up high with a graying sky developing in the distance. The mall was one of our favorites in the city.

As we entered the central shopping area, Jennifer poked and prodded at me to spill the beans about my secret. I was about to share it with her soon, once we were sitting down with a coffee so I could focus, but she couldn't wait. She wouldn't give up on trying to extract the truth from me. I needed the time to rustle up the courage just to tell my friend, let alone John.

"Come on, Grace. You can't do this to me. You know I love gossip and secrets. Please, just give me something. I'm dying here."

"Tell you what: I'll buy you a coffee if you wait for me to tell you."

"Fine," she replied. "You know my one weakness. But I'll need it up front. I'm already coming down from the one I had at home."

I giggled at Jennifer as we approached a coffee shop we both frequented. There was a bit of a line to order that would only add to my friend's impatience. I turned my head to see a nearby store that would help me reveal my idea. I grabbed Jennifer by the elbow. "Come on. We'll grab a coffee in a minute. I want to show you something first. This will be much better."

"Are you serious? I could smell the coffee beans. You can't do this to me."

"You'll get your coffee." I dragged Jennifer toward a small boutique that had clothing inside that neither of us could ever afford. A lady inside was rummaging through some new items she was putting on display when we walked through the entrance. She gave us the quick up and down and by the way she went back to her merchandising must have concluded that we weren't there to buy anything.

"What are we doing in here?" Jennifer complained, her shoulders slumping.

"I'm telling you my big secret. Well, showing it to you, at least."

Jennifer brightened up and straightened her back. "What is it?"

We stopped near the limited children's section of the store to Jennifer's confusion. Her brows twisted inward as she gave me a frown. "What are we...?"

I moved past her and rifled through some clothing until I found what I was looking for. I spun around and held up a bodysuit that would snuggly fit an average newborn.

Jennifer took a moment, but the cogs started to turn in her head as she threw her hands over her mouth to contain a scream. "Oh my God, are you pregnant?"

"Not yet. I'm going to ask John if he wants to start a family."

"This is amazing. I can't believe it. So, when are you asking him? Please tell me it will be soon."

"I'm telling him tonight."

"Anniversary dinner?"

I nodded.

"That is just perfect. I'm so happy for you guys." Jennifer clutched her hands together, interlacing her fingers as she stared at me with glee. She was more excited about the idea than I could ever be. So much so that she grabbed the bodysuit and took it up to the counter to purchase it.

I stared at Jennifer as she paid way too much for a bodysuit from a boutique. I studied her face and thought if my friend could be so positive about the future then so could I. John was going to say yes and be happy about the whole thing. We were going to move forward and take our marriage to the next level.

Nothing could stop us from our happy future.

CHAPTER 7

Now

I sit in silence and gaze out the window of Jennifer's sedan as she takes me back home from the lawyer's office in Portland. The drive goes by painfully slow and gives me too much time to think about what Thomas Hart had just told me and more importantly, who I thought I saw in the street.

Did I really see John staring at me from across the way? It couldn't have been. I saw him die. I saw the life fade from his eyes. I saw his lungs give up. It can't have been him.

John's face is quickly replaced by Thomas Hart's, telling me about the million-dollar payout that will most likely go to John's estate a short time after I sign the documents he gave me. The words on the paper regarding my husband's life stir in my handbag, eager to be read, acknowledged and signed off. However, I can't do it. I can't sign away John's existence. Not yet. I can't move forward and leave him behind dead and buried in the ground, not while I'm seeing him in the streets of Portland.

The image of that night six weeks ago inevitably flashes into my mind. I see the pickup run John down at a speed no person could ever manage to survive. I see myself drop to my knees over his twisted, bloodied body, doing what little I could to comfort him in his dying moments as he tried to tell me something important.

I know John is dead. I just buried him, dammit. So why am I imagining him alive and well stalking me outside a lawyer's office?

"Is everything okay?" Jennifer asks for the tenth time. "You've barely touched your coffee. Since when do you not drink your coffee, huh?" Jennifer laughs at me for a second as she rubs the back of her neck.

"I'm sorry," I say, trying to think of an excuse. "I guess I've gone off the stuff." I realize that I haven't been drinking coffees since the accident. I used to drink too many per day like clockwork, thriving on the aroma of ground beans alone.

The cappuccino I ordered the night John died was the last one I ever tasted. If I hadn't have needed that damn drink and just gone straight home with him, he'd have taken that call on his cell in his car and would still be alive today. No light-blue pickup would have had the opportunity to run anyone down in the street.

"Fair enough. I'll remember that for next time," Jennifer says, cutting off my memories.

"I should have told you not to get me one, sorry." I don't want to tell her why, but maybe I should.

"No, it's fine," Jennifer says as her spare leg bounces up and down. "I should have asked first. It's not like a cup of Joe is going to fix anything. That was stupid of me."

I turn to Jennifer, averting my eyes away from the emptiness outside. "No, it wasn't. Don't beat yourself up because of me. I know you are just trying to help. It's just in the last moment I had with John I..." I can't even bring myself to say it as I see a flash of his final words in my head saying "Grace, I have to tell you—" seconds before his body gives up and dies. That flash transitions to a stupid look on Thomas Hart's face as he tells me about the life insurance documents I need to sign. Seconds later, I'm seeing John in the street.

"I know," Jennifer says. "It's just I want to help you through all of this. I want to be there for you, but I don't know what to do or say. If I'm honest, I hate this. I hate that I can't fix your problems. I always could in the past. We both always managed to help one another through all kinds of crazy things. It was simple."

Simple. The word no longer applies to my life. I've spent the last six weeks in a void, hiding away from the world and its endless difficulties. Now I have to crawl out of the shadows and face reality. However, reality is throwing curve balls at me left and right. My problems are too complex to fix with a few words.

John's million-dollar life insurance policy gnaws at my brain, mocking me with its mere existence while simultaneously giving me hope that I can get through to the next phase of my life without needing to worry about money. He opened a secret account to pay for this policy he knew I would never agree to. Why? What was he hiding from me? It might be nice that my money problems will be taken care of, but I'll never know why my late husband felt the need to cover such a thing as his death in such an extreme way.

At the same time, though, I think about the fact that I don't deserve a single cent of the money. Why should I get to live in comfort and luxury all the while knowing that my husband died without ever realizing I was finally ready to start a family with him?

A peek in the side mirror distracts me from my thoughts as I see a familiar car trailing behind Jennifer's Toyota in the distance. I can't quite put my finger on it at first, but it hits me that it's the same year and color Nissan Altima that John had. I sit up in my seat and focus my eyes on the vehicle as it follows our path a short distance behind. Before I can get a good look at the driver, the car speeds straight past us, overtaking on a long straight of the I-5. I trace the vehicle as it passes and see a man inside. I can't see his eyes, but that doesn't matter. I know it's not John in there. It can't be; he's dead.

A glimpse at the license plate confirms I'm not seeing John's car. I slump back down in my seat as I realize I'm staring at a car that just happens to be the same model and color as the one John drove. It's just a coincidence. I shake my head with closed eyes. One day out from the fortress that was my bedroom and I've already cracked.

"I want you to know again, Grace, that I'm here for you. No matter what. If there's anything you need to talk about, tell me."

I contemplate telling Jennifer what I thought I saw in Portland. More importantly, who I saw. I wonder, though, what good it will do to say to my only friend in the world that I thought my dead husband might have been watching me from across the street from his lawyer's office. Will she think I've lost it? Will she think the weeks of solitude have broken my brain?

My mouth opens to speak, but I quickly shut it to rethink my words. "Thank you," I say after a delay. It's all I can handle saying at the moment. Anything else won't help.

"So, did you want to head back home? Maybe we could stop off and get a bite to eat?" Jennifer asks me.

A stab of guilt hits my stomach at the mention of going somewhere for a meal. It doesn't even occur to me that Jennifer might be hungry. The funeral and the meeting seemed like big enough tasks to wrap my head around. Given it is now lunchtime and that Jennifer has taken time out of her day to help me, I figure I owe her.

"We could go to the café," I say, speaking of our once regular spot near home. "My treat."

"Sounds amazing to me, but you don't have to go there if you don't want to, Grace. I'm happy to take you home instead."

"No, I owe you. You're wasting part of your weekend to babysit me. A free meal won't even begin to pay you back for the burden."

"It's no burden, okay? I'm here to help. If you want to go to the café, do it because you're hungry, not to thank me."

A few seconds of silence pass by as I give Jennifer a weak smile. The best I can generate. I wonder if I'll ever smile again for more than a fading moment. I wonder if I'll ever want to.

"So?" Jennifer asks.

"Let's eat." Food is the last thing on my mind, but I have to eat and thank my friend for her efforts.

We drive on down the highway and reach our town of Sherbrook. It's not the biggest town in Oregon, but it has a quiet dignity about it that I could never leave. At least it used to. Now it seems different. The sign welcoming me into town has aged over the last month and a half. The whole area feels distant and foreign. Despite spending all of my time locked away in my house within the town's borders, there is something off about the place. It no longer feels like home.

A permanent network of gray clouds hangs low over the region, rendering all color dull and lifeless. The rain isn't helping to quash the feeling in any way. Is it always like this?

Jennifer drives through the town center and heads for our café spot on autopilot, taking the quickest route there. Before I can get a word out, I realize where we are. How could I not remember?

"Oh, God," Jennifer blurts as she brings the car to a stop on the side of the road. "I'm so sorry. I forgot. Please forgive me, Grace."

"It's fine," I say as I stare out the windshield at the very spot where John was run down on one of the main streets. A stack of flowers and condolence cards placed by the patch of road he died on are starting to wither and fade as life moves on. The rain has destroyed a lot of the kind messages the locals had left for John. How long would it be until the shrine became a nuisance that needed cleaning?

There wasn't much nightlife in town, but there was a strip of restaurants and even the odd bar here and there to keep the small population happy. Of course, this meant I could never revisit that part of town without seeing the accident over and over in my head on some kind of cruel loop.

"I'll take us the back way to the—"

"No, don't. It's fine. I need to face this. I need to be able to go through these streets if I'm ever going to move on. It's okay."

Jennifer stares at me from the driver's seat with a furrowed brow. "Are you sure? I don't mind going the long way."

I do what I can to hide my trembling lips. As much as I want to curl up into a ball and hide away forever, I have to face the world. "I'm sure," I say with a voice that's too quiet. I continue to stare out of the windshield of Jennifer's car wondering who it was John was speaking to on the phone. Why did his conversation stop so suddenly? Why did he freeze in the middle of the damn road? What was he going to tell me?

I fail to think of anything else as if I'm determined to punish myself for that night. Everyone tells me it wasn't my fault. I know I didn't run John over and drive off. But I also know that my actions didn't help him to take better care when he crossed the road. I only served to allow that pickup the perfect timing to run him down.

I can't convince myself to stop absorbing the guilt that flows over the street like a river, especially when I think of every moment I ever failed John in our marriage. I don't think I'll feel guilt-free again.

I keep expecting to see him walking around Sherbrook without a care in the world as if he had just been out on a six-week-long walk around Oregon. Maybe I did today, but I know I couldn't have. I can only ever break the cycle by asking myself the one question I know I don't have an answer for:

Will I ever accept that John is dead?

CHAPTER 8

We drive past the spot where John met his end. It sends a shudder down my spine, reaching out to me, trying to grab hold to pull me down into the abyss. I attempt to ignore the images in my head of the few seconds it took for everything to change my life, but I can't.

Time slows down as I imagine John staring at me from the street, the pickup a short distance away. His eyes pierce through mine, condemning my every action taken since that moment. I shouldn't have waited six weeks to bury him. I shouldn't have avoided his lawyer's calls. I shouldn't have gone to see Thomas Hart on the same day as the second funeral.

A shadow of guilt casts itself over me until I see John mouth those words at me again. "Grace, I have to tell you..." His eyebrows pull tightly together as he tries to speak but blood quickly washes over his teeth.

"What were you trying to tell me, John?" I whisper.

"Here we are," Jennifer says, saving me from the street. She climbs out of her sedan and opens my door for me while I try to recompose myself and focus on the now.

"You good?" she asks.

I'm not good. I'll never be again, but I nod as I climb out of the car. I then follow Jennifer's lead toward our destination like a lost child.

The café seems different to me when we walk in, and I can't quite put my finger on it beyond a gut feeling. I study the decor, dreading the challenge of remembering what the establishment looked like only six weeks ago. I fail to recall any particular detail from my last visit. All I know for sure is that things have changed. It's just the way the world presents itself to me now. Nothing feels right anymore.

"Go grab a seat," Jennifer says. "I'll order us the usual, minus the coffee for you. Okay?"

My eyes snap from staring around the café to Jennifer's eager eyes. "The usual?" I ask her, my mind a blank.

Jennifer responds by raising her brows at me as if I've just asked her what year it is. "Yeah, the usual. Turkey wrap with Swiss cheese and bacon. I get the chicken salad."

"Oh, right," I say feeling a flash of embarrassment. How could I possibly forget? "That will be fine." I'd forgotten about the meal we ate here as regularly as clockwork. I'd unintentionally blanked out most things about my life before that night like nothing else mattered. There were, however, some moments that could not be forgotten, but in general routines, food, entertainment, all seemed to fall by the wayside when John's life ended in front of mine. Something as arbitrary as a turkey wrap held less importance to me now than it would have before. Would I ever crave the regularity of a café meal again? Would I ever see a normal life?

I take a seat by a window along the side of the restaurant, away from the front of the building, not wanting to see the road connected to the main street where it all happened. I still see the flashing lights of the ambulance and police cruiser as a small crowd of onlookers gathered around to get a good look at John's lifeless body. They all stood there staring, smartphones out recording the authorities as they responded and failed to resuscitate John. "Vultures," I mutter to myself unintentionally.

I wonder how many images and videos ended up on the web for all to see? How many people had viewed the shots of John in a brief moment of their jaded day only to forget about it in the next second?

"Just be a few minutes," Jennifer says as she sits down, bringing me back to the present. "I got you a glass of water to drink. Is that okay?"

"Perfect. Thank you."

Jennifer settles in and does her best not to stare at me. I've noticed her trying hard not to gawk at me with the same eyes that most people can't help but give me now that I'm out and about in the world again.

"It's okay," I say to her. "You don't have to keep looking at me like I'm a fragile little bird."

"I'm sorry. I didn't mean to, it's just..." she trails off.

"What is it? Come on; I won't take offense. Nothing you say can make me feel any worse than this day already has made me feel. Trust me."

Jennifer lets out a long-winded sigh. "That right there is what I'm struggling to say to you."

"What do you mean?"

"Your feelings," she says.

I squint back at her and suppress a scoff. It almost hurts to do so. "My feelings?"

"Yes. I know it sounds stupid, but I can see you're trying to push everything that happened that night down into the pit of your soul and hide it there forever. You should be doing just the opposite and—"

"And what? Telling you every detail of John's death? Spilling to you exactly how much blood he lost before he finally gave up and died? Or would you like to hear about the half dozen compound fractures my husband had that tore through his skin and clothing?"

Jennifer sits back as far away from me as possible with her hand over her open mouth, eyes wide. I'm standing up, leaning over the two-person table, both hands flat on the wooden surface. I can feel the heaviness of my breath as the sneer on my face subsides. I remember where I am and who I'm talking to. What have I done? Everyone in the café has stopped talking, eating, drinking, and staring at their devices.

All eyes are on me.

CHAPTER 9

I sit down with a thump and collapse into myself away from the judgmental eyes of the café. My hands cover my face, attempting to hide the shame overwhelming me, as I try to shrink away and stop the tears from flowing. They come anyway. I can't stop them. What the hell is wrong with me?

"Is everything okay?" a passing waiter asks.

"It's fine," Jennifer whispers to the man who I can't bring myself to address or even look at. "We're sorry for any disturbance caused." The waiter slinks away.

I shake my head, keeping my face covered for as long as I can. Where did that anger come from? Me, or from the grief I'm suffering through? I force myself to look up to Jennifer without an answer. What could I possibly say to make things right? "I'm so sorry," I say. "I don't know what came over me just now."

"It's fine."

"No, it's not fine. I just bit your head off for no reason."

Jennifer gives me a quick smile that fades in front of me. "It's okay. I can take it. You obviously still have a lot going on in there that you need to deal with. I just have to back away and let you work it out on your own instead of trying to interfere the way I always do."

I close my eyes and feel a sudden thickness of tension run its way through to my legs. "You haven't done anything wrong, Jennifer. You're not interfering. I promise you. It's just..." I trail off again and open my eyes as I direct my head away from her gaze. I can only imagine what Jennifer must think of me. I can't stand even the thought of her staring at me and hating me like I'm some sort of freak.

"You can talk to me, Grace. You can tell me anything. Hell, you can yell at me some more if it will help, just please don't bottle up what's going on inside your head."

I face Jennifer and give her the courtesy of full eye contact. "I'll try, I promise," I say as I force a smile for a brief moment. It's all I can muster up. She deserves more for putting up with me. Our friendship has become a one-sided mess centered around my pathetic existence.

"The turkey wrap," the waiter says, his voice slightly shaky.

I look in his direction, confused. I guess my outburst got things moving in the kitchen. The owner probably wants me out the door as quickly as possible without causing another scene. "Thank you," I mutter the second the plate hits the table. I stare at the food and know it will be a tremendous effort to eat even half of the meal. No matter how much time and care the chef did or did not put into making the lunchtime treat, it won't taste right. It won't have a flavor beyond the basic, bland cardboard taste I have come to accept. But, I have to eat. I have to survive. I can't let these emotions overtake my life.

"The chicken salad," is the waiter's follow-up, as he places Jennifer's meal down with care. "Is that everything, ma'am?" he asks Jennifer. No doubt he wants to avoid interacting with me. I don't blame him.

"Yes, thank you. That's all of it."

The waiter hands over the bill. I reach out to take care of it, but Jennifer beats me to the punch.

"I'll sort this one out, Grace."

"But I—"

"Seriously, just enjoy your meal. You can get the next one, okay?"

I pull my hand back in without argument. I should fight her on this seeing that I already owe Jennifer for today, but I don't have the energy. Instead, I thank her and withdraw back into the invisible shell made of guilt I imagine surrounds my body.

Jennifer handles the bill including the tip. Considering the money I'm about to come into, I should be the one to pay for the meal along with the next dozen or so outings I owe my friend after today.

As Jennifer starts to eat, I glance up and begin the process of forcing my meal down, taking large bites to get it over with as soon as possible. It all tastes as bland as cardboard. Jennifer isn't interested in matching my approach and takes small, manageable bites as she savors each mouthful.

"So when do you start back at the hospital?" she asks.

I hear her words and shudder. I shake my head at the thought of the hospital and the faces that work there. The place I once loved now seems like the last building on earth I want to step foot in. I'd been putting off telling them when I planned on returning for as long as I could. Now, they were leaving me voice messages and emails, asking me for a meeting to no doubt discuss my future.

"I'm not sure. They keep calling me to find out. Frankly, it's the last thing I want to think about. I guess I'll talk to them about it eventually." I think about the large payment that could possibly be coming my way the second I sign John's paperwork. With the stroke of a pen, I could have enough money to leave the hospital I once considered a second home that I shared with John.

There are too many memories of John in that building for comfort. I don't know what I'll do about my career, either. Will I ever nurse again? The second I come across someone bleeding—hospital or not—I know in my heart I'll freak out. I might never work in the industry again whether I want to or not.

Jennifer continues to chat with me. I slip into autopilot, taking in only half of her words as I contemplate telling her about the money. Would it make her happy or jealous? Would she think less of me if I were able to quit my job and never work again?

"Are you going to eat the rest of that?"

I look down at my meal and feel my stomach churn in disgust. I pick it up and polish off the wrap, swallowing it down with a hurried gulp. "Finished."

"You didn't have to eat it because of me. I wasn't going to force you to."

"It's fine. I need to eat." John's pending funeral had consumed my every thought and need for the last day. I'm pretty sure I forgot to eat breakfast. I almost had to remind myself to breathe on occasion. It was beyond exhausting.

"Grace, I need to ask you something, and you don't have to answer me, but I have to ask: What happened in your meeting with the lawyer?"

I stop breathing for a second as Jennifer's words drill into my brain. I almost draw a blank as I try to decide how best to reply to her question. I realize at that moment that she deserves to know everything. All of it: The last thing John said to me, the money he'd potentially left behind, and the sighting of a man in Portland who looked exactly like John. She's the only real friend I have left in this world. I need her on my side armed with the truth.

"Jennifer, I..." My mouth closes before I can form the words in my head. More than anything else I want to put them in the right order and spit them out, but each letter jumbles up into a mess. My head starts to spin as I see John's eyes staring at mine from across the street before they disappear into the crowd.

"What are you trying to say?" Jennifer asks me.

"John, he..." My jaw slackens as I fail to speak and instead gawk at her like a clueless idiot. My mouth freezes open as dizziness overtakes my ability to think straight. A quiver runs down my chest and into my stomach. I close my mouth and feel my teeth jitter. Sweat dots my forehead. Jennifer must think I'm losing my mind.

"Grace? Do you need some air?"

I shove my chair back and jump to my feet. I'm about to vomit all over the table. I rush past the busy waiter, narrowly missing his large tray, as I charge across the café to the bathroom toward the back of the building. I smash through the door to the women's and run into the first stall, falling to my knees. In less than a second, I am vomiting into the bowl.

My body heaves for the next two minutes, ignoring my pleas for it to stop until I feel Jennifer holding my hair back behind my head like we are in high school at the prom. How pathetic.

I turn around when I finally stop and gaze up into her supportive eyes and say, "I'm sorry."

"It's fine, Grace. Just take your time. This is a big day for you. I should have taken you straight home after the meeting. So stupid of me."

"No, you're not stupid. I am. I should have realized this was going to fail." I lean against the wall of the toilet's cubicle and drop my gaze to the floor. I don't know what else to say.

Jennifer doesn't accept this and drops down to my side with the glass of water she ordered for me, proving to me yet again what a good friend she is—one I'm not worthy of having in my life.

My mind drifts back to John. I want to tell Jennifer about everything and unload the last six weeks of hell onto her, but I can barely believe any of it myself. Is this real? Is this my life now? It can't be.

I stare at Jennifer as she bites her lip. She has something to say to me instead, and I can tell I'm not going to like a word of it. "What is it?" I ask.

Her brows wrinkle in together. "I think you need to go see your psychiatrist."

CHAPTER 10

Then

After cruising around the long sweeping aviary-like halls of the Floyd Center mall, Jennifer and I parted ways. She took the bus back home so she could head to work. I would have taken her back myself but I decided to visit John at work on my day off with a tasty doughnut from the mall. It would be a nice anniversary surprise, I figured, provided he could get a few moments to himself. If I couldn't get him alone, I'd leave the doughnut for him to eat when he had the chance. It all depended on how slammed his team would be in the ICU.

Being a Saturday afternoon would mean the ward would already be recovering from a Friday night of car crashes, assaults, and God knows what else the weekend period decided to throw at the medical staff of a large metropolitan hospital. I was probably pushing my luck going in there, but I was in the area and I missed him.

Jennifer didn't mind taking the bus back to Sherbrook. She rarely drove anywhere unless she absolutely had to. I mostly picked her up when we ventured out of town. It didn't bother me; she wasn't the best driver.

I arrived at the hospital and parked in the multi-level employee parking lot that was situated toward the back of the main buildings. I sat in my car for a moment, alternating between checking my makeup in the mirror and staring out the side of the structure toward the many buildings of the hospital. The place never stopped moving. Patients flowed in and out of the gates day and night. Most left in better condition than when they came in while other less fortunate individuals left via the morgue. The longer I spent working in a hospital of such a size, the harder my shell became. It had to stay that way if I was to continue being a nurse.

When I left my car and walked toward the stairs that would take me to the ground level, I thought about the good and the bad that I'd seen in my time servicing the area. Flashes of blood and pain washed over me along with the rare smile a patient had when they finally got to leave the hospital in the right way. I could never take any praise that came my way as I knew a patient's recovery was a collective effort. I would instead accept the appreciation on behalf of the hospital staff. It did, however, make all the effort we nurses put in worth the struggle.

It was going to be challenging for me to stroll on into the ICU and find him for my impromptu visit. The second he did stop and take some time for himself, I only hoped I could be there to wrap my arms around him or give him a chocolatey surprise. I wanted to build up this day as much as I could before I finally asked him the one question I know he'd been keen to hear from me for a few years now. I only hoped I didn't wuss out.

After a long walk across the hospital grounds via the pedestrian pathways that littered the roads, I arrived at the front of the ICU. I glanced to the side of the building to the helipad that I'd seen welcome the worst of the worst into the hospital's arms. Those were the patients whose lives were either close to the end or would be forever changed. How many people that landed on that small patch of ground survived this place?

I shrugged off the thought and moved in through the automatic double doors of the building and came to the desk to find two nurses on duty manning the staff entrance. Beyond the security door was access to the ICU and ER. One of the nurses I'd only spoken to on occasion while the other I'd worked with for three or four years.

"Grace?" Deborah said as she saw me approach the tall counter. "What brings you here? Are you working today?"

I matched the smile on Deb's face and placed both hands on the counter.

"Got the day off, so I thought I'd see if John was free for a minute."

Deb twisted her brows at me for a second before a crash boomed off the cold, sterile walls. Everyone in the room turned their heads to see a wheeled stretcher come barreling through and bounce over the slight lip on the ground beyond the double doors of the ICU entrance. "Coming through," an EMT shouted as he and a few other medical professionals crowded around a new patient that was about to be admitted to the ward, bypassing the emergency department's triage process.

I glanced at the patient and saw the telltale signs of a car crash victim. A man in his mid-thirties was lying on his back unconscious in a neck brace. Blood and cuts scarred his clothing. Another patient in a similar condition wasn't far behind him. From my assessment, just one of the pair would make it. Some patients had that indescribable look about them that told you if they'd pull through or not.

Deborah buzzed the busy crews through the security doors of the ICU that were necessary to keep the general public out and away from the chaos inside. Car crash victims with such injuries often didn't need to go via the ER first. Once the teams had cleared the area, we went back to our conversation as if we hadn't just seen two individuals whose lives would never be the same again. It was the delicate balance we had to strike to function in such a facility efficiently.

I went to speak again with Deborah, but a tap on my shoulder grabbed my attention. With a narrowed brow, I spun around and saw my colleague Layton standing behind me with a smile on his face. What did he want?

"Hi, Grace. Got a minute?"

My mouth fell open, but I uttered a garbled bit of confused nonsense in response to his question. Layton worked in the hospital's server room and maintained its vast network. We'd known each other for three years and first met in the hospital's cafeteria one day.

"What are you doing here?" I asked him. The server room was on the opposite side of the hospital.

"I could ask you the same thing," he said with a grin.

I shook my head at Layton and pulled him away from Deb. "What do you want?" I asked.

He huffed out of his nostrils with a smirk. "Can we talk outside? In private?"

I crossed my arms and shrugged. This was unlike him. He led the way out through the entrance of the ICU. I followed along, shaking my head, until we came to an empty park bench I had sat on a few times with John.

"Take a seat," he said.

I groaned under my breath and sat down on one end of the bench that could comfortably seat three people. Layton sat at the other, leaving a decent gap between us. "Grace, I wanted to talk to you al—"

"Well, here I am," I said interrupting.

Layton closed his eyes for a second and shook his head. "I know you're upset with me, but you don't have to be like that. I'm trying to help you."

"Help me? I'm not asking for your help."

Layton closed his mouth and exhaled. "I'm not here to argue with you, Grace; I'm here to tell you something."

"Please," I said, "I don't want to hear anything you have to say."

Layton leaned toward me with a sneer. "Oh, I think you will."

"Is that right?"

He nodded.

What was he on about? What was sitting on the edge of his tongue? I didn't want to lose any potential window I had to surprise John, but at the same time, I had to know what Layton was going to say before it ate me up. "Okay. What is it?"

He took in a deep breath and looked away. "It's about John."

"What about him?" I asked as my brows tightened. My heart picked up its pace.

Layton faced me, looking straight into my eyes. "I've been doing some maintenance in the ICU. There's a nurse in there I've seen him talking to."

"So what? That's part of his job."

"I know that," Layton said. "But this is different. The two of them haven't just been talking on a professional level. I saw John take down her cell number. I think that there could be something going on there. I think John might be—"

"Don't you dare say it," I said, cutting Layton off. "John isn't like that, and you know it."

His arms flared out wide in defense as he raised his brows. "Just telling you what I saw. Don't shoot the messenger."

I shook my head slowly as I felt my arms squeeze even tighter over my chest. "Is that all?" I huffed at him. I was about ready to scream.

"Ah, yeah."

"Good. I'll see you around." I pushed up off the bench and rushed away from Layton without looking back. I couldn't believe he had the audacity to tell me he thought John was being unfaithful. I knew my husband. He would never do such a thing, especially in the same place he worked. He was probably just getting her number for professional reasons, if at all.

I rushed through the double doors of the ICU and moved up to the counter again, shaking off the negativity Layton had sprayed me with.

"Everything okay?" Deborah asked.

I pushed out the anger brewing inside and gave her a quick smile. "Yeah, fine. Nothing to worry about."

Deb stared at me with a hint of confusion as she had before we were interrupted. I didn't want to explain any of it to her, so I powered through. "Anyway, I need to see John. Can you buzz me through?"

Deb squinted at me as her head flinched back. "What do you mean 'see John'?"

"Sorry?" I asked, trying to understand her confusion. Was everyone losing their mind today?

"It's just I figured you already knew."

"Knew what?"

Deborah frowned at me and lowered her voice. "That John has called in sick this morning."

CHAPTER 11

Now

Doctor Millard Sylvain is the first psychiatrist I have ever seen in my entire life. More accurately, he is the first psychiatrist I've ever *spoken* to, as we have only ever conversed over the phone.

Up until John's death, I felt like a well-adjusted adult who coped fine with the stress and pressure of life. I never imagined ever needing therapy to get me through the day. Working as a nurse in a busy hospital while being married to an eager resident had thrown a few challenges in my direction, but I'd always pushed through. I'd seen the best and worst of myself as well as what other people could offer me. To be blunt, I could handle more than the average person. At least I thought I could.

Jennifer looked up Doctor Sylvain online and made a booking for the next day at his office, paying a higher amount for what she deemed to be an emergency session. She didn't give me an option after I refused to talk about the meeting in Portland with her. How could I?

I didn't know what to say. I couldn't tell her about seeing someone who I swear was John across the street. I couldn't tell her about the money or John's other bank account without it sounding like he was keeping secrets from me. Despite the insurance money being a blessing, I didn't like the secrecy behind it, and Jennifer would pick up on that fact in a heartbeat. I don't want my friend to think ill of his memory.

"Okay, you're all set for tomorrow," Jennifer says.

I let out a huff. "I can just wait for my scheduled call to Doctor Sylvain in three days," I say with stiff arms that hang by my sides. I'm sitting on the sofa in the living room of my home. Jennifer got me here in one piece but refused to let go of the idea of booking me in to see Doctor Sylvain in person.

"Grace, believe me when I say this: you need to see him. You are single-handedly trying to deal with everything that has happened to you in one go. This can't wait."

I roll my head to the side on the sofa. Jennifer doesn't know the half of it, and she is convinced that I need emergency therapy. I'm not suicidal or a danger to myself, yet she is acting like something serious is just around the corner. I don't know if it's her personal bias driving her decision or if I'm really that bad. I guess I don't know myself anymore.

"You've tortured yourself for the last six weeks over John's death as if you were the one driving that damn pickup. Now, something happened when you met with that lawyer, and you won't even tell me about it."

I force my eyes closed and see John. He's there in the street as plain as day. I open my eyes again in a hurry to wash his image away. "Jenn, please. I want to tell you, but I can't. I just—"

She holds up a palm to quiet me down. I feel nothing but shame in an instant.

"You don't have to tell me anything, okay? I understand that you're not ready to talk, but you need to stop blaming yourself for everything and take a positive step in the right direction."

I nod at my friend, wondering how she is so articulate on the subject.

"Will you see Doctor Sylvain tomorrow?" Jennifer asks.

What choice do I have? "Yes, but I don't know how much good it's going to do."

"That's fine. You can think whatever you like about seeing him as long as you go to your session. I think seeing the doctor in person will be better than over the phone. Also, I can drive you there."

"No, it's fine. I'll get there on my own."

"Nonsense. I'm happy to drive."

Jennifer never drives me anywhere, but I don't know how the meeting will go down, so I accept her offer. "Okay, thanks."

She smiles from the corner of her mouth, clearly pleased with her efforts. "Anytime. Now, I know tomorrow is going to cost a lot, but it will be worth every cent, I promise."

The immediacy of the session will prevent me from using my HMO to cover it. I am going to be up for several hundred dollars tomorrow to see Doctor Sylvain. As soon as I think about money, I instantly think about the life insurance policy sitting in my handbag waiting to be signed. Why did John keep it a secret from me, and why did he insure our lives for so much? These are two questions along with many others I'll never get an answer to. The one person that can provide me with the truth is dead.

"Do you want some more water?" Jennifer asks as she rises from the sofa opposite me.

I gaze around my dark living room. I keep all of the shades closed and the lights off. I'm so used to sitting in a dim place like this it's the only thing that gives me comfort.

"Grace?"

I glance at Jennifer. I know she asked me something, but my mind was elsewhere. I have to stop doing this. "Yeah?"

"Water? Do you want some?"

"Uh, sorry. No, thanks." I watch Jennifer as she continues to move toward the kitchen across my open-plan house. We thought we were so smart picking a design with a space that felt much bigger than it really was. Would I ever find myself in that situation again with another man? It's far too early to be thinking about such a thing, but I can't help but wonder where the future will take me.

I follow Jennifer with my eyes as she enters the kitchen and opens my fridge. I cringe at the inevitable response I am about to hear when she sees the inside of the refrigerator. How could I have forgotten to make a semblance of normality?

"Oh my God, Grace, you have no food whatsoever. What have you been eating for the last few weeks?"

"It's not as bad as you think." It's worse.

"It has to be. You've got next to no food in this fridge. And what is here is either off or not something you can eat on its own. Not to mention the near empty bottles of wine."

I think about the night those wine bottles came from before John died. Those were just the bottles that didn't get finished.

Jennifer closes the door and stares at me with her mouth open and one hand on her hip. I feel like a kid who has been caught doing everything wrong by her mom.

"I have a walk-in pantry, too, you know," I say. "Plus, I've been getting groceries delivered."

She raises her brows and tilts her head at me. "Is that right? So you won't mind me taking a look in your pantry then?"

"Be my guest," I say, bluffing. I have no idea what's in there. It's the last place I look anymore. I know I haven't been eating enough food each day. I can't help it, though. The thought of forcing food down my throat adds to the nausea I'm still reeling from after my meal at the café.

Jennifer's mouth drops open when she inspects the walk-in. "This is almost as bad. I can even see dust on the few cans of food you do have in here."

I shrug. How else am I supposed to respond? I realized on some level that I hadn't been taking good care of myself. Some days I questioned why I should even get out of bed. I guess I never knew how bad I'd let things become.

"That's it," Jennifer says. "I'm going to have to buy you some groceries. Come on; we're going back out."

My eyes go wide as my head lifts itself from the sofa. "What?" I don't want to leave the house again.

"You heard me. We need to get some food in this house right now."

I need to stop this now. "No, it's fine, Jenn. I can pick up a few things myself."

She shakes her head at me as she closes the pantry door. How can I stop this? "I don't think I can trust you to do that. We should go now and—"

"Jennifer, please," I say. "I can take care of myself." I'm standing up; arms flared out wide.

She remains tall in return, both hands on her hips as she gives me a heavy sigh. "Is that so? Tell me then: how much weight have you lost?"

There it is. She knows. Is it that obvious? "That's none of your business," I say.

Jennifer scoffs. "You don't know yourself, do you?"

"It's just a few pounds. Nothing crazy." I know it's more.

She shakes her head slowly at me. "Have you been to the doctor's about this?"

I go to respond, but nothing comes out. I can't keep lying to her.

"Grace, honey, the second I saw you, I didn't recognize your face. You wouldn't let me come over until now. The vomit at the café told me the rest. When are you going to go see a doctor to get a checkup?"

I close my eyes and try to ignore her question, but I realize Jennifer won't give up that easily. She never has. She never will. I grin away, but it's not a happy smile.

"Come on, Grace. This isn't a joke."

"I know it's not a damn joke," I say. "Do you think I want to live this way? Sitting around in the dark, hardly eating a thing while my husband remains dead and buried?"

"Of course I don't think that. But when I can see that's what you are doing, I have no choice but to intervene. I know you'd do the same for me if..."

"If what?" I almost yell.

"If I were in the same situation."

I stare right through her, my mouth partly open. I'm about to break. "You don't know what it's like, Jenn. You never will. The sooner you recognize that fact, the quicker you'll understand how little you can do to make things better." I sit back down and slump on the sofa.

Jennifer walks over to me and sits down on the seat opposite. I can feel her gaze on me without looking. It burns into my skin, but we sit in silence. Only the ticking of the minimalist clock that sits on the far wall makes a sound. All I can do is shake my head to stop myself from shouting out to the world.

"You can go," I say. "You don't have to waste your day here with me."

"I'm not going anywhere, Grace. Not until you can accept one thing for me."

I raise my head, curious to listen to the words of wisdom she thinks she is about to deliver. Nothing can help me. "What is it?"

Jennifer clears her throat and takes a moment to breathe. She stares into my eyes as she answers. "That you will get through this."

CHAPTER 12

The next day, I sit in silence in the reception area of Doctor Millard Sylvain's office. It's nothing like I imagined every time I spoke with him on the phone. I don't know what he looks like either, but I have a predetermined image of him in my head. From our conversations, I pictured a medium build man in his late sixties with a finely kept gray beard that compensates for some thinning hair on the top of his head. I imagined round reading glasses balanced on the end of his nose purely for taking notes and nothing else. Meeting him will shatter it all. Meeting him will shatter a lot of the things I've told him.

I hardly slept last night. I guess I was nervous about today and had a million thoughts clouding my head from the previous day. I couldn't help but check to see if John's car was still in the garage where it has been for more than six weeks after one of the police officers dropped it back home for me after John was killed. I know the car I saw had different plates but seeing it still freaked me out.

At least three or four times I woke up and ventured my way in the dark to the interior garage door to see if his car had moved an inch. Every time I looked, I found it sitting correctly in its place with a tennis ball hanging from the ceiling on a piece of string resting against the windshield. John had attached the ball himself to make sure he always did the perfect park. That's just how he was with most things.

I didn't know what it was I was expecting to find each time I looked or what prompted me to head into the garage to begin with, but there was a feeling in the pit of my stomach each time I stared at John's Nissan Altima. It almost felt like he was still alive when I ran my fingers over the surface of his sedan. I knew he wasn't, of course, but the waning moment of possibility that came over me was too much to ignore when I swear I saw him in Portland.

My mind snaps to the present. Jennifer is by my side in the waiting room, keeping an eye on me. I almost feel like she has thought about handcuffing me to the chair. If I were to bolt for the door, I'm confident she'd tackle me to the ground first. She even put her smartphone away in her bag to remove all distractions. She's not messing around.

"Grace?" a tall man says from an open beige door. I look up and see who I presume to be Doctor Sylvain. He is nothing like I imagined. He has a full head of brown hair and no beard. No glasses frame his face, and his voice sounds different than it does on the phone. I suddenly feel like I'm a stranger meeting him for the first time. All and any confidence I could have brought to this session evaporates.

"Grace Dalton?" he asks again to clarify.

"Yes, Doctor Sylvain. I'm Grace."

He nods with pursed lips and ushers me toward his office. I get up on two shaky legs and make my way over with caution. I glance back at Jennifer and see her supportive smile urging me on. I feel like holding my breath for as long as I can but resist the temptation to do so.

"Right this way," Sylvain says.

"Okay," I reply with a whisper. Nerves cloud my every move. I step into his office and stop to take it all in. I see an arrangement of furniture designed entirely around the endless hours of conversation that must take place within these walls. The doctor's desk is tucked away at the rear side wall while two armchairs sit opposite one another in the middle of the room. A large rug spans the gap between each seat. A window that looks out onto a garden is the only source of light filling the space, which suits me fine. I don't want a brightly lit room holding me in a spotlight.

"It's good to finally meet you in person, Grace. Why don't you take a seat."

Each of the two armchairs has a side table. One holds a telephone, so I take the other seat instead, knowing my place. As I lower myself into the plush chair with wooden armrests, I realize just how qualified Doctor Sylvain really is when I see the half-dozen framed credentials on his wall. It overwhelms me slightly to learn he is not just some person I'm speaking to but a trained professional.

"So, what brings you here today?" he asks as he picks up a folder from his desk and brings it over with him. He sits down opposite me with raised brows that are eager to hear why a patient felt the need to book in an emergency session.

"Well, if I'm honest, I didn't book this in today. I was happy to wait until our scheduled call to talk about everything, but my friend out there was a bit concerned for me."

Sylvain purses his lips again and hums out a thought. Can he see through me? "Why don't you tell me why you think your friend made this booking."

"I can't answer for her."

"Try it. Humor me, if you will. There are no wrong answers."

I feel like cringing a little to that piece of cliché. I hoped to never hear phrases like that from him. I glance away quickly to think of a suitable answer to his request and instantly feel my pupils darting around. What am I supposed to say? That Jennifer possibly believes I might harm myself? That she knows I've lost too much weight? We both know there's nothing I can say to get me out of this room. I shake my head with doubt as I avoid the doctor's eyes.

"It's okay if you can't answer me. Sometimes silence says more than words ever can."

I push the air out of my lungs harder than is necessary, muting my response. I think about the dread of coming here when I could have been at home, tucked away safely in my bed with the lights off and the curtains closed. The thought almost calms me. Is this really what I needed?

"I'm sorry," I blurt out, "but I don't think this session was necessary. Would you mind if I waited until our phone call to speak?"

"We're already speaking, Grace. Granted there have only been a few words exchanged, but we are talking. Why don't we continue this chat in any way you see fit. We don't have to get into specifics. We can simply talk about whatever you'd like."

I fight back a heavy sigh and reluctantly nod my agreement. I'm fully aware we are not having a casual chat, but I go with it. "Okay, fine. Let's chat."

"Good. Why don't you tell me what you've been up to."

I scoff at his request. "You really want to know?"

"Of course," he says as he taps his pen sideways against his notepad.

"Okay then. I haven't left the house for six weeks until yesterday to finally bury my dead husband. In that time I haven't watched TV, read a book, or been online for more than a few minutes. I've mostly sat in the dark of my bedroom sleeping twelve to fifteen hours per day waiting for the world to somehow go back to the way it used to be."

Doctor Sylvain does his best to hide any emotional or physical response to my ranting. It impresses me despite everything.

"So," he says, "you've been lying to me on the phone then."

"I didn't want to, but how could you think I was all fine and dandy after witnessing John..." I trail off, unable to complete the words to that sentence. I take a quick breath and try again. "After John..." I falter. "After he..." I can't do it.

"It's okay, Grace. I've known you haven't been entirely honest with me from the first conversation we had. It wasn't hard for me to hear it in your voice."

"You knew?" I say, tears falling down my cheeks. "Why didn't you—"

"Bring you in? Force you to admit the truth? I didn't want to spook you into making yourself worse. In most cases, time is all a person needs to push through the grief of losing a loved one unexpectedly. Letting you omit a few things to me over the phone was helping you to slowly get better."

"Was? What do you mean by that?"

"Well, up until last week I was feeling confident with your progress. I was about to take you through to the next phase of therapy, once we'd met, of course."

"But?"

"But this emergency session changes a few things. I'm guessing its very existence is centered around you getting up the courage to bury John."

I think about the funeral. I think about the money. I think about the man I saw across the street. My eyes go wide as my chest tightens. The walls feel like they are closing in, ready to seal off my ability to breathe. This can't be happening now. The window seems to be more open than it should. I can't think straight. I hold both hands to my face and feel my heart race.

"Calm down, Grace. Take a deep breath in through your nose and slowly release it out of your mouth."

I try to do as he says, but my heart keeps pounding faster and faster, tricking my breathing.

"Try it again, but this time when you suck in that air, I want you to hold it for a count of three seconds before you slowly let it all out, okay?"

"Okay," I say with a sharp nod. Three seconds seems impossible, but I do as the doctor instructs and repeat the process again and again until I can feel everything begin to fall back into place.

"That's it, Grace. Keep going. You're doing well. Everything is going to be okay. You are going to be okay. You will get through this."

I hear Jennifer's words repeated by the doctor and wonder if any of this ever works. Will I ever be able to return to society as a functional person?

CHAPTER 13

After I narrowly avoid having a full-blown panic attack, Doctor Sylvain continues the session. I take a huge gulp of water and close my eyes for a few minutes until I am ready to proceed. Not that I want to. I'd be happy to run out the door and never come back, but something tells me that won't ever be an option.

"Okay, Grace. I'm sorry you had to go through that, but in a way, it showed me a lot of things."

I'll bet it did. "Like what?" I ask.

"Well, for one, you are far from being able to cope on your own when something triggers you. We need to get to the bottom of what has sent you spiraling back down to day one."

"And you want to continue to drill down into that today? Even after what just happened?"

Doctor Sylvain stands up for a moment and heads back to his desk in the corner. He looks at something on his laptop that mustn't have been written in his notes. "You buried John yesterday in the morning. You then traveled to Portland with Jennifer to see your lawyer regarding John's estate. By the afternoon your friend had to intervene and book you in for an emergency session. What changed in less than six hours to make that happen?"

What happened? It's a damning question. One I don't want to answer but know in my heart I have no choice but to. I don't know where to start, but one aspect sticks out to me more than anything else rattling around in my brain.

"I thought I saw him."

"Saw him? Who?"

I feel a stab of sweat in the faint wrinkles on my forehead that forces my eyes to the ground. I shouldn't have said anything. Nausea from yesterday returns as if it is on a strict schedule.

"Who did you see, Grace? You don't have to answer if you—"

"John," I say. "I thought I saw him across the street from the lawyer's office without a care in the world."

"Did you see his face?"

"Yes. I swear it was him. He was wearing a black hooded sweatshirt and glasses, but I could see John underneath it all. At least I thought I did."

Doctor Sylvain fumbles with his notes as his narrowed eyes blink over and over. "It's understandable that you would try and find ways to see John again."

"I wasn't trying to find ways to see him again. I just saw him."

"How you came to see him is irrelevant. John is no longer with us. I understand that death can be a hard thing to accept. It's a grieving process that can take years to push through."

"Years?" I ask. "I can't keep living like this for years. It's too much." I stare up at the ceiling to compose myself.

"I'm afraid none of this is optional."

"I know it's not, but—"

"Take your time," he reminds me.

I stare back down and look the doctor in the eyes. "Look, I know John is gone. I saw him die in front of me as close as we are right now. I can't deny that ever happened because it did. But at the same time, I would give anything to be able to see him again or hear his voice."

"I understand, Grace. The sudden loss of your husband has only made this desire stronger within you. It's not going to be an easy bond to break."

I stare at him for a moment before I start slapping my hands to my head. "I have to break it."

Sylvain raises both hands, even the one clutching his notebook and pen. "Take a moment to breathe again, Grace. Just like before."

"I'm breathing."

"That's good. Take some time to calm yourself down because there's something else we need to discuss first to get to the root of what has potentially caused this, let's call it a glitch."

"A glitch?" What the hell?

"Bear with me. From what I can see, several other issues are attempting to hide away underneath it all. I'm wondering exactly how much you realize that these other issues are contributing to your overall problem."

"Problem. This isn't just one problem, Doctor."

He gives me his defensive hands again. "Please. I'm getting to my point. Trust me."

Trust him? I don't trust anyone. How can I? But I know I need to eventually.

"If you decide to chase this feeling and bring John back from the dead in your mind, there's potential to do some real damage."

"Damage? Like to my mental state?"

"Yes. There's a name for it."

I exhale and close my eyes a moment before I refocus on Doctor Sylvain. "Just say whatever it is, Doctor."

"Okay, Grace. If you want it straight, here it is: it could lead to a severe case of major depression."

"Major depression? Anyone can see I'm already depressed."

"No, I didn't say depression; I said major depression. There are some sharp differences on top of your common depression symptoms. Let's go through them, shall we?"

I roll my eyes away with a scoff. "Fine. List away."

"You feel worthless and out of control. You feel guilt over witnessing John die while you remain alive. You don't trust people or think they can't help you. You feel lethargic and sleep a lot more as if your body has slowed down."

There's nothing here I didn't already know. I can't believe I'm paying extra for this session today.

"You can't handle the day-to-day problems of life such as eating enough food. Jennifer told my receptionist that you aren't eating right. Is that correct?"

I wonder what else she's told him. "I just need to eat better food, is all. Is there anything else?"

"We'll discuss that further." Sylvain stares at me, holding my gaze. He has something in that head of his he's been holding back.

"There are two symptoms of major depression that could come about. Delusions and hallucinations."

"What?" I utter. My voice chokes in my throat. "I don't understand."

"It's right here, Grace." He walks over to me and holds up a printout he's had hidden away inside his computer of the symptoms of major depression. He taps one of the lines that talks about hallucinations and visions of seeing a deceased loved one for brief moments as if they are alive.

I shake my head out of pure embarrassment and shame. How could I let myself reach such a low point? I focus in on the doctor. "How can I stop this? How can I stop seeing him?"

Doctor Sylvain lowers his notebook. "The first step in defeating this is to acknowledge that John really is dead and that you are possibly seeing hallucinations of him. If you can get past this point then you can begin to claw back and win the battle."

I begin to breathe a sigh of relief, if only for a moment.

"But be warned, Grace," Doctor Sylvain says. "This won't be easy."

CHAPTER 14

Then

It took me almost ten minutes to leave the hospital after my run-in with Layton. I sat in my car, gripping the steering wheel while staring out into space. He'd gotten me so annoyed with his little made-up story about John and some nurse that I couldn't think straight. The next thing I realized was that my surprise visit to see John was a complete waste of time considering he never went into work. I had to look like a complete idiot in front of Deb.

Why did John take the day off without telling me? He had apparently called in sick, but there was nothing wrong with him this morning.

I got back on the highway and headed for home, my foot heavy on the gas. I tapped the interface on my car's dashboard and called the first person on my list of recent calls. It went straight to voicemail. "John, it's me. We need to talk. Call me the second you get this." I pressed the end call button on the steering wheel and started muttering under my breath.

Was I being silly calling him? I eased up on the gas. Maybe he just needed a day to himself for some reason? God knows I did from time to time. It wasn't like I needed a break from John, but some days I just needed to be alone. We all did.

For all I knew, John could have been out somewhere buying me an anniversary gift. The task would not be a simple one for any guy like my husband who was hopeless at finding things in a busy mall. If he was out there shopping, I was almost surprised he didn't just come out and ask for my help. I decided not to assume the worst and headed back home to get on with the rest of my day off with a smile on my face. I still needed to tidy up the house and get ready for our anniversary dinner that night.

I drove through the middle of town and arrived back at the house after the usual commute home from work. It felt odd doing so in the middle of the day. Most of my shifts ended in the evening or early in the morning. I hated night shifts more than anything else. They left my body clock out of sync and always took me a few grouchy days to get over.

I rolled into our garage with plenty of time up my sleeve left for the day. After I ate some lunch and cleaned a few rooms in the house, I decided to try on some different outfits for our dinner. John would make it home from his secret day off in time. I trusted him to do so and had all but forced the worry out of my thinking.

Layton was wrong. John wouldn't do something so crazy as cheat on me with a co-worker. He was smarter than that, plus he loved and respected me. I knew he did. The real culprit was Layton. It was no secret he wanted to break John and I up so he could swoop in and take his place. I knew Layton would do or say whatever he thought was necessary to win me over. It was never going to happen, though. Ever.

Once I'd decided what dress I was going to wear to the restaurant, I laid it out for ironing in the limited space of our laundry. I would later iron out every crease and fold until that dress was perfect for my baby question for John.

On my way back to our bedroom, I saw John's study out of the corner of my eye. I don't know why, but I took a few steps toward it and gazed inside. A thought suddenly hit me. The room's proximity to our bedroom would make the small space the perfect nursery for our first baby. Sure it would mean John would be losing his study, but it was important for a newborn to be close to their mother for the first six months to a year.

I wondered how John would take the news when I asked him about it. Would he refuse? Or would he do whatever was needed for our baby? I knew I could count on him, but lately, he had been spending a lot of time in that small room. He'd spend all of his available hours in there studying for his residency, cursing away at his computer until the early hours of the morning. He seemed so determined to become a physician. Anytime I tried to come in and help him, he got upset with me. He had a particular way he needed to study and didn't like my interruptions. He'd also been to a lot of conferences lately as part of his residency. He told me how much he hated to leave me on my own at home, but at the same time he seemed eager to go.

I still had to ask him if he wanted to start a family in the first place before I went about stealing his study away from him. I shouldn't have been thinking too far beyond that moment, but I knew what his answer would be tonight when I finally got around to asking him about having a baby. He'd say yes and want to get started right away. I knew that much going in. I had to think ahead to the future.

I left the study and checked my cell in our bedroom. John hadn't called back or so much as sent me a text. I guess if he wanted me to think he was at work that was the best approach. John never had too much spare time in the ICU to play around with his cell. I hovered my thumbs over the screen, debating whether I should send him a text of my own to remind him to call me when he could. I just wanted to know he was okay and that nothing was wrong. He wasn't actually sick, was he?

My cell rang in my hand and startled me, so much so that I dropped it onto my bed like an idiot. I fumbled for the device and saw who was calling: it was John returning my call from earlier. "Hello, honey," I said. "How are you? Is everything okay?" I cringed at my words. I tried my hardest not to lay it on thick, but I couldn't help myself.

"Everything is fine. Why are you calling me at work?"

My heart skipped a beat as I caught John in an outright lie. I'd never done that before. Was he pretending to be at work so he could surprise me later with an anniversary gift? Or was this something else? My brain didn't want to think of the possibilities as Layton's stupid words echoed in my head. I had to answer him.

"No reason. I just missed you, is all. I wanted to hear your voice."

"I miss you, too, honey," he replied.

He didn't sound all that genuine, but I didn't call him on it. I tried to pinpoint the background noise I could hear down the line. Wherever it was, there was a decent amount of people chatting away. It had to be one of the malls. I smiled as I realized what a great husband I had. He really wanted to surprise me. He just had an odd way of going about it.

"So when do you think you'll be home? From work?"

John huffed down the phone. "You know what? Sooner than expected. I think I'll be in by five."

Five in the afternoon. He'd never been home before six or seven, ever. Residents weren't let out of work early like school kids breaking for summer. Again, I had to respond.

"Uh, that's great. It'll give you some extra time to get ready for tonight."

"Yeah it will," he said. "I'll have plenty of time to do what needs to be done."

John's voice was flat. I didn't know what to make of it. I said the first thing that came to mind. "Are you okay, honey? Have you had a bad day or something?"

John didn't reply for a few moments. All I could hear was the busy mall trying to compete with his voice. I instantly regretted my questions.

"Everything is fine. I'll see you soon, honey," he said.

The line went dead.

CHAPTER 15

Now

I walk out of Doctor Sylvain's session feeling like a balloon that has been drained of all its air. Did I really just confess seeing John to him? It all seems like a bad dream. My skin is weighing me down, pulling me toward the ground with every step as I recall the looks the doctor gave me when he mentioned the worst symptom of major depression: hallucinations.

Could it be true? Could the stress of John's funeral and the meeting with his lawyer in Portland have made me start seeing something that wasn't real? I know I saw a man who looked like my dead husband. But he was wearing a black hooded sweatshirt. I'd never seen John dressed that way. I have to stop thinking about that moment. Otherwise, I'll start seeing John in more places. Is that how this works?

I've dealt with a lot of pain over the last six weeks. And when I came out the other side of it, I felt as if I'd forgotten a lot of things about my life before that night, before that moment John tried to tell me something. Maybe it was time I started remembering my life.

Did he even say those words to me: "*Grace, I have to tell you...*"? Was that a false memory my brain created to mess with me? I shake my head. It couldn't have been. My mind wouldn't be so cruel. I remember that night in full. Every last detail down to the smell of the burning rubber tires. It's the days before that have become a blur.

"Are you okay?" Jennifer asks.

I half jump out of my skin as I turn to face her. I'd forgotten she brought me to the session, that she had taken time out of her day to help me. I must look completely insane.

"I, um..." I couldn't answer her question. How did one tell a friend that a psychiatrist thinks they might be hallucinating that their dead husband is alive?

"Grace? What happened in there? Is there anything I can do to help?"

I shake my head at her, my brow twisted. There's nothing anyone can do to help me. Including the doctor.

Sylvain told me to go back home and rest, that this sighting of John was hopefully a one-time event due to what he called acute stress. It was a key part of any hallucination. Burying John and going over his estate forced me to think about the night of his death over and over on some kind of sick loop. It's possible I became overwhelmed by it all and imagined John was still alive as a coping strategy.

He also told me that if I did see my dead husband again to contact him immediately. I'm far from being out of the woods, mentally. I need to get my eating back on track as well. I also now have to see Doctor Sylvain at least twice per week in person for the next month before he will consider letting me manage things on my own. I don't know how I feel about the extra session and the burden of having to see him in person.

"Let's get you home," Jennifer says.

"Okay," I reply, not arguing. I'm out of arguments. The doctor ate all of mine up. Jennifer holds me by my elbow like I'm too injured to walk by myself. I let her help me back to her car, where she opens the door. I climb in and burst into tears within a second.

"Hey, hey, hey. What is this? What's going on?" Jennifer asks.

I hold up a hand to her standing outside of the car as she lowers herself down to me. What has the session done to me?

"Everything is going to be okay, Grace. You just have to work through this time and keep fighting until you make it out the other side. I promise you things will get better."

The tears don't stop. It all takes over. I feel like a little girl who has done something wrong and has upset her parents. The last six weeks roll into one big ball of pain that floods my heart and tightens my chest. I clutch at my pants and grip a handful of fabric tight.

"Take it easy, Grace. Just remember to breathe. I'm sure the doctor told you about that. Just go through the process."

I nod at Jennifer with wide eyes and start going through the method Doctor Sylvain showed me to fend off a panic attack.

After a few deep breaths in and out, I begin to calm down enough to stop my blubbering. I wipe the tears away and close my eyes as I lean back in the passenger seat and focus on my breathing.

"Better?"

"Much," I say as I rotate my neck toward Jennifer. "Thank you for your help. I don't know what I would do without you here."

"Anytime. We gotta look out for each other, you know?"

"I'll pay you back for all of this garbage one day."

"Forget it. I'm happy to help."

I chuckle at her. It's not a happy laugh. "Who would want to help me? I'm a damn mess."

"You're not a mess. Stop saying bad things about yourself, okay? Anyway, we better get a move on. I gotta go back to work soon. I'll drop you home after we raid the grocery store for some much-needed supplies. I'm going to fill that fridge and pantry of yours with good food whether you like it or not."

"Okay," I say, welcoming the idea. I've been eating so terribly over the last few weeks. I need better sustenance than I'm currently giving myself. I was at a reasonable level of health before all this hell began.

We hit the road and head for home. Doctor Sylvain's office isn't too far away from town so we'll be back at my place quite soon. While I gaze out the window of Jennifer's car, I think about the final piece of advice Doctor Sylvain had for me before our session expired.

"I know this might sound a tad unconventional, but I feel it would be best for you to revisit John's grave next weekend. This will help remind your subconscious that he has indeed passed on and that his body is buried there. I know it seems like that might cause you more stress and trigger something else, but if you do it with the help of a friend—say Jennifer out there—it will only stand to benefit your progress."

"What if that doesn't help? What if it only makes things worse?" I asked.

"I don't think it will."

"But what if it does? What if I lose it out there?"

"You'll be okay, Grace. You just need to push through the pain and see his grave. Trust me, not doing so could lead to worse problems."

I don't like the idea one bit. I've just buried John and look what happened. Would seeing his grave again really help me? Would it help give me closure after the sighting of John in Portland? I am yet to run the idea by Jennifer. She's already done so much for me. I don't want to lump another trip onto her plate, but I have no choice. I have to get things under control.

On top of the favor, I also have to tell Jennifer about seeing John. At least, that's what Doctor Sylvain suggested. I'll try to rustle up the courage to tell her on this short trip home. There's also still the insurance money hovering over my head, but I can continue to push it out of my mind for now and keep it as my own secret. I know I should have told the doctor or Jenn about John's secret account and insurance policy to get it off my chest, but I don't want to face their judgment of John.

I find the courage to speak from deep down in my soul, hoping Jenn will somehow understand and say yes. I feel stupid needing to bother her with my strange problems. How did our relationship get so one sided with me needing constant favors from her? My fingers tremble as I turn to face her in the car.

"Grace. What is it?"

"Jenn, there's something else. I need to ask if you are free to take me to see John's grave next weekend. The doctor recommended I go see it again to help with my progress." I don't know how else to put it. I hope my rambling will be enough of an explanation for her to lend me a hand, but, then again, I know Jennifer will be able to do more if she knows the full truth. I have to tell her about Portland.

"Of course. Not a problem," she says.

"Thank you. I promise this won't become your life or anything. I just need to get through this month and show the doctor some progress. Then I can leave you alone."

"It's no bother," she says. "I'll do my part and see you through this time. You know I'm good for it."

I smile for a moment, relieved that she isn't asking more questions. I could use this moment to get out of telling her about John, but I know what needs to be done. It has to be said. "There's one other thing."

"Name it."

"The reason I need to see John's grave again is that..." I fade away with closed eyes. I hold one hand over my face. I can feel the panic coming in the distance, but I keep it at bay.

"Grace. It's okay. You can tell me."

I take a deep breath in and let it slowly out after a count. "Alright. Here goes. The reason I need to see John's grave again is to confirm he is actually dead. When I came out of the lawyer's office in Portland, I swear I saw him across the street staring at me."

"You saw him? Who's him?"

"John. I saw my dead husband standing on the opposite sidewalk without a care in the world."

Jennifer goes silent for a few seconds too many.

"You think I'm nuts, don't you?" I ask.

"No, not at all. I just feel so sorry for you. This whole thing has been so intense, and now it's starting to mess with you. How can this get any worse?"

"Hopefully it doesn't. The doctor thinks the pressure of burying John and handling his estate at the same time caused me too much stress and triggered a hallucination."

"A hallucination? Wow, I didn't think that was even possible. The things our brains are capable of doing."

"Yeah, it's great," I say with a forced smile.

"Don't worry," Jennifer says. "I'll do everything in my power to help you, okay?"

"Thank you."

"Don't mention it."

"No, seriously. Thank you," I say. "Because I don't want to end up having to volunteer myself to a psychiatric facility if this doesn't help."

"That's not going to happen. We won't let it, will we?"

"No," I mutter as we reach the outskirts of town. All I can hope now is that I don't see John again no matter how much I want to.

CHAPTER 16

The next few days creep slowly by. In that time, I try to establish some sort of routine that balances cooking, cleaning, eating, and relaxing that will get me through each day until Jennifer stops by at night to check in on me. I feel like an unstable shut-in who needs to be constantly checked on. Jennifer didn't have to help me like this but insisted upon the task. After she leaves, I head to bed, forcing myself to be ready for sleep by ten at the latest. I have to get a good night's sleep in to help wash away any stress.

In the two somewhat productive days—good by my new low standards—I also manage to get out of a phone call with the hospital until they try again in another week or so. I wonder what Doctor Sylvain would think about me dodging their calls in such a way. I have a follow-up session with him the next day and am determined to drive myself to his office for a change.

With no more entitlements left to keep my pay check coming in, I will soon be on unpaid leave. I know without a doubt that eventually the board at the hospital will take action and have me fired by some means. Frankly, I wouldn't be overly devastated if they had to let me go. There's too much of John tied up in that place. There always will be.

But the threat of losing my job does force me to think about John's estate paperwork. It won't be long until I run out of money. The house will go soon after once I fail to make repayments on the mortgage. I could prevent all that by signing the paperwork and mailing it all to Thomas Hart's office in a flash. That terrible lawyer would have what he needs within a day or so. But I know I won't send it today. The thought makes me nauseous. I can't let go of my husband. Not yet. Not until I have no other choice.

The rest of my week rolls together into one monotonous, but necessary, blur of repetition, broken up only by the visit to Doctor Sylvain. He notices my improvement straight away and almost seems impressed by it. I feel a sense of pride that I have managed to stick to a routine regardless of how dull it has now made my life. At least this way I'm not tempted to start thinking about John being alive. The doctor still recommends for me to go to John's grave despite my efforts to regain control of my life. I still don't know how I feel about the idea, but I agreed with him all the same. I have to.

The night before Jennifer is scheduled to pick me up and take me to the cemetery doesn't go as well as planned. My friend couldn't come round the way she had every other night this week to check on me. She had to help out her brother across town. I know it's silly and that I don't need her here checking on me like I'm a child, but the stability her visits provide are too much of a loss to deal with.

I find myself alone on the couch in my living room, laptop on my knees as I scour over every form of social media John once took part in. Part of my new regime had involved a strict ban on social media. Without Jennifer here to see me through to my bedtime, I cave like a house of cards and do what I can to find any photos of John online.

I scroll through John's Facebook timeline and his Instagram photos, taking in every word he ever typed while gazing at each picture he took. I go back through several years of selfies of the two us. In every photo we are happy. Even in some of the newer ones I can find the sparkle in both of our eyes that only a couple in love has. I can see the younger versions of us madly keen to spend our nights at clubs and bars in and around Portland. Things seemed simpler then. We didn't have a mortgage and weren't thinking about starting a family. Our studies and professional goals weren't the focus of our very existence the way they came to be.

The more time I spend in this virtual memory scape of our relationship, the more alive John feels in my heart. I'm treading on dangerous ground that I know Jennifer and Doctor Sylvain would not approve of. Not in the slightest. Still, I can't help myself. I have to keep looking. I can't stop for one simple reason: I almost feel happy.

My eyes dance between each post and photo as the corners of my lips curl into a smile no one can stop. On occasion, I look at the Facebook contacts list that shows me who is online. I know I should hide my presence away in case Jennifer sees me, but I figure she's too busy.

I catch sight of John's profile and see it remains grayed out. It will be like this forever until I request to have his profile turned into a memorial page. That won't happen for a long time. I can't bring myself to make such a final decision yet even on his profile.

I turn to the clock on the wall and realize the time. It's two in the morning. I've ruined my new schedule completely and broken several rules. I might be able to turn things around if I go to bed right now and promise myself to never do this again. But like a drug, this feeling will be hard to break.

Tired, I slap the lid shut, not properly closing my laptop down, and head to bed. After I stumble through my bedtime routine of brushing my teeth and tying my hair back, I fall into bed exhausted. Sleep eludes me.

Instead of falling into a deep REM cycle, I toss and turn with both eyes wired and awake from hours spent staring at a bright screen. What was I thinking? I should have stuck to the plan regardless of Jennifer's availability. What am I going to do when she can no longer stand to look after me like this?

After hours of frustration, I get up at around six in the morning and head back to my laptop in the living room. I power it on from sleep mode, so I can wipe my browsing history in case Jennifer decides to check in on what I got up to in her absence.

I see Facebook and Instagram still active on the screen and can't help myself. I start scrolling through it all again from the beginning. I've got a few hours before Jennifer will arrive to pick me up for the visit to John's grave, so I know exactly what I'll be doing to pass the time until then.

I go through John's online history again and absorb the dopamine hit I get from allowing myself to believe he is somehow still alive. Every time I see his smile or take in his laugh in a video, it feels like I could reach out and touch him, that he is just there waiting for me. It isn't fair to know that it's just a trick my brain is playing on me.

I stop where I am with Facebook still open. I can't keep doing this to myself, especially at the cost of my sleep. I glance at the time in the bottom corner of my laptop and realize that Jennifer will be here soon. "Crap," I let out.

Just as I am about to close Facebook and scrub my history, I notice something flash up in the corner of my eye. A single green dot. Typically, such a thing wouldn't mean much, but it shows up right next to a specific name, one which is impossible for it to be logged into.

I stare at my screen as the computer tells me that John Dalton is online. This can't be real.

A knock at the front door startles me. It takes me a few seconds to get my bearings as I realize Jennifer is at my door and I still have my laptop open. John's Facebook page stares back at me. I quickly check his status and discover he is offline. He's gone. "What the hell?" I blurt out with a croaky voice.

Was he ever online? Did I dream that John was active on Facebook or did that really happen? I can't tell. Maybe it was something else. I'd heard of hackers targeting dead profiles to exploit money from loved ones through various means. Could that have been it? We were, after all, in an age when even the dead got no respect. This felt different, somehow. At least that's what I want to tell myself.

Another knock at the door startles me into action. I quickly tidy up my laptop and hide it under the sofa. I feel a pit in my stomach weighing me down as I step out the short distance to the front door. I must look like hell. I can't shake the nerves swimming around in my gut as I transition my thinking from a terrible night's sleep to the prospect of going to the very place that may help me get better—or send me over the edge. I'm just glad Jennifer has the time to help me through the day. I can only hope she doesn't work out what I spent my night doing.

I open the door and see her standing neatly with her handbag held in both hands at the front of her body. "Hi," she says with a smile.

"Hey," I say. "Come in." I swing the door wider to invite Jennifer into the new version of my home I've been working on over the past week. The shades aren't drawn shut the way they used to be, but I let her down immediately when she sees me dressed in my slacks and a stained sweater. It's the same thing I wore for most of the time I spent moping around in the dark on my laptop.

"Sorry," I say with a croaky voice again. "I overslept. Had some bad dreams."

"That's okay," Jennifer says. "What kind of dreams?"

I turn toward the living room and stare at the sofa. I still don't know what was real and what was a dream.

"Nothing to worry about. I'll go get ready. Make yourself at home. I'll be as fast as I can."

I run to my room and rush through my usual process of getting dressed. I only put on half of my makeup and do what I can with my hair. I don't want to waste a second more of Jennifer's time, but I also don't want to go out there looking the way I do. It's not a good start to the day.

"What a week," Jennifer calls from the kitchen as I come back down the corridor. "Just went by in a blur." She undoes her coat and hangs it off the back of one of the breakfast bar stools John and I rarely used. She locks eyes on mine and asks, "How have you been?"

"Better. Still not great but getting there." I can't tell her about last night.

"That's good. Did your session with Doctor Sylvain help?"

"Yeah. It got me through to today, that's for sure." Almost.

Jennifer nods her head, eyes glued to mine as she takes a few steps toward me. "That's amazing. Really, I mean that. We just need to survive today, and then we can think about next week and how to tackle it."

I feel like a failing business the government is trying to pick up by its bootstraps and save. It makes me wonder why Jennifer cares so much. Surely, I'm not worth wasting time on. She deserves a better friend.

I shake my head. I can't start thinking that way. I have to see that I have worth, that I deserve to move on from what happened. I hear Doctor Sylvain's words echoing in my head. They sound right, but his advice is easier said than done, like most things in life. I feel so confused.

"You ready?" Jennifer asks as she scoops up her coat.

"Ready as I'll ever be." I smile my false smile at Jennifer, unable to give her a genuine expression yet. I don't want to offend her or get so emotional that I push her away with the real me again. No one wants to meet that woman. I have no one else who will do these kinds of things for me. Technically, I could ask my mom or a few other people I know to help me, but I don't trust them the same way I trust Jennifer. She doesn't even know half of the things that are going through my head or traumatizing me at the moment, and she is still willing to make sacrifices to help out. I'm lucky to have her in my life. Without a doubt.

I lock up the house and follow Jennifer out to her sedan. I don't know if it's a good thing or not, but we don't have far to drive to reach John's grave. If he were buried an hour away, I'd spend the whole time obsessing and thinking about this visit. But him being buried this close to home prevents me from having time to prepare myself for what comes next and how best to deal with it.

"Cold one today," Jennifer says.

I figure she's just trying to fill the silence. She's not wrong, though. I tug at my thick coat and wrap it tighter around my body as I huddle into myself for warmth. "Let's get this over with so we can get back inside."

"There's no need to rush," Jennifer says. "We need to do this right, no matter the weather."

I stop at the passenger side of the car and cast my gaze toward her. "I know. And with you by my side, I'll do this the right way."

"You will. There won't be any more hallucinated Johns in your life."

I let the thought sink in for a moment, letting my eyes slowly roll down to the car's roof. Maybe things are going to improve. Perhaps I will be able to start over without John. But is that what I want right now? John to be gone and forgotten, never to be thought of again in the same way out of a fear of losing my mind?

"Come on," Jennifer says, tapping her many rings on the metal roof of her car. "Time to get going."

I snap out of my daydream and open the door. I settle into the car and keep my eyes forward. I can't look back.

CHAPTER 17

Before I know it, we arrive at the cemetery. It looks different than it did from my previous visit, somehow bleaker despite a lack of rain. The graying weather overhead only serves to make the task of revisiting John's grave a tough one. It may not be raining down, soaking me to my core, but it will be soon.

"Are you certain you can do this?" Jennifer asks as we sit in her car staring out at the numerous headstones, old and new.

"I have to," I say without looking at her. I run a finger over her dashboard in a circle and gather a fine layer of dust. "Doctor's orders."

"I know."

"But?"

"No but. Just hoping this is the right thing to do. I didn't want to bring this up, and I swore to myself that I wouldn't."

"But?"

"But, I've been thinking about this, and I keep wondering if seeing his grave again so soon will, you know, make you hallucinate again."

I let out a long breath of air and face Jennifer. I think about John's Facebook page and seeing him across the street in Portland. Did I want to see him? Would I be happy to see John off in the distance staring at me? "I thought about that too. And it may be a possibility. The thing is, I have to face facts and allow myself to understand that John is dead. Until my mind can accept that, I can't move forward."

Jennifer absorbs my words for a moment. "Okay, then. Let's do this."

I nod to my friend and open the passenger door. We both leave the car at the same time and walk side by side up the small hill toward John's headstone. Jennifer interlocks my elbow with hers for support. Her presence is already helping to keep me on my feet and focused. The warmth and closeness of her body makes me feel human for a moment.

John's grave is near the back of the cemetery where all of the newly deceased are buried. We couldn't afford to give him anything more than a basic headstone in the ground, unlike some of the oversized ones that jut out of the field and point skyward. I never understood the appeal of wasting money on things like headstones and caskets, but I know John would have wanted something a tad more appealing than what I gave him. Still, I'm sure he would be happy knowing that I hadn't wasted money I desperately needed to keep me going. It wasn't like a fancy grave was going to bring him back from the dead.

I trip on the uneven ground but feel Jennifer's strength guide me right. I shouldn't be thinking about bringing people back from the dead in any capacity. Not with what's been going on lately. John wasn't online. He couldn't have been. Just as much as he wasn't in the street a week ago. My brain just did what it had to so I could cope with what the day was throwing at me. All I could hope for was that it righted itself sooner than later.

Those lines of therapy sounded good, but they were about as reassuring as the lies I continue telling myself on an hourly basis. This trip has to help me think clearly and accept the truth. Otherwise, I don't know what may happen next.

We move closer to the most recent headstones. I can see there is a newer one next to John's that is littered with alcohol bottles. A flash of laughter enters my mind, the memory of a blurry night spent drinking and celebrating before John had died. I shouldn't be thinking about that evening now.

I shake off the thought and inspect the new grave. Someone had died and had been buried while I was away. It had only been a week. Death never stopped. It couldn't be stopped. For some reason, the idea resonates within and pushes me on.

We reach John's final resting place and stand over the headstone. I stare down at the same words I read to myself seven days ago:

Beloved by family. Cherished by friends.
John Dalton
1982—2018

The inscription already seems different like it had been etched into the headstone years prior. "Life moves on," I say out loud.

"It does," Jennifer agrees. "Whether we want it to or not."

I purse my lips and nod. "You know what, I think I can do this on my own. You can wait for me by the car if you'd like."

Jennifer's mouth falls half open. "Are you sure about that? I mean I'm here to help you through this. I don't want anything bad to happen to you because—"

"It's okay. I've got this. I promise. If you see me acting nuts from the car, you can step in and bring me back to safety, okay?"

"Okay, I guess. Just yell out the second you don't feel right. Got it?"

"Got it."

I watch Jennifer as she cautiously backs away and turns to head for her car. She glances over her shoulders several times on her way down to check on me. I don't mean to send her away like this. She's a good friend, but I should be doing this on my own. I have to. I'll never move on if I need to rely on everyone around me just to do something so basic as visiting my dead husband's grave.

I start to acknowledge that John is dead by using certain words when I think about him. I have to. I can't cling to these thoughts about what I thought I saw or who I thought I saw. No matter how badly I want for John to somehow be alive, I have to say goodbye to him and really mean it.

"John. Here we are again. I know my last visit didn't go so well, but this time I'm here to do things right. What I am here to say to you is that I have to think about my future and let go of the past. I have to accept that you are gone. It's not going to be easy, but I know I have to do these things."

I close my eyes as a wave of thoughts hit me all at once. They settle on the money John left me by dying. That huge sum of funds will change my life, but it will never buy back what we had or what we could have had.

Tears streak down my cheeks as I imagine the life with John that will never be. The two-bedroom home I live in will never be filled with the joys of a child's laughter. It will never hold the happiness of a thriving family home that John and I could have provided together. We will never grow old as one.

I fall to my knees and weep. "John. I love you. Always, you got that? I don't care about anything else. Whatever it is you were trying to tell me, I don't care. I don't care about the money you left me or your secret bank account or the way you were acting that day. I don't care about any of it. I just want you to know how much I love and miss you. You will be in my heart forever. Always."

His headstone says nothing in return. Was I expecting anything else? Instead, it just sits there, lifeless and immovable. I feel like an idiot talking to a piece of slate and stone, but at the same time, it's starting to help.

"Okay, John. I gotta go. But I'll be back to visit you. Next time, I'll even drive here on my own. I promise. No more forcing other people to face my problems for me." I take a moment to breathe in deep and let the crisp morning air flow back out again. "Goodbye, my love."

I turn away from John's grave and slowly make my way back down to Jennifer. She waits for me with open arms and embraces me the second I'm within hugging distance. I sob uncontrollably to the point where I can feel everything coming out at once. I can't help it. The six weeks, the visit to Thomas Hart, seeing John in Portland, and finally seeing his profile come online. It all hits me hard. I feel my legs buckle until Jennifer is forced to take over and guide me down and into her car. I can't even stand on my own without her.

"We better get you home, Grace." She buckles me in like I'm a toddler who is incapable of handling her own safety. I feel so pathetic and useless, but at the same time, I welcome Jennifer's care. It's the only thing keeping me going.

As we drive away from the cemetery, I pull out my cell when I feel it vibrate in my coat pocket. I almost forget I have the thing on me. I slide it out and look at the display to see a single notification on the screen, wondering who could be sending me a message. I whisper the text message out loud, feeling each word as it falls out of my mouth:

It's time to move on.

CHAPTER 18

Then

John seemed weird on the phone, to say the least. Something was troubling him, and I had no idea what it could be. Today should have been a happy day considering we would be going out to dinner to celebrate our fifth wedding anniversary. Maybe he was just tired from shopping at the mall.

I wanted so badly to tell him not to bother, that he didn't need to buy me a single thing. I just wanted him to come home to me and enjoy his day off instead of him being out there busting his butt trying to find me the perfect gift. It's funny how much value we placed on physical items over simple time together.

Besides, nothing was going to top the present I had for him. Nothing. I almost wished I had the guts to give it to him this morning instead of waiting until tonight, but I wanted the moment to be right. I wanted everything to be perfect. I wanted to be able to look back on this dinner with a smile and remember it to be the very night we decided to start a family together.

It was silly of me to try and orchestrate perfection in such a way. I knew it was simply an excuse to delay the task at hand, as past experiences had shown me that things never worked out the way you planned them. I was confident, however, that this time things would be different. John and I would have our perfect evening made ever more full and complete when

I handed him that wooden pacifier. Nothing could possibly ruin that, right?

There was still some time before John got in, so I took a moment to relax on the sofa in the living room. I sat on my cell, scrolling like mad through my Facebook feed, looking for anything to distract myself with. A few funny videos kept me going for some time along with a discussion or two in one of the nursing groups I belonged to. I realized after too long a time that I was wasting my day off the way I always did, so I got off my phone and decided to do something more productive.

I pushed myself up off the sofa and stopped halfway across the room when I heard a knock at the door. "What the?" I said out loud. I had no idea who it could be coming to see me in the middle of the afternoon on a Saturday, so I headed for the front door. I could make out the shadow of a figure through one of the window panes by the door.

I squinted and held my eye up to the peephole and almost cursed out loud when I saw who was on the other side of the door. "Layton?" I unlocked everything and twisted the handle in a hurry. I stood with the front door wide open, my hand firmly gripping the lever. I was ready to slam the door shut. Layton stared back at me with his shiny blue eyes, long hair, and a smile he couldn't seem to contain.

"Layton? What are you doing here?" He looked different in his casual clothing, wearing jeans, a white shirt, and an open brown suede jacket. I was used to only seeing him in a suit with no tie at the hospital. I'd only seen him dressed like this a few times. It gave him an extra layer of confidence.

"I was just in the area and thought I'd drop in."

Alarm bells rang inside my head. "In the area? Are you serious? You live in Portland."

"I was visiting my cousin, Pete. He happens to live in Sherbrook, too."

I'd heard of his cousin before. Not once had Layton mentioned that he also lived in the same town as me. It sounded like a lie, but I wasn't going to get into that with him. Not yet.

"Are you going to let me in, or should I continue to stand out here like this?"

I shook my head with closed eyes for half a second. "Of course not. Come in." I released the handle and stepped to the side, gesturing for him to enter. I didn't exactly feel like entertaining a guest, especially Layton. But I couldn't send him away without a valid reason.

Layton slowly strolled into my house with a smug look plastered across his face like he owned the place. He'd been to our home before when we'd thrown a big barbeque one year, and knew the layout. Casually, he took it all in, absorbing the decor like he was thinking of moving in sometime soon.

We got halfway toward the kitchen when he slowed right down to compliment the space. "Nice house. I like what you and John have done with it. Oh, and what do we have here?" he asked as he leaned in toward a wall that was covered in framed photos of John and me on our wedding day. He stared at each one for a few moments with both hands on his leather belt, pushing back his jacket, as if he were in an art gallery.

"What are you doing?" I asked him. I didn't need him in my house, looking at those pictures, making things awkward.

"What? Just taking in the beauty of your home."

I shook my head. "No, what are you doing here? You were working earlier today."

"I was. I decided to head home. Told them all I was sick."

"You don't look ill."

He faced me. "I'm not. But I hear the excuse is working well today."

I shook my head at him. Did he overhear Deb telling me that John called in sick? Did he think me not knowing about it was some sort of joke?

"Isn't that a curious thing about working in a hospital," Layton said, continuing on before I could work anything out. "You stay at home and as far away as possible from the place when you're not feeling well. Makes you think."

I breathed out loud through my nose as I crossed my arms over my chest. "That's a fascinating thought and all, but it doesn't tell me why you are here in my house."

"Fair enough question, Grace. I'd want to know a few answers myself."

I clenched my fingers and suppressed the urge to yell. "I don't have time for this, Layton."

"Oh, I think you do. You see, I wasn't too happy with how things went between us back at the hospital. I think we need to talk about it, don't you?"

I resisted the urge to roll my eyes. "There's nothing to talk about. You told me about some rumor you made up. If you've come here to apologize, I don't want to hear it; I've got other things I need to do."

Layton chuckled at me with a sneering grin, keeping his eyes lowered. He brushed his long hair out of his face. "I was trying to warn you about the truth, Grace."

"The truth? There's no truth to any of what you have to say. You're still just trying to drive a wedge between John and me. For the last time it's not going to work."

Layton didn't listen to my words. He continued to hold his ground and laughed to himself, like there was a joke no one else knew about. None of this was funny, though. And I didn't care what was giving him so much joy. I'd had enough of his interruption.

"I think it's time for you to go." I brushed past him and stomped to the front door. I opened it back up and held out a hand and ushered for him to leave.

Layton walked toward me and nodded with a grin. "So, where's John? I heard he called in sick today. I figured he'd be here seeing as you guys are celebrating your five-year wedding anniversary and all."

I slammed the door shut before he had a chance to walk through it. "What the hell is your problem?" I took a step toward him, eyes wide. I was about ready to strike.

Layton held my stare. "You know exactly what my problem is. And you think you can just ignore it, but I got news for you, Grace: some things can't be avoided."

I opened the door up without taking my eyes off Layton. "Don't ever show up like this again. Got it?"

Layton didn't say a word and stepped slowly out the door. I followed him through and down the drive to make sure he was really leaving. I watched him with my arms crossed firmly over my chest as he climbed into his sedan and left.

With clenched fists, I waited by the curb until his car disappeared around the corner. I was surging with anger, unable to move until my mind shifted focus away from Layton and toward John. He would be home soon enough and make everything better. He always made things better.

CHAPTER 19

Now

I stare down at the text message as Jennifer drives me home. I read it again and again to myself as if there is more to the message other than "It's time to move on."

I can't help but remember the box of chocolates that had the exact same message accompanying them. All along I figured it was Jennifer who sent me that package as her way of getting me up and moving again and back to my life. I give her a quick sideways glance. Could she have sent this text message? No, impossible. She would never do that to me. Ever. Besides, she was too far away from me to even know what I said to John's headstone.

I check the number the message was sent from. It's not from my contacts list and looks like nothing I've ever seen before. What the hell? How could someone have sent me this message a moment after I said goodbye to John at his grave? Especially the part about moving on. It doesn't make sense and seems impossible. What was happening?

After a short drive, we're back at my house, sitting inside on my sofa. The drive was a blur. I haven't said a word to Jennifer. I don't know what to say to her or if I should be telling her about this message. I couldn't even send her on her way. Instead I had to allow her to come inside so I could say thank you for her support today. Really, I wanted her to leave in a hurry so I could get to the bottom of the strange text message.

I can't tell Jennifer a thing about it. She wouldn't believe me, would she? No one heard what I said at John's grave. I was there alone. At least I thought I was.

"Everything okay?" Jennifer asks me as I sneak a look at my cell for the hundredth time.

"Ah, yeah. I'm fine, I think. Just a bit shaken up by the visit to John's grave, I guess."

"That's understandable, Grace. No one expected this to be a walk in the park. Besides, you should be proud of yourself. You did it. You got through the visit without anything bad happening. Doctor Sylvain will be so happy to hear it."

I give her a weak smile. "Yeah, he will, won't he?" The doctor is the last person I'm thinking of in this moment. I stare away from Jenn's eyes before they beg me to tell her what I'm hiding in my hands. I need to move away from her. "I'm just going off to use the bathroom real quick. Back in a sec."

"Take your time," she says as I rush across the living room. "Can I get you anything while you're up?"

I think about requesting something strong and alcoholic but decide not to. She will assume I'm not coping and possibly relay the bit of information to Doctor Sylvain. "Just a glass of water, thanks."

I continue along past the bathroom to grab a notebook and pen from John's study. Once I've retrieved the notepad, I head to the bathroom. Inside, I run the tap in the sink and pull out my cell. I stare at the text message and copy the number down to the notepad while I pretend to use the toilet. As soon as I can, I plan on finding out whose number the message belonged to. Maybe it was only a wrong number and an unfortunate coincidence, but I can't convince myself of that. Not yet, anyway.

"Grace? Are you okay in there?" Jennifer calls from outside the bathroom door.

"Uh, yeah. Be out in a second," I say. Is she following me? Checking up on me like I'm too stupid to use the toilet? I ignore Jennifer's eagerness and keep my eyes glued to my cell as I try to decipher it some more.

Time ticks on, running out and making me more nervous with every second. I know I have little choice but to lock my phone and put it in my pocket and get back out to my friend. But this message can't be real, can it? It has to be a cruel joke someone is playing.

I shut off the tap and move toward the door, taking a deep breath in and out as I go. I gently open the bathroom door and poke my head out first. Jennifer has moved on back to the living area, fortunately. I breathe a sigh of relief.

I decide to duck off to my bedroom and stash my cell under my pillow. I don't want Jenn to catch me looking at my phone and see the message. I need to understand what it is first before I go showing a single person, especially one that is willing to pass along my paranoid thoughts to my therapist.

"Everything okay, Grace?" Jennifer asks when I come back through to the kitchen. I can see my glass of water sitting on the island bench. I take it in both hands and drink it down in a flash.

"Sorry. I'm fine," I say as I catch my breath. "Just needed a minute to freshen up." I give her a smile I know is too much and can feel myself blinking a lot. I need to get it together or else Jennifer will see right through me. How does a normal person act?

"So, what did you want to do now?" she asks.

"Oh, I hadn't thought too far ahead, sorry. But, to be honest, I'm feeling kind of tired." I rub the back of my neck and try to force a yawn. Something half-baked comes out instead. I need to work on my acting.

"You probably need to rest then," she says.

"I do. Thanks, Jenn, for everything. You've been wonderful as always. I owe you."

"You want me to go?" she asks with narrowed brows.

I freeze. What the hell do I say to that? If I say yes then she'll think I don't want her here. It won't come across all that grateful given what she's done for me lately. But at the same time, I want to find out who sent me that message. I can't have her here while I'm doing that. I can feel the dilemma eating away at me from the inside, taking me apart, piece by piece, until I can find an answer.

"Grace? Do you want me to leave you be? Because I can stay out here while you go and take a nap."

"No, that would be a waste of your day. I'll be fine on my own, I promise. But we could meet up later, though. After lunch, if that suits? I just need a few hours to rest."

Jennifer holds her gaze on me, analyzing the way Doctor Sylvain does. Her eyes sting like laser beams. I fight the urge to show my frustration and instead attempt to throw her off the scent.

"Okay," Jenn says. "I can do that. I'll swing by around two in the afternoon. I've got a few things I need to sort out in town, anyway."

Whether I mean to or not, I let out a sigh of relief. Fortunately, Jennifer was distracted momentarily by the process of gathering her handbag and coat up from one of the breakfast bar stools to notice. I smile at her and open my arms to give her a quick hug goodbye. I hope it's not too much or too little.

Jennifer accepts my half-hearted excuse to be alone and leaves soon after. I lock the front door as I hold my breath the second I see her disappear down the drive and then let it out. I take a second to close my eyes as I lean against the solid entry into my home and remember to control my breathing. I can't let myself get overwhelmed by this message. It could bring me crashing down considering how much of a mess I already am.

I charge to my room like a kid at Christmas, stopping by the lounge to grab my laptop first. When I'm close to my bedroom, I bump into a small hallway table that is mostly for decoration and knock over an empty vase. It once held flowers given to me after John's first funeral, but now it shatters to pieces and scatters itself across my path.

"Dammit," I shout at myself. I stop and run a hand through my hair, trying to focus on finding out who sent me that text. I can sort the vase out later.

Ignoring the mess, I tiptoe over the shards and walk into my room toward the large bed I'd grown used to sleeping in on my own. For the first two weeks after John died, I'd stuck to my side of the bed, convinced I wasn't allowed past that invisible threshold in the middle. It took me all that time to realize I could sleep wherever I wanted to. John would never need it again. I'd give anything to have to share my bed with him again.

I shake off the thought before it grabs hold and place my computer down on my bedside table, then reach under the pillow. I almost expect my cell not to be there, secretly praying that the message is something my loopy brain has dreamed up in another moment of stress. But no, that would have been too easy. I hold the device in my hand and unlock the display to see the message there again.

Nothing has changed. I contemplate again if this is just some sick joke someone has decided to pull on me, figuring I'd be visiting the grave at some point. But it dawns on me that this would have been done by someone who knew I would be visiting John's grave today. Only Jennifer and the doctor had any knowledge about it. What reason would they have to mess with me?

"This has to be real," I say out loud almost like a mantra. I shake my head and place my cell down on my bed and reach for my laptop. I plug in its power adapter, knowing the battery will be dead after my session on Facebook and Instagram last night. After a delayed loading screen adds to my anxiety, I am greeted with a series of pop-up messages telling me a million things that are wrong with my aging computer. I close them all instantly with a huff, wishing I'd shelled out for a tablet instead. I open a browser and wait a frustrating amount of time for the homepage to load.

With my cell by my side, I enter the number into the search bar along with the words "cell number." I get too many results of pages claiming to be able to tell me who owned the cell number. I enter it and am met with a message that blocks the results until I pay a fee. "Dammit," I mutter. Without another thought, I rush out of my bedroom, bypassing the shards, to find my purse to retrieve my credit card. I stare at the card and think about John and his secret account. What other secrets was he hiding?

I charge back to my laptop in my bedroom, determined to not let thoughts of John distract me and enter my details. I'd pay any fee right now to get to the bottom of this message.

Once my order is processed, I am met with a loading screen that pushes me to my limits. Finally, the information comes up. I read the results out loud.

> *This number is not known to our database. You have not been charged for this search.*

CHAPTER 20

I spend ten minutes cleaning up the broken vase outside of my bedroom in an attempt to distract myself from disappointment. The online search to try and determine the owner of the cell number is proving to be impossible. I'm half tempted to call Jennifer back to my house so I can tell her everything. In one morning, my world has gone from messed up to crazy with a single text message. It takes a bit of convincing, but I force myself to deal with the problem alone. At least for now.

The response I got from the website doesn't help me in any way. I search online for an explanation as to why I got the result I did, but all anyone can say is that the number is most likely unregistered. I'm left feeling more annoyed than when I started.

Instead of calling Jennifer back, I continue to stare at the message. I can feel myself becoming obsessed with the single sentence.

It's time to move on.

After ten minutes of this, I still can't work out if I received this message on purpose or not, although I'm leaning heavily toward the text being a deliberate move.

I try to understand why someone would want me to get this message. What would be in it for them? I say the words out loud again as if the hundredth time will make the difference. "It's time to move on."

I spoke to John's headstone about moving on. Had someone been close by, listening in to me? I close my eyes and picture the cemetery. It's quite open, even at the top of the hill where John is buried. How could anyone have heard those words without me seeing them?

I push away an overwhelming desire to freak out, and remember to breathe. In and out. In and out. The calm starts to kick in. I begin to quiet down enough to think a little clearer. I decide that I am reading too much into the message and figure my best bet is to ignore it for now. What else can I do?

As I discard the broken shards into the bin in my kitchen, I fight back the urge to fix myself the kind of drink you shouldn't have on your own on a Saturday morning. I think about the late nights I once spent drinking with friends, celebrating life. It had become something John and I did less and less before he died.

I don't want to start any bad habits, so I forget about drowning my sorrows and ignoring the truth with a bottle of wine. I managed to survive my six weeks of near solitude by avoiding alcohol. It was the only achievement I managed in the dark time. I knew even a single sip of alcohol could have caused me to start depending on the liquid to get through each day. I'd seen it at the hospital. If I had foolishly added in drinking to my horrible depression, who knows how long I would have stayed inside my bedroom for? I doubted I would have ever emerged.

I pull out my cell from the pocket of the slacks I decided to change into and glance down at the message again. Maybe I could pretend I never received it. I could just delete the thing and forget it ever found its way into my cell. But I can't. With the sighting of John and seeing his profile online on Facebook, I'm starting to question my own sanity levels.

The thought makes me grab a pen and paper and write down each event that has messed with my head. I start a list of sorts, not knowing what else to call it. It's brief and only makes sense to me.

- I saw John in Portland across the street outside Thomas Hart's office.
- I saw John come online on Facebook.
- I got a message from someone that read "It's time to move on." Same message found on the box of chocolates.

The message is the only item on the list that I can see is proof that I'm not losing it. It's proof that someone is messing with me. But who and for what reason?

A chill runs down my spine. I move away from the kitchen and move around the corridor and reach the gap toward the front door. The entrance to my home has a lot of glass windows that I had previously covered up with the shades. In my attempt to heal by letting in the light, I have left large openings in my home. Large portals for anyone to see inside.

Am I being watched right now? Could a person be staring at me through a telescopic lens as I gaze out into the street? I freeze on the spot, halfway to the door, crippled by the very idea. My eyes fall shut, but my feet keep going, determined not to let fear win.

I force myself to continue to the door. As long as I don't look outside, I can make the short trip to close the curtains and regain control. If I open my eyes and see a car parked in the street watching my house, I'll be too paralyzed with terror to do anything.

My feet shuffle, one step at a time. "Don't stop," I whisper. "Don't open your eyes." It's working. Slowly but surely, I'm going to make it, I hope. My hands reach out as I bump into the wall by the entrance. The pain opens my eyes enough to let the sunlight from outside into my retinas. I quickly seal them shut again and roughly pull across the curtains over the window panels.

My mouth billows open as I realize I'd been holding my breath. I suck in a rapid lungful of air and reach out to the front door. I double check the latch. It's locked, so when I feel the tension of the deadbolt I press into the wood and slide down the paneling of the door into a heap on the floor.

I land on my butt and plant both hands on my head. I shake my head and wonder how in the hell I have managed to get myself into such a state. I can't move.

My hand falls to my pocket and pulls out my cell again as an overwhelming sense of fatigue kicks in.

I call Jennifer.

CHAPTER 21

Jennifer knocks to come inside, waking me. Somehow, I fell asleep in the time it took her to reach me. She said she'd be over in under an hour. Apparently, it was enough time for my body to shut down and fall asleep. My cell sits in one hand where I left it as I nodded off, so I place it in my pocket before I drop the damn thing.

I feel the impact of Jenn's knuckles through the wood of the front door vibrating down my back as she continues to knock. I haven't moved from the pathetic spot I made for myself on the floor since I called her, but now I need to get up.

I roll away from the door and push up to stand. I need to put my game face on before I open up. I don't know what I'm going to say to Jennifer or how much I'll let her in on what I've discovered. All I said over the phone was that I needed her right now. It's the truth.

I go over my options. On the one hand, I need to tell someone about the million thoughts running through my head, but on the other, well, I don't want Jennifer to think I'm losing the plot once she hears about me scouring through John's social media. She'll have no choice but to let Doctor Sylvain know that I had been actively looking at photos of John on Facebook and Instagram. I still can't believe I saw him come online and have no idea if I was merely dreaming.

I take a peek through the peephole in the door before doing anything. Jennifer is standing on the other side, worry clouding her face. I undo the lock and turn the handle as guilt sets in. When I open the door just a crack, Jennifer bursts inside, eager to see what is wrong.

"Are you alright? What happened?"

Her concern does wonders to reassure me already, but what I told her on the phone has left her with too many questions. I should have thought this through a little better and not panicked.

"Grace? Talk to me."

"I'm okay. Physically. It's just, well..."

She leans forward at me as I quickly shut the door without looking outside. I lock everything and check the handle three times like I have OCD. It doesn't encourage Jennifer to back up from me.

"Well?" Jennifer asks.

"I'm not coping. I thought I could handle today, but clearly, that was a mistake."

Jennifer tilts her head slightly to the side and furrows her brows in at me. "And?"

"And I needed you here to help me."

"Nothing else, though? There's nothing else that's happened?"

She knows I'm lying to her. How does she do this? It doesn't matter; I should be able to tell her the truth. I feel stupid forcing her to come back like this again for no reason other than for my own comfort. "I'm sorry to be a giant pain, Jenn. I don't know what came over me. I didn't mean to waste your time. You can go. I'll be okay."

"Go? I'm not going anywhere until you tell me what the heck is going on. I think I've been patient enough. It's time you let me in on some of what's upsetting you."

"You're right," I blurt. I didn't want things to come to this, but I no longer have a choice in the matter. "Come and sit with me on the sofa and I'll tell you what's been happening."

Jennifer nods. "Good, because you should start telling me more. It will help to get some things off your chest. I don't need to hear everything but tell me a few things at least. I think you'll find it will lift some of your burdens."

How right she is. The list I created is going to consume me if I let it. I can feel its words eating at my soul. But even the list doesn't hold all of my thoughts.

We reach the sofa in the lounge room, and both sit down. Jennifer stares straight at me and crosses her arms. "So, tell me. Why did you call me here in such a hurry?"

Her gaze rushes straight through me. "I had to," I say. "It was an emergency."

"Okay," she says. "What kind of emergency?"

"The kind that forces you to call a perfect friend back to come and save you."

Jennifer smiles at my strange compliment. "I'm far from perfect, Grace. We all are, so why don't you tell me what this perfect friend is here to save you from."

"Okay," I say, letting out the word with a long breath. I still don't know what to tell her or in what order. I decide to start with something small and work my way up. I'll get to that message on my cell eventually. I just need to give Jennifer my problems one at a time. "The visit to see John's grave today. Well, it got to me more than I ever thought it would. I'm worried that I'm on a slippery slope as a result, and that I won't pull through to the other side of it all."

Jennifer seems a tad frustrated by my vague response, but she keeps her disappointment to herself. Soon she'll wish she didn't know the truth. "Grace, it's okay to feel that way."

I smile out of the corner of my mouth. It's not a happy face coming out of me, but one that is trying to cope with what exactly it is that has me so frazzled, as Jennifer says. Is it the words John said to me a second before he died that are eating me up? Is it the burial of my dead husband that's niggling at my brain? Is it the life insurance policy that needs addressing? Or the damn text message telling me to move on?

Jennifer leans toward me on the couch and places a hand on my forearm. "You can tell me, Grace. I'm not going to blab anything to anyone. Anything you say is purely between the two of us."

I stare into her eyes, unsure where to go from here. Maybe I should tell her every waking thought in my head and see how she handles it. But is it too much at once? There's a lot in there swimming around.

"I need to show you something," I blurt out with closed eyes.

"Okay?" Jenn says, dragging out the word.

"I got a text as we left the cemetery this morning."

"A text? From who?"

"That's the thing. I don't know who sent it," I say as I pull my cell out of my pocket.

"What does it say?" Jennifer asks.

I navigate to my text app and bring up the most recent messages. Instead of seeing the text in question staring back at me, I see Jennifer's name as the most recent. As my heart skips a beat, I scroll down through the list, sailing past texts sent to me by family and friends giving me their condolences until I reach John's name. There's no message that reads, "It's time to move on."

"What?" I hear myself say out loud. "Where is it?" This can't be happening.

"Where's what?" Jenn asks.

I glance up to her eyes, mouth agape. "There was a message here that said one sentence."

"One sentence? What do you mean?"

I close the app and reopen it. Nothing. It's gone. "No, God. Please. It has to be here."

"What is it, Grace?" Jenn asks.

I place one hand on her shoulder. I can feel my eyes doubling in size as a panic sets in. "You don't understand. I got a message from someone. It was here a minute ago, I swear it."

"It's okay, Grace. Just calm down for a moment. Let me take a look with you."

"Okay," I say, hopeful Jennifer knows how to find it. Maybe I accidently deleted it when I fell asleep. She can find it. I hand over my cell and watch as she does a full close on the app and tries again. She can't find any texts from a strange phone number. She tries the deleted folder of the app as well. Empty. I feel a sting of fear cover my forehead.

"There's nothing here, I'm afraid. Are you sure about this?" Jenn tilts her head at me like I'm a confused little kid.

A flicker of hope runs into my head as I remember writing down the number on a piece of paper.

"I wrote it down." I run to my bedroom, knowing the note should be somewhere in there. I tear off my sheets and go through both of my bedside tables. Nothing.

"My laptop," I yell as I think to check my browser history. I power it on from sleep mode, avoiding a lengthy boot time and open my browser. I immediately go to the history panel with a wild grin across my face. "This will show her what I mean," I mutter aloud. My grin soon freezes and slowly fades as I see that my history has been completely cleared. Did I do that? I have been wiping it lately, but I couldn't have this time. I back away from my computer.

I return to Jennifer with both hands on my head, ready to burst into tears.

"Dammit."

"Any luck?" Jenn asks.

I shake my head. "It's disappeared, too. I thought it was in my room on my computer and a piece of paper." Tears streak across my face as I realize the number is entirely gone.

"What did the message say?" she asks.

My eyes find Jennifer's. I don't know if I can tell her without sounding nuts, but I have to. "It's time to move on."

CHAPTER 22

Then

The unexpected visit from Layton left me shaking as I charged back into my house. I found myself pacing around the living area, muttering away at the sheer nerve of the guy to show up like that and lay more suspicion on John for taking a day off. I decided to take a hot shower to calm myself down.

As I stood under the enveloping warmth of the hot water, I felt my shoulders lower as my neck muscles released any pent-up anger this day had caused me. In the dreamlike rhythm of the water's flow, I almost forgot Layton was ever here, but I couldn't entirely shake him.

I thought back to the hospital and Layton trying to tell me that John was flirting with one of the nurses and taking down her number. I knew it was just a plot to create a bit of doubt in my head, but at the same time, I couldn't silence the voice in the back of my head that wanted to believe the lie. Could John have been out all day with someone else? It didn't seem plausible. He wouldn't cheat on me, right? It wasn't in him to do such a thing, was it? I could feel the lies burrowing their way down into my subconscious. I had to fight back and not let them in.

I finished in the shower and quickly threw a towel around my head and wrapped my body in a dressing gown. I would dry myself off properly once I'd completed one task that was starting to eat away at my brain and wouldn't let go. I rushed out of the bathroom, through my bedroom, to John's study, pushing away any guilt that came over me in the process. If I were going to find anything to suggest there was a problem with my husband of five years, it would be in his office. The place he spent all of his spare time in.

I stopped at the open space of the small area and saw his desk covered in papers. I let out a sigh at the mess. It was not the way I would keep such an area. I vaguely remembered him messing around in there for a few hours last night. I had to be careful not to put anything out of order in case he remembered where he left each item on the desk.

I did all of my personal development in our bedroom using my laptop. I stayed on top of it most of the time and never felt that overwhelmed by my studies. John, on the other hand, seemed to always be drowning in his work. I don't know how he did it. He managed to work sixty-plus hours a week while studying and maintaining a somewhat active social life. He also had to squeeze in time with his wife. How would he handle a child on top of all that? Would a baby ruin the delicate balance we'd struck up?

I sat down in John's squeaky desk chair. I resisted straightening up his medical journals no matter how loud the voice in my head demanded me to do so. The one time I did, John got mad at me, saying he had things in a certain order I couldn't understand.

I leaned my head around some of his medical journals. Most had an abundance of sticky notes jutting out of their pages with scrawled words only John understood. Eventually, these resources would become outdated by the medical community and end up being discarded like trash.

I began to wonder how John could have time to cheat on me given his workload. It almost seemed impossible, but the doubt Layton injected into my bloodstream said otherwise. It wasn't just Layton's words making me search John's private study. Lately, he'd been in here more than normal. He took phone calls late at night in a hushed tone, and always seemed to be a touch grouchy whenever I came over to offer to make him a coffee. I didn't want to intrude like this, but I felt like now I had to.

Once I'd checked and carefully placed back every scrap of paper on the desk, I started on the drawers. The left side of his oak table was almost empty with only a few pens inside rattling around. When I opened the right-hand drawer, I found more rubbish and pens. How many of them actually worked? I felt like replacing them all with functioning pens. It was an odd thought to have when snooping on my husband.

Just as I was about to close the right drawer back up, I noticed something seemed off: the bottom of the drawer was higher up than the left side. I pulled open the left one again and confirmed that the right was a few inches higher up.

"What is this?" I asked myself with a scrunched brow. I reached into the right drawer again and felt around for what could only be a false bottom. I found an edge and jammed my fingernail in to lift up the floor of the drawer. What I saw made little sense.

Scrap after scrap of random bits of torn paper littered the hidden section of the drawer. I pulled the first one out and saw a few numbers scribbled down in John's handwriting. But the piece of paper was only a tiny section of something that had been torn up in an attempt to destroy it. I looked through the rest, wondering if they could be pieced together, wondering why they were sitting in a hidden part of John's desk I had no idea existed.

I took every scrap of paper out and soon realized that none of the pieces fitted together. All I found were fragments of numbers. What did these remnants represent?

I saw John take down her cell number. Layton's voice echoed in my brain. Every word stabbed my heart. Could there have been some truth to what he was saying? I swept the scraps into my palm and took them with me. I didn't even bother to close the open drawer. I was too furious to think straight.

John was going to have to answer a few questions the second he got home, questions I was sure he thought he'd never hear in his life. In a matter of words, he would determine our future and whether or not we would ever have a baby together.

CHAPTER 23

Now

"What do you think it means?" Jennifer asks me.

I take in a deep breath and slowly release it back out. The breathing technique doesn't work. "Okay, here's the full story. When we visited John's grave this morning, I spoke to his headstone and told him that I needed to think about my future and that I needed to move forward and let him go. I said my goodbyes and then came down to see you. The next minute, my phone buzzes and I get a text from a strange number saying, 'It's time to move on.'"

"And that text is gone now, right?"

I try not to search for any tones in her voice that suggest she might not believe me. "Somehow, yes. Along with a note I made of the number the text came from." I let a moment pass as I shake my head. Would I believe Jennifer if she were telling me such a story? I continue before I give up. "I even tried to trace the number with one of those websites before it was deleted from my cell. The results came back as a number not listed in their database."

"Did you try any other websites?"

I shake my head. "I didn't think to. And now my browser history has been wiped."

Jenn's brows raise and lower in thought. I don't need her to say it. I can see there's doubt in her eyes.

"Okay, so let's just say someone is telling you to move on. In what way exactly?"

I've never thought of this until now. I figured someone was just messing with me. I never thought there was a purpose to their words. I'm so naïve. Was it Layton trying to tell me to move on so he could make a move? Could he be that desperate? He was one of the few people who hadn't offered me their condolences. In fact, I hadn't heard from him at all since John died. I never thought anything of it until now.

There has to be another reason, though. I'm simply failing to see it. Maybe I just need to tell Jennifer more, or I need to tell her everything.

"I don't know exactly, but maybe you can help me once I fill in a few blanks for you."

Jenn leans forward. "Are you about to tell me everything that's been going on?"

"Yes. And I'm sorry I haven't done so sooner. I wanted to, but this isn't easy."

"I realize that, Grace, but you have to understand, again, that I'm here for you and will do what it takes to help. I can't do that if I don't know what's happened. So please, tell me everything. Get it all off your chest."

※

It all came out; well, most of it. I told Jennifer the things I could stand her to know: the last words John ever spoke to me, the meeting with Thomas Hart, the life insurance policy, John's secret bank account, and the foolish time I spent on social media that lead to me seeing John online. My embarrassing life has been thrown onto the table for consumption.

Jennifer takes it all in without a single piece of judgment on her face. Either she's really good at this, or she just wants to know what's been going on with me.

"So, there. That's everything I can think of. You probably think I'm nuts, don't you?" I ask.

"What? No. Don't be silly, Grace. What you did now took a lot of courage and heart. It couldn't have been easy."

I take a deep breath and focus. "So what do you make of the text with all of that out in the open?" I ask her.

Jenn gives me a slight sigh. "Well, I guess a few things jump out at me."

"Like what?"

"Like the insurance money. You signing that document is the perfect way to 'move on' and start over. It will mean financial freedom and a new life. Seems like a good thing to me."

"Okay. But why would anyone send me a reminder about it in the form of a text message? What's in it for them?"

Jennifer smiles at me, but not with her usual calming expression that fills a person with hope. It's the face you give a person when you have something awkward you want to say without harming their feelings.

"What is it?" I ask.

"You're not going to want to hear this, but..."

"But what?"

Jennifer stares away from me for a moment as she exhales. She refocuses on me. "What if you sent yourself that text? What if it never existed in the first place?"

"Are you serious?" I ask.

"Hear me out. You've been under a lot of stress lately. Maybe your subconscious was trying to tell you what to do. Maybe it is trying to get you to move forward and think about what happens next. God knows John made the right call having that insurance in place. Sure, he didn't tell you about it, but I'm glad for your sake that he took the cautionary step to cover you both."

I squint my eyes closed, not wanting to hear John praised regarding the insurance money. I still wasn't comfortable with the hidden bank account he opened to fund the policy.

"Grace? Are you okay?" Jenn asks.

"It can't be that simple, can it?" I ask, ignoring her question.

"Maybe it is. Maybe one part of you is fighting it off by trying to find John online while another part of you is saying 'it's time to move on.'"

It sounds crazy to think she could be right, but Doctor Sylvain did say I was potentially suffering from major depression. Hallucinations are one of the symptoms. Maybe part of me wants to take a step forward while the other half is fighting for the past? I don't say much else. I don't get upset either. I've done enough of that for one day. Her words make sense. I just don't want to hear them right now. So much so that I try to change the subject.

"Enough about me and my strange life. What's been happening with you?" I ask.

"We should keep talking about everything, Grace. Don't worry about me."

"No, I need to get out of my head for a few minutes. Tell me about you. Please."

Jenn seems pleasantly surprised by my request and starts telling me about her life and her problems for a change. It's so easy to get wrapped up in my world that I forget other people have difficulties in their lives as well.

"I'm getting really sick of it," Jennifer says, talking about her boss and his habit of forcing her to work back thirty minutes every day without any extra pay. "And it's never my fault the day gets away from him. He's the one who is always messing around making jokes."

I nod away at Jennifer, letting her get it all out. Jennifer has been talking about quitting for at least a year now, but we both know she won't do it without a big enough push.

With the gossip in my system, I feel my anxiety begin to lessen a slight amount, but not enough. It can never ease up enough for me to forget my problems. I start to wonder if Jenn is right about it all. Was the text real? Or did my brain create it as a way to communicate what needs to be done? I know that insurance form is the last thing keeping me tied to John. I know I have to sign it to properly let him go. Maybe once that task is done, I'll stop having these hallucinations. I'll stop seeing John.

This is all too much and I feel a layer of sweat coat my palms.

I tell Jennifer that I need to use the bathroom, but I head for my bedroom instead. I pace around, crippled with doubt. Am I overreacting? Should I just ignore the world and continue with my life? Should I do whatever I have to to move on?

I stop pacing by my bedroom window and glance down into the street. In the distance, I see a man on the corner staring straight at my house. He's wearing a black hood up from his sweatshirt in the same way the man in the street who I swore was John did. Why is he staring at me? Is he watching me? The man is so far away that I can't see his eyes. He could be waiting for a friend. Or, he could be waiting for me.

"There you are," Jennifer says from the doorway.

I almost leap back from the window.

"Whoa, didn't mean to disturb you, Grace. I was just a bit concerned when you didn't answer my call."

"Oh, sorry. I mustn't have heard you." I couldn't hear a thing.

"It's fine, honey. But, um, you seem a bit jumpy just now."

My wide eyes dance around the room trying to dream up an excuse. I glance back out the window and see that the man is gone. My jaw drops open.

"Grace?"

I snap my head towards Jennifer and say the first dumb thing that my brain thinks of. "I was paying a bill real quick. It was overdue and needed to be paid straight away. I keep forgetting things like that, these days. So stupid."

"What a pain," she says with a laugh. "Don't stress. I hate when that happens."

"Yeah," I say in return. An awkward silence cuts across the air. Does she know I'm lying? I stare at Jennifer's face and can tell she is about to grill me further on why I'm really up here. She does know I'm lying to her. How many more times can I get away with it before she really cracks down on me?

"So, Grace, I was thinking—"

"I'm sorry," I blurt out loud, cutting her off.

"You're sorry? For what?"

"For this. For everything." I shake my head. "I keep dragging you to my house or making you drive me around town just to waste your time."

"It's not a waste of time. None of this is. I'm here to help you. It's time to heal, Grace. You do need to move on."

Her words almost haunt me. Move on. Did Jennifer send the chocolates? Did she send the text? She couldn't have, right? Not her. The easy move worked on me before, but not now. Not when there are so many unanswered questions. Plus, I don't even know how safe I am right now. Can I even go outside?

"How about we go take a walk? It'll do you good to get some fresh air into your system."

"A walk, you say? As in outside?" Is she reading my mind?

Jennifer squints her eyes at me with flat lips. "That's generally where you go for a walk."

I try to think of an excuse. Anything to get me out of this, but I draw a blank. My brain is too overwhelmed.

"Come on," Jennifer says as she moves toward me and grabs my elbow. "You know it will help." She guides me out of my bedroom. I don't stop her.

Before I realize what is happening, Jennifer has taken me to the front door for the walk she so badly wants. Is this part of something else? It can't be. The sight of the front door instantly reminds me of the vanishing man out there. Just the outline of his body sends chills down my spine. What was he doing?

My legs freeze up before we reach the door, bringing us both to a halt. We almost trip over one another as I dig in.

"What's going on?" she asks me when she releases her grip on my arm.

"I can't do it. I can't go out there."

"Why not?" she says, her hands splaying out wide.

I can see I'm pushing her patience to the limit, but I can't do what she wants me to do. "I can't explain why—"

"You can't explain? I thought you were going to tell me everything? I thought we were being honest with each other?"

"I have. I am. Just you don't understand, Jenn."

"Please then, for the love of God, tell me exactly what it is that I don't understand."

My mouth falls open to answer, but I don't know if anything will come out.

CHAPTER 24

Jennifer takes me back to my bedroom as if she knows it's the one place I might be able to calm down. With the man I saw in the street out of my window, I don't know how true that really is, but I feel somehow safer in this space. Jenn stares at me, waiting for an answer to my odd behavior. With raised brows, she leans forward toward me, eager to understand why I've been acting so strange.

My jaw bobs up and down as I try with all of my heart to force the words to come up from the pit of my soul. I get out a half-garbled bit of nonsense and quickly close my mouth. I can't say anything. What's wrong with me?

"So?" she asks.

"I'm sorry," I say. "I can't tell you."

Jennifer shakes her head as she exhales. "So be it," she says. Without another word, she turns away from me and walks out of my bedroom and down the corridor toward the front door.

"Wait, where are you going?" I ask. She can't leave me like this.

Jennifer doesn't turn back to face me. "I don't want us to fight over this, Grace, so I'm going to go. It's clear to me that you need space."

I take a step toward her and try to argue against her point, but I have nothing at my disposal that won't sound forced. There's nothing short of the truth I can say that will keep her here, and I don't know what that is anymore. I don't know if that man out there was real. If I tell her about him and he isn't real, where does that leave me with Doctor Sylvain? I lower my head, defeated, and let Jennifer go.

The front door opens and shuts a moment later. The slight thud sends a jolt through my body like I'm a fragile bird that gets startled easily. I basically am now. I fall to my knees and hold both hands over my face. I can feel an overwhelming wave of pressure build inside my skull. And it's not just because of Jennifer. It's everything. What have I become? I remind myself I used to be a strong person, one that could handle the pain of the world. As a nurse, I'd seen the worst of humanity, but I'd also seen how resilient people could be at defying the odds. That strength had once been my own, absorbed through years of hard work. I've lost my intensity. I've lost my spirit. In their places exist nothing but a jumbled mess. I sicken myself.

The only bit of power I display is when I manage to pull myself off the floor toward the front door that needs to be locked. I have no choice but to secure it. My brain won't allow me to be in this house without the knowledge that I am safe from the potential dangers that lurk outside, ready to strike, even if they aren't real. Maybe the real dangers are within these walls instead.

Finally, I reach the front door and slide the lock across. I follow that up with the deadbolt by twisting the key I keep in the door. The clicks and sounds of metal sliding over metal reward me instantly. The part of my mind demanding me to put my pity party on hold to safeguard the house releases its grasp if only for a second.

Once again, I slide to the floor, defeated by my own self. I feel the list in my pocket, folded up. I pull it out and grab a pen from the small console table that sits by my front door. I add a new point to the piece of paper: I spotted a man staring at me from a street corner near my house. He was wearing the same hooded sweatshirt as the man in Portland.

I fold the list up and put it back in my pocket with the pen. As I sit against the door, I see something I'd thought I'd lost:

the wooden pacifier I was supposed to give John at our wedding anniversary dinner. It had fallen behind the small table.

I reached over and slide the present out. It's still in its felt box. I think about the fact that John never knew about this gift. He died before I gave it to him all because I got nervous and took too long. If John were here right now and I gave him the same gift, would he even want to raise a child with me? I honestly don't know. So much has changed since that night. I only wish I'd dared to give it to him sooner.

I shake my head at the thought as I bring myself to stand up and face the rest of my day without Jennifer.

I'm not mad at her for leaving me. I doubt anyone else would have lasted this long given the number of things I wouldn't divulge. I don't know if I will be able to continue by myself, but what choice do I have? I have to survive until she comes round. No one else out there cares or understands me better than Jennifer.

※

The rest of my day passes by in a blur. I spend most of it on the couch half-watching some endless TV drama that only gets more and more over the top with time. I eventually turn it off and head to the kitchen again to eat. I had to put myself on a schedule to remember to provide myself with enough nutrition.

I fix myself a BLT and half force it down with a big glass of water. After thirty minutes of staring at the walls in my kitchen, I get the desire to pee, so I head to the bathroom attached to my bedroom. When I finish, I walk by John's study. Determined to keep myself distracted from the world outside, I decide it's time to cleanse this small room of all things related to John. Whether I imagined the text message or not, its words rang true in my mind when I wasn't trying to hold onto John. It is time to move on.

I grab an empty box from the garage along with a big trash bag. I don't hold back when I clean his desk. It's the only way I can do this without breaking down. If I don't do this now, I might run the risk of turning the messy room into some sort of shrine to John.

Everything that isn't a textbook goes straight into the bag. I don't even bother to see what each item is. It's easier this way. I could find some connection to John. I just want this space clear. His journals and textbooks all go in a box to be donated to a charity bin. I like to think he would want that for his expensive resources.

Something falls out of the last textbook and lands on the desk. I scoop up a business card into my hand and read the name of a local bar in town: Hernandez. "What the—?" I ask out loud. I've never heard of the establishment. I flip the card over and discover the name "Felix" in John's handwriting on the back above a phone number. I don't know what to make of it, never knowing anyone by the name of Felix or hearing John mention this person before. I throw the card into the bag of rubbish.

When I'm done clearing the mess, I wipe down every surface with a damp cloth and clean out all of the dust. Six weeks of neglect has built up a thick layer of the stuff. All that is left when I finish dusting is John's laptop. I shove it to the side to clear some room for a task I need to complete no matter what. After a deep breath in and out, I place one item down in the middle of the desk: the insurance form. I set a pen beside it and take a deep breath in and out.

I have to do this. It's time, despite that niggling force that doesn't want me to do this. I've waited too long as it is to sign. I know that in doing this one simple act, it will mean the end of John's affairs. It will signify the end of our marriage by acknowledging that he is dead and will never come back. And what do I get for signing some document? A lump sum of money that I don't deserve.

I turn the pages and attempt to read through the text, hoping to make sense of what's written. I read the same sentence three times and realize I'm never going to fully understand any of it.

When I see a page I need to sign, my heart skips a beat. I think of the text to my cell, of John showing up online on Facebook, of the sight of him in Portland. And finally, I think about the man staring at my house from afar.

The words from the text jump out at me, clearly telling me what to do. It's so simple. I hold the pen in my hand and press the tip to the paper. "Come on," I tell myself with closed eyes and a shaky wrist. But the pen drops out of my hand and rolls toward the back of the desk. It clatters onto the floor.

I can't do it. I can't sign John's life away. Not yet.

CHAPTER 25

I pace around the small study, both hands on my hips as I furrow my brows with worry. If I can't bring myself to sign the release form, I will reach a point where I run out of money and have no choice but to sell the house. Considering the amount I owe on the mortgage and what the house is worth, there wouldn't be enough money left for me to start over. My best bet is to claim the life insurance. But logic doesn't seem to be winning at the moment.

All I have to do is sign the document and send the paperwork over to Thomas Hart. He would then get the ball rolling so the insurance company could start their investigation. Why is that so hard for me to do? Not signing won't bring John back. I know that, but I can't seem to make the simple task happen.

I think about the investigation Thomas mentioned. Am I afraid of what it may turn up? I seem to be discovering things about John that he had kept from me. The policy and the bank account that funded it are one combined secret I don't have an answer for. I can't even explain how he managed to pay for it, secret account or not. A joint life insurance policy with such a large payout would have been beyond our means to afford. He had to have gotten the money to fund it from somewhere other than our income.

My late husband's laptop sits to the right of where he read and wrote his medical notes. John seemed a little old-fashioned when it came to studying. He preferred writing everything down with pen and paper over typing away at a laptop. He only used it for research. At least that's what I assumed he used it for. I had to stop assuming such things given what I'd discovered lately. I wonder what else sits on his computer's hard drive.

I take in a deep breath and power it on. His system is much faster than mine. I could have been using his computer instead of my slow machine up until now, but I try to avoid anything of John's. I can't stand the reminder that comes with each of his possessions. They all scream at me and say that he is no longer here, that we'll never have another conversation again. It was part of the motivation in getting me to clean his study out.

The computer finishes powering up and reaches the login screen. I know the password is Shadow123—something John said was easy to remember but not something personal a hacker could guess. Failing that, it was written down on a sticky note attached to the computer. I type in the password as I had a few times in the past and receive an error message.

"Dammit," I say. I try again, typing a little slower this time. I get the same error message. "What?" I try the password again, making sure caps lock is off and that I type each letter one at a time.

Incorrect password.

"John," I say. He must have changed it. He was acting somehow off that day he came home before we went to dinner. He even sat in this room while I got ready and refused to come out when I asked him to switch the machine off. I didn't think anything of it at the time.

There is only one person I know that can help me unlock this laptop, and I haven't spoken to him in over six weeks.

"Layton," I say, shaking my head. Saying his name out loud makes me cringe.

Layton knows a lot about computers. His job in the hospital was primarily to run and maintain the vast server network that allowed the medical systems to operate flawlessly. There was nothing worse than a vital machine failing during an operation. He could break into this thing without looking.

But how could I ask him to help me unlock John's laptop? He might see this as a golden opportunity to make a move on me. I wouldn't put it past him to do so despite John only being dead for such a short time. Still, I have to know why John felt the need to take out such an expensive insurance policy. His laptop has to hold something of importance for him to change the password in the time leading up to his death.

How did John fund his secret account? How did he keep the money hidden from me? As a resident at a busy hospital, I find it insane to think that he managed to keep any secrets at all. Was I so wrapped up in my own world to not notice anything, or was John just really good at hiding the truth? I hate to think I was so self-centered that I didn't notice what was happening around me.

But I don't have time to dwell on what could have been. What's done is done. John is dead, and for reasons I may never know, he left me with a life insurance policy that will save me from bankruptcy. Which leaves me to wonder if I'll even see a cent of the money once an investigation takes place. I can't explain why, but I feel it in my gut that John was up to something. What that was I have no clue, but I can't help but fear the worst.

I've been so distracted with stress that I've been seeing things that can't be real, receiving texts that don't exist, dreaming of things that can't have happened. Now, though, I need to push past anything that might stop me. I have to find out the truth.

Whether I lose my mind in the process or not, I am going to learn why John felt the need to take out a joint life insurance policy worth one million dollars with secret money once and for all.

CHAPTER 26

Then

I laid out the scraps of paper I found in John's study on the kitchen bench. The fragments of numbers didn't seem to fit together in any sort of cohesive way. Despite my frustrations and swelling anger, I tried, again and again, to match them all up like I was spending the afternoon working on a jigsaw puzzle, but nothing fit. Irritated, I left the pile where it was. John would have to fill me in on what these were the second he got home. It would be an interesting conversation, to say the least.

I wanted to believe these numbers weren't from a woman he'd picked up in some sleazy club or bar out of town. John just didn't seem the type of guy who would ever think of doing such a thing. It was beyond him. He wasn't weak like most people. He wasn't like Layton. I rarely saw John give in to temptation. Ever. He never ate more food than he needed, never had too many drinks when we went out, and he rarely ever afforded himself much in the way of luxury. I suspected this all had to do with his upbringing in the foster homes, not that I could ever get much out of him about that life. If only.

I could count on one hand how many times John had told me about his childhood. I tried to get him to open up whenever I could. I remembered one time when he was in a particularly nostalgic mood and actually had something to say to me about his youth. We were staying on the waterfront for a few days over east at Cannon Beach. The resort overlooked the sandy bay and was a pleasant two-hour drive from home. On our first day in town, we decided to have a look at some of the quirky antique stores located at the end of the main street.

As John and I perused the store, not looking for anything in particular, John stumbled across an old wooden toy. It was a vintage race car that looked like it had seen better days. The paint was peeling, and every bit of the toy was scratched. None of that mattered, though. John held up the toy with a gleeful smile, one I hadn't seen come from him in my life.

"What is it, honey?" I asked him, curious.

He almost seemed startled by my voice at first, but he wrapped his arm around me and showed me the toy. "I used to have this exact toy when I was a kid."

"Back in one of the homes?" I asked, some hesitation in my voice. I instantly regretted bringing up the foster homes. It was always a no-go zone. Always.

His smile dropped for a moment. "Ah, yeah. The main one in fact. I used to play with this thing like crazy, so much so I had to hide it from the other kids." He chuckled to himself as his eyes drifted off to a memory. I only wished I could have seen what his brain was showing him.

I rubbed his bicep. "Was it hard growing up in those homes?" I had to ask him, now that for once I was going to get a bit about his past out of him.

"They weren't exactly a walk in the park. It's funny, you'd get thrown into these places with other kids who all had the same defeated look on their faces that told you they were scared, but that didn't stop them from being cruel to one another. You'd think we'd be united by our common enemy, but no, we were too busy hurting each other to realize we were just hurting ourselves."

I felt my heart pound in my chest as I absorbed John's pain. I felt for him. I held him tight and rubbed his bicep, encouraging him to keep going. It would do him a world of good to get some of these things off his chest.

"None of us ever knew what was going to happen next or when we'd be put into a place that we could truly call home. We just went from one hellhole to the next. You'd see a few familiar faces when you got transferred, but there were just as many fresh-faced kids who were new to the system. We didn't welcome them with open arms. No one had done that for us when we arrived. We weren't about to break the mold and change things for the better. Stupid, right?"

"I'm sorry, honey," I said. What else could I say? I felt useless.

John held up the toy for a moment and then tossed it back onto the shelf without another thought. His smile vanished. He moved on. The memory was either over, or he didn't want to think about it.

"Wait, John. Why don't we buy this toy? It's only three dollars."

"No, it's fine. I'll never use it. It'll just gather dust somewhere in our house." He started to walk away from me, heading for the exit.

"John? Where are you going?"

He didn't answer me. I grabbed the car and paid the store owner five dollars and told her to keep the change. I rushed outside to find John sitting on an empty park bench beside the main road. I slowly approached him and sat down beside my husband for a chat he desperately needed to have.

"Are you alright?" I asked, hopeful he would answer.

His eyes were fixed on the distance. Where was he?

"John?" I said. I held up the race car. "I got you this."

His eyes snapped out of their daze and met mine. He took the toy out of my hand and ran his fingers over the surface until anger overcame him. He shook his head and handed the toy back to me without looking. "Take it back or throw it away. I don't want to see that thing."

"Why not?" I asked as I took back the toy and stowed it away.

"Too many memories around it. I don't want to think about any of that."

"Well, maybe that's a good thing. You never talk about the past. Maybe this will help."

He smiled out of the corner of his mouth. "Some things are best left alone, you know?"

"Come on, John. It's me. Tell me what's got you so bummed out about this toy. Why does it bring you happiness and sadness at the same time?"

John let out his breath and ran his fingers through his hair. He slowly turned his face to me. "You want to know why? Are you sure about that?"

"I am," I said. I was ready.

"Because I used to beat up anyone who touched this thing. Yeah, this car brought me a lot of joy and happiness, but it also turned me into a wild beast when it came to such things as a possession."

Keeping any reaction from my face, I nodded at John. I tried to reassure him that I understood by rubbing his back. "That's not your fault. You didn't choose to be put into those homes. It was forced upon you. You were just trying to survive."

"Survive? That's rich. I didn't need toys to survive. I had my wits about me. I didn't let a single kid take that thing from me. No matter the cost. They all knew what I was capable of."

I could see John was starting to get angry about the toy, so I shoved it away into my handbag. I didn't want to trigger something within. I didn't know how I would cope if he lost the plot. My weakness failed to push him.

John blinked rapidly and rolled his head around. "Sorry for that. I don't know what came over me."

"It's fine, honey," I said. "There's nothing to be sorry for, okay?"

We managed to get back on track a little with our vacation after that moment and avoided any significant existential crisis.

The last thing we needed was for John to become unhinged on our first vacation together in at least three years. We both needed this time.

We'd been working hard at the hospital. Too hard, in fact. A string of staff shortages saw us both filling in wherever we were needed. It was too much. I pulled one double shift after the other, as did John. We were exhausted and demanded some time off by reminding our superiors how tired we were, and how likely we were to make a mistake. By some miracle, we'd got a weekend off together. We left the antique store and headed for the beach. I figured a nice stroll toward the water would do us both some good and allow John a moment to decompress. Me as well.

We took off our shoes and allowed the tide to sweep over our bare toes. John started to relax and forget all about his past. At least at that moment.

That night and the next morning felt like heaven. We spent most of the remaining time in our hotel bed watching TV, having sex, and ordering room service. It was the perfect ending to a weekend away that had started out a little rough.

When we went back home, I decided to keep the race car. I would one day get more out of John. He'd willingly tell me all about the homes and accept that I only wanted to help him.

As the clock in my living room hit four in the afternoon, I drifted out of my daydream and back into reality. John was still an hour from home. I remembered the fragments of numbers I'd found and quickly scooped them back up again. They didn't look like phone numbers once I had a closer look. For all I could tell, they were just scraps of paper from when John had been studying. I took them to the drawer and put them back inside the false bottom.

I decided John could have his secrets—if they even were secrets. I trusted him. I had to. I knew he would never do a thing to harm me. I wasn't about to let someone like Layton get into my head and change things between us. It was exactly what he wanted. I knew all too well to think this was anything other than Layton trying to find another excuse to be closer to me.

I glanced up at the clock on the wall. John would be home soon. Layton had better not show his face again at the worst possible time.

CHAPTER 27

Now

I'm back in my bed, back where I spent six weeks of my life in a dark, inescapable hole. There's nowhere else to turn to right now, plus I fit into this space perfectly. It would be so easy to find myself falling back into my old routine. I have to be careful.

I've moved away from John's laptop and am yet to think of a way to get Layton to help me with my password problem. He is the only one I can simultaneously trust and not trust to help me access John's PC. I know that the last time we spoke I yelled at him to leave my house, but that was only because of what he said about John. Layton and I used to be good friends at one time. I can only hope he remembers that and doesn't think this means anything else.

I understand what I plan on doing isn't strictly right, but I have to find out why John changed his password leading up to his death.

Instead of using my mattress as a numb escape from the world that forces itself upon me, I am starting to worry about the mistakes I have made recently. I give up on thinking about John, the list, and my future for a moment, and start to stress about Jennifer. How severely have I compromised our relationship? I can't lose her from my life. Not now.

I lift my cell to my face and scroll through my contacts. I find Layton's number with ease and stare at it for far too long. Do I text him? Call him? I'd never done anything like this before. It feels wrong. It feels like I am digging up John's grave, but I have to know. I couldn't continue to live in this state of painful limbo.

I hit the call button on Layton's contact card, not knowing what else to do. I can feel my breath quicken its pace. My cell begins to ring out immediately, sending my heart into overdrive.

"Grace? Is that you?" Layton says, confusion wrapped around his voice.

I think about hanging up for a moment, but I force myself forward. "Hi, Layton," I say softly.

"What's going on, Grace? Why are you calling me?"

I pause for a moment as all of my words get caught in my throat. "I, uh, well. I didn't mean to bother you, but I need a favor."

"A favor? Are you serious? From me?"

"Please, Layton. This is serious. I wouldn't be calling you if I had a choice." I slam my eyes shut, cringing at my own words. I must sound like the worst person in the world.

"Oh, well when you say it like that, of course, I'll do you a favor," he says, laying on the sarcasm as much as possible.

"That came out wrong, sorry."

"Forget it, Grace. I'm hanging up."

"No, please, don't. I seriously need your help. This isn't a joke, and you're the only one I can trust to help me."

Layton huffs down the line. "And what is it exactly that you need help with?"

"I can't tell you over the phone. Can you come over?"

Layton had probably been dying to hear those words once upon a time. Would they still hold their strength after all this time?

"Okay," he says. "I can be there in the next hour."

"Thank you," I say, relieved. "And please bring your computer with you. You're going to need it."

※

Almost an hour later, Layton knocks on my door softly. It's been seven weeks since he showed up unannounced on my doorstep. This time, I asked him here and actually want to invite him in.

"Hello," he says to me when I open the door. I give him an awkward smile and say the same in return. I never thought I'd see him anywhere near my house again. I figured we'd only see each other at the hospital as colleagues, assuming I decided to continue my employment at Bellflower General.

"Come on in," I say, gesturing for him to walk through in front of me. He does so with a hint of caution.

"So what's this all about?" Layton asks over his shoulder before we're even halfway down the corridor.

I don't blame him for getting straight down to business. I try to think of the best way to ask him what I need to, but nothing comes out.

Layton comes to a stop and faces me. "Well, Grace?"

I stare into his wide eyes. "It'll be easier if I show you."

"Show me?" he asks with a frown. "Listen, Grace, if this is about the last time I was here—"

"It's not, okay? And just forget about that day. I just need your help with something, and you're the only person I could think to ask who I can also trust."

My words bring a smile to Layton's face. He continues on to the kitchen and turns around. "Okay, what are you showing me?"

"Through here," I say. "In John's study."

Layton follows and narrows his gaze at me. He takes a quick look at the laptop he's holding in a messenger bag over his shoulder. "Wait, is this a computer problem?"

"You could say that," I reply.

Layton sighs. He's probably been called around to his friends' and family's homes to solve basic computer issues more times than was polite. "I thought this was something serious. Alright, let's get this over with then."

I point him along toward the study.

Layton gives me a laugh. "So, what did you do? Get a virus?"

"Nothing like that. Through here," I say pointing him into the study. John's laptop sits on the login screen.

"This the one?" Layton asks. "What's the problem? Forgotten the WiFi password?" He settles into the desk chair and hovers his fingers over the keyboard.

"You could say that, but no. I can't remember the password to login to John's laptop."

Layton looks at me sideways. "And you want me to get you in?"

"Yes."

His hands shift away from the laptop to a sticky note that says John's old password. "Did you try this?"

"No, wait—" I say too late. I forgot to remove the sticky note. Layton has already typed the old password in and hit Enter. He gets an error message and turns to me with a furrowed brow. "Why doesn't this work, Grace?"

"Oh, that. I think it got there by mistake."

Layton purses his lips at me and crosses his arms. "Is that so? So let me get this right: you need to get into John's laptop for reasons you haven't told me, and you've somehow forgotten his password."

I close my eyes for a moment and exhale. "That password worked for as long as I can remember. John gave it to me so I could use his laptop when I wanted. For some reason, he changed it before he died. I need your help to get into his system."

Layton holds his gaze on me, not looking away for one moment. I can see exactly what he is thinking and what he is about to say. I cut him off before he gets a chance to speak. "Can you help me?"

"The question isn't whether or not I can help you; I can crack through this thing in a matter of minutes." Layton leans forward. "The real problem here, Grace, is why should I help you?"

CHAPTER 28

I stare at Layton's face with my mouth open as he swivels in the desk chair in John's office left and right. He throws back his chin and studies my reaction to his statement as if he is waiting for the perfect moment to strike.

"So, you won't do it?" I ask. "You won't help me unlock John's computer."

"Never said that I wouldn't; I asked you why I should. You and I haven't exactly been friendly to one another as we once were, which leaves me to wonder why I should get involved in whatever it is that you are trying to find out about John."

I can't hold back what I'm about to say. "You don't understand. He wasn't quite himself the night he died. He was acting different. After it all went down, when I finally buried John and met with his lawyer, I found something out about my late husband; something that only left me with more questions."

Layton leans forward in the chair. "What did you find out?"

I draw back away from him. "I can't tell you. It's private."

"So you're asking me to respect your privacy?"

"Yes, yes I am."

"Even though John changed the password on this computer?"

"That's different," I say as my hands instinctively fly up to my face. I squeeze my head for a moment and run a few fingers through my hair. I refocus on Layton. "Please. You have to help me." I move in closer to him.

"Actually, I don't. Just because you say so, doesn't mean—"

I charge at him, dropping to my knees. I grab hold of Layton by the sleeves of his jacket and lean up toward his face. "This isn't a joke, Layton," I yell. "This is my life we're talking about. My husband is dead and may have left something on that computer that will help to explain to me why he felt the need to take out a secret million-dollar life insurance policy a few months before he died."

"A million dollars? That's what this is all about?"

I nod. "Yes. Because the policy is so young, the insurance company will have to investigate John's life before they can give me a cent of the money I need to survive. There could be something on this computer that could tell me why he took out such an expensive policy without telling me."

Layton nods as he turned away. I let go of his jacket and slid down. He faces me again. "They could also use it against you."

"Use what?"

"Anything you find on John's computer that tells you why he took out a life insurance policy. The investigator could use it to end your claim."

I shake my head and squash down my body. "I know. I realize that. I guess I'm just hoping whatever is on that laptop will reassure me John was the man I thought he was and that it isn't as bad as I'm imagining."

"Maybe it won't be," Layton says, lowering down to my level. "John seemed like an okay person to me."

A glimmer of hope registers in my eyes. "Does that mean—"

"Yes, I'll help you. But I'm telling you now, if this is anything too crazy, I'm out, got it?"

I rise to my feet. "Got it. I understand."

"Okay," Layton says with a huff. "Then I guess we'd better get to work."

I watch as Layton spins to the laptop and resets the system. He presses some buttons and gets the computer into some strange mode I never knew existed. Before I know it, he has reset John's username and password. It seemed all too easy. "Okay. What do you want the password to be?"

"Don't set one. Make it as quick as possible for anyone to access."

I could see Layton wanted to protest out of habit but instead he complied. "Okay, it's done."

"Thank you!" I say as we watch the computer load up. It bypasses the login screen and goes straight to John's messy desktop. His study matched the organization levels he had on the display.

"May I?" I ask.

"Go for it," Layton says. He steps out of the way and gestures for me to take over. I sit down and feel the heat he left behind. "Let's do this," I say.

I start searching in all of the usual places. His browsing history, his files, and his general documents. All I find are items related to his residency studies. There's nothing here that can tell me anything special. I'm about to give up when I see his email app sitting on the desktop waiting to be opened. Jackpot.

"Wait, Grace. Are you sure you are ready for this? You don't know what we are going to find in his email."

"I don't care. I have to know," I say as I turn to Layton.

He holds up his hands defensively and backs up a step.

I refocus on the laptop and click to open his email. It takes a few minutes to load as seven weeks of email floods into his system. There are emails that have been automatically sent relating to his residency. There are the usual junk emails and newsletter subscriptions that plague the system. There doesn't seem to be anything here of use, or that can shed some light as to why John felt it necessary to take out such an expensive policy and pay for it with cash I also never knew existed.

I'm about to give up when Layton points something out to me. "Wait. Don't close anything just yet."

My hand moves away from the mouse. "Why?"

"I'll show you." Layton motions for me to get out of his way. I let him through without protest. He takes a seat at the desk and makes a few adjustments.

I watch as he clicks around the screen and types a few commands. I have no idea what it is that he's up to, but it seems like he knows what he is doing.

"Right there. You see that?"

"Not really. It just looks like his emails."

Layton chuckles under his breath. "Take another look again. There are no old emails."

"What do you mean? These are all new emails John couldn't answer as they came in after he died."

"Yes, but take a look at any emails before he last used his laptop."

I lean in as Layton shows me what he is talking about. I look at the timestamps and dates. There are no old emails before the time we left for dinner. "Oh," I say.

"You see what I mean. There's nothing there. The deleted folder is empty. The junk folder has even been emptied before that time."

"What does this mean?" I ask, trying not to let the information overwhelm me.

Layton's eyes fall away from the screen. "He wiped it clean and changed the password. Whatever it was John didn't want you to see is gone."

"No, he wouldn't do that. He wouldn't keep something from me." I think about the strange numbers hidden in the drawer in this desk. Were they connected to this? Why didn't I confront him about those pieces of paper when I had the chance?

I pull open the right-hand drawer and lift up the false bottom. The scraps of paper are gone. He must have cleared them out before we went to dinner along with everything else of importance.

Layton taps away furiously at the keyboard, going into screens I don't understand. "Just as I thought," he says.

"What is it?" I can't take much else.

He shakes his head at the screen. "Not only did he delete his emails from this computer, but he also wiped them from the email server so no one could possibly restore them. He knew what he was doing. His browsing history is also gone across the cloud."

My hands find their way to my face as I turn away from Layton and fight back the tears. What was John hiding? What was so bad that he didn't want me to ever find out about it?

CHAPTER 29

I stand out in the living room wiping away tears from my eyes with a tissue. Layton is still in John's study but emerges a moment later with a somber face, stopping by the kitchen. Both of his hands are in his jacket pockets.

"Are you okay, Grace?"

I pull out my cell and spin away from Layton, pretending to use the device, so he doesn't see me crying. It fails to hide my tears. I place my cell down on the armrest of my sofa and walk past him and into the kitchen. "No, I'm not okay. My husband is dead and seemed to be living some sort of double life I have no idea about and apparently never will."

"It's not ideal, is it? I wish I could tell you more, but there's nothing there. He really didn't want you to know what was going on."

"Why that night?" I blurt.

"What do you mean?" Layton asks, his brows tight to the bridge of his nose.

"Deleting his emails. Clearing his computer. Changing the password, I assume. Why did he do it literally moments before we went out to celebrate our five-year wedding anniversary?"

Layton shakes his head as he looks at the floor. "Maybe he had plans for that night, but they never came to be because... well, you know why."

I think to myself what that pickup stopped from happening. A moment of silence forms between us. "So you think he never got to finish what he started. Could it have been related to the life insurance policy he took out several months prior?"

"I don't know, Grace," he says with a shrug. "If I knew, I swear I'd tell you." He comes closer to me and puts an arm on my shoulder. "Maybe you just need to move on. Take the insurance money and start over, you know?"

I turn away from him and plant a hand on my forehead. "I can't. Not yet. I need to know the truth. I need to know what he was up to. I can't move on with my life with this hanging over my head."

Layton sighs. It's not just a sigh of frustration, either. It's one full of regret. I turn and face him. He knows something. "What is it?"

The corner of his mouth curls up. "I shouldn't show you this, but I found something underneath John's laptop. It slid out and fell to the floor." Layton pulls both hands out of his pockets and places something down on the island bench in my kitchen.

"What is that?" I ask. "How could there have been anything under John's laptop? I cleaned the desk and moved it around."

"It was partially taped to the bottom of the laptop. The glue must have dried up over time. I'm not one hundred percent sure what this is, but it might explain why John went through his computer the way he did."

I furrow my brow at Layton as he picks up and hands me a folded piece of paper no bigger than a napkin. I take it and carefully unfold the note as if it might explode. A find a list of four names, each with a dollar amount next to them. I read each one to myself.

Stefano—$40,000
Marvin—$50,000
Jimmie—$60,000
Felix—$100,000

"Felix?" I whisper as I think of the business card I found in John's study.

"John must have forgotten about it in his rush to wipe everything," Layton says, interrupting my train of thought.

"Do you know what this is?" I ask Layton as I stare into his eyes, my mouth half open.

"I'm just guessing, but it looks like he might have owed these people money."

"That much money? You can't be serious?"

"Like I said, I'm just guessing. Hopefully I'm wrong, but maybe you should just leave this alone. If it means anything, you could be stumbling onto something that you might never be able to unlearn about John. Do you really want to ruin your memory of him? Do you really want that kind of stress on top of everything else?"

I stare at Layton for a few seconds too long as I try to size him up. "Why do you care? John is dead. You should be happy that he wasn't perfect, that something like this might turn up."

He shakes his head at me. "Are you serious? I'm not a monster, Grace. I'm not about to hit on a widow and take advantage of her just because it turns out her dead husband may or may not have been hiding secrets. I knew I shouldn't have gotten involved."

I shake my head and feel stupid. I'm lashing out at the nearest person. "Layton, I'm sorry. I didn't mean to imply that—"

"It's fine. I've been a jerk to you in the past. I shouldn't expect any different. Anyway, I need to go." He starts to walk toward the front door.

"Wait," I say. "I'll see you out." I follow Layton. He doesn't slow up for me. I really managed to cross a line with my comment. It seemed to be my specialty of late. He opens the door on his own and steps out into the afternoon light. Gray clouds have rolled over the town and seem to be flattening out across the region. Layton half turns to me. "Take it easy,

Grace, and please, be careful. You don't know what you could be getting yourself into."

"Okay," I mutter as my eyes drop to the ground for a few seconds. I can feel a weight crushing me down. "Thank you for today. Maybe I'll see you around the hospital."

He gives me a nod. "Yeah, maybe. Goodbye, Grace."

"Wait," I say. I open my arms to him for a hug. He accepts it after a moment's hesitation. We embrace for a few seconds. I welcome the comfort of another human being.

"I have to go, Grace," he whispers to me.

"Okay," I reply. I let him go and follow Layton with my eyes as he walks down my driveway to his car. He gets inside and starts the engine without looking back at me. I pull the door shut and lock the entry before he leaves. The potential list of debt, a new list I need to worry about, stirs in my hand. I hold it up to the light while Layton's car idles in the background. I reread the names and settle on the last one. Who the hell is Felix? What did he have to do with John and a bar named Hernandez? I know that Layton's right, I shouldn't follow this lead, but it's all I have. My brain won't allow me not to.

I rush to John's study and rummage through the trash bags in the corner until I can find the business card again. I'm lucky I hadn't thrown them out just yet. I have to make sure it was real and not some imagined object to torture myself with. I see the card after only a minute and dig it out from the pile of papers.

Hernandez. The card is real. I'm not crazy. I flip it over and see the name "Felix" and a phone number. I can't ignore this name. Whoever it belongs to, they must know something about John's list of names, especially if he owed them up to a hundred thousand dollars. I bring the card along with me. I now have two lists and a business card that I will never throw away.

I rush back to the kitchen and hear my cell buzzing away in the distance. I remember leaving it on one end of the sofa, so I quickly head back to the lounge to see who is calling me.

When I get there, I see that an unknown caller is on the other end. It's probably someone trying to sell me something, so I don't answer, deciding if they really want to contact me they will leave a message. I have too much to think about to allow any distractions into my head.

My phone stops vibrating and displays a missed-call notification. I sit down beside it and let out a sigh of relief, not wanting to speak to another soul after my fight with Jennifer and my meeting with Layton. It's been a long day, and it's only early in the afternoon.

But then it buzzes again with another unknown number. This person didn't leave a message but insists on calling again. Frustrated, I snatch up my phone and answer it. "Hello?" I don't hide the annoyance in my voice. Someone is about to get yelled at.

The person on the other end grunts down the line. I can hear them breathing.

"Hello?" I say again. "Who is this?"

They laugh softly to themselves, doing little to make their exhales less audible.

"Whoever you are, this isn't funny, you sick son—"

The caller hangs up. "What the hell?" I ask myself. I don't need this.

I hold my cell up, unsure if I had just experienced something real or not. Is this another sick joke someone is playing on me? It's probably only a wrong number and I'm overreacting to it. Either way, it has me on edge.

I clutch my cell in my hand as I look over my shoulder and listen out for anything. My phone buzzes again, unnaturally vibrating my hand. It's another unknown caller trying to screw with me. I go to answer, but I stop myself when I realize I can still hear Layton's car idling in the background.

Could he be calling me from his car? He wouldn't do that to me, would he? We seemed to have bridged a gap today when I wasn't putting my foot in my mouth. I stand and move across the room to the corridor that leads to my bedroom. I should be able to see him out the window quite easily from there without him realizing. As I run into my room. I answer my cell. "Hello?" I say.

"Hello, Grace," someone says.

I freeze instantly, gripped to the carpet as if my feet are nailed down.

"Who is this?" I try to demand with a weak voice. I even manage to continue to the window, but I'm too late; Layton begins to drive off.

"This is Ben from Verizon Wireless. How are you doing today?"

"What? No."

"I'm sorry, Grace? Can you hear me?"

I let my cell fall to my side. It's just a telemarketer trying to sign me up to their network. I can hear the man speaking, his voice barely a whisper. I let him continue to give out his pitch and bring me back from the brink, but my jaw is locked shut.

All I know at that moment is that I need Jennifer, and I need her now.

CHAPTER 30

Then

Time seemed to come to a halt as I waited for John, especially after Layton's little visit. But now, there were only ten minutes left before he came home from skipping work to spend the day buying me a present.

I know he wouldn't have spent the entire day doing so, but he clearly needed the opportunity to get me an anniversary gift and had no doubt forgotten to allow himself the time to do so until now. I knew it meant more to me than it did to him to celebrate five years of marriage as I was far more sentimental than him, so I could forgive his forgetful brain just this once if he responded positively to my gift.

I grabbed the wooden pacifier in its box and placed it in a gift bag in my handbag in preparation for our dinner reservations. We weren't booked in until eight, seeing as I was expecting John to be home at his usual work time. It didn't bother me that we'd have to wait. The extra time would allow us a moment to catch up. I still had some doubts kicking around in my head about the day's discoveries, but there was nothing that made me fear the worst about our marriage. At least not yet.

I wondered where John had spent his non-shopping hours. Did he meet up with some friends? Did he stop off at a coffee shop and read? He rarely had time alone to himself. I bet it would have been nice for once that he could disconnect from the hospital and just be himself without having to worry about friends or me. Wherever he had gone, I figured he needed the time. We all did some days.

My thoughts transitioned to the next few years of our lives. I didn't usually like to plan things out in my head, but lately I had begun to as a coping mechanism. I'd fall pregnant, have the baby, take a long time off work, and watch our child grow. Would we have a boy or a girl? I hadn't thought about names yet. Just arriving at the decision to finally agree to start trying for a baby was enough to freak me out. It was a lot to think about and imagine. Would I be able to handle it?

What happened when John wanted another baby? Where would our first child sleep once it outgrew the nursery? Suddenly, our two-bedroom home began to shrink all around me. We'd need a bigger house with a bigger mortgage if we ever wanted more than one. It would all come down to John becoming a physician if we ever planned on buying a bigger home.

I had to stop myself. My imagination was speeding away from itself. Even though I knew John would be over the moon to start a family with me, I had to take things slow. Falling pregnant wouldn't magically happen overnight, nor did I want it to. There were a thousand things to organize for the arrival of a baby, and I knew in my heart that I would want to be on top of it all. Everything perfect. I never understood these people who let the nine months sail by without giving much thought to what would happen once the baby was born.

As I sat on the edge of our bed, eagerly waiting for John to arrive, I began to feel strange. I don't know why, but I was nervous. Almost overwhelmed by nothing. Maybe I was just excited, but the thought of John coming home was enough to send butterflies to the pit of my stomach. Deep down, I knew it was the gift that was doing this to me. I hadn't quite figured out how I would give it to him, but I knew it had to be picture-perfect.

I'd changed my outfit no less than six times throughout the day, leaving the previous outfits carefully laid on my bed in case I changed my mind. I'd tried out three different ways to wear my hair and finally settled on something I knew John loved more than anything else. After all, wasn't he the one I was trying to impress for once? I usually dressed for other women, hoping they'd see the effort I'd gone to in my attempts to appear somewhat decent. After all, they were the ones who cared.

Five o'clock came and went. John hadn't gotten home yet. Where was he? I knew I should give him a few minutes before I started to panic, but I was already bouncing on the edge of the bed as it was. This couldn't be good. I grabbed my cell up from my side. Unconsciously, I unlocked it and checked every notification I could. I checked my messages, my voicemail, the various social media accounts that were apparently needed these days to stay in touch with the world. There was nothing from John. Would he actually come home as promised? Why wouldn't he? He wouldn't lie about that.

Something had to be wrong. John was always punctual and never skipped a beat. The thought pulled me up to my feet. What exactly was it I was going to do to get him here? Clap my hands and make a wish? Before I made it to the bedroom door, I felt the rumble of the garage door. The engine was pulling its metal panels along a track to allow a car to enter the space. John was home. Finally. Thank God.

I rushed out of our room and charged along toward the kitchen and then on to the single door that divided the house from the garage. I stared at the knob, eager to see it twist open and allow my husband inside to hold me in his strong arms again.

It had felt like a long day without John. Finally, we'd get to spend some time alone together to celebrate. We'd get to have our dinner and drink our wine and celebrate our decision.

If only I'd known the truth back then. If only I'd seen the signs that were placed there for all to see.

CHAPTER 31

Now

"Is everything okay?" Jennifer asks over the phone. I dialed her only a moment ago and can barely get any words out like a stuttering child. I called her from my bedroom where I have sat frozen for the last ten minutes.

"Um, yeah, fine. No, not fine. Things aren't great."

"What's going on?"

I don't know what to say. I just want to shout out for her to come over and never leave. I know I can't expect her to come running, though. She has her own life and her own problems. "It's nothing. I'm sorry I disturbed you."

"You want me to come over again, don't you?" Jennifer asks.

"I do, sorry. And I know I have no right to ask, either. Wait, how did you…?"

"You won't believe this, but I'm just around the corner. I was coming over to check in on you. I didn't like how our conversation ended before. If anything happened to you, I would never forgive myself."

"Thank you," I say. I let out a sigh of relief.

"I'll be there in a few minutes."

"Thank you, Jenn," I say again. I hang up and climb to my feet. I feel like I've just gotten back from running a marathon. I use whatever I can to guide my body along and out of my bedroom through to the kitchen. It takes me a few moments to get my bearings and for the world to stop spinning. Why do I feel like I am about to hurl?

I shake off the overwhelming urge to vomit and instead straighten myself up. Jennifer knocks on the door a second later. I turn around and will my body to the front door, despite the crippling fear it is casting in my direction. I keep seeing and hearing things that aren't real. The phone ringing before has thrown uncertainty over my every thought. I don't know if I can trust my brain anymore.

I gulp with a dry throat and slowly make my way down the corridor. I can't see Jennifer out there with both of the side curtains closed, and my front door is one solid piece of timber.

"Grace? Are you coming?" Jenn calls through the door. "It's too cold for me to be standing out here. Get a move on, please."

I take some relief in hearing her voice. Of course, my mind begins to wonder if it really is her voice I'm hearing. It has to be. It can't be some imagined call coming through the house, can it? I haven't lost the plot yet.

"Grace?"

"I'm coming," I say, three feet from the door. I slowly reach out and, one at a time, unlock each bolt that protects me from any perceived dangers lurking outside. I turn the deadbolt key and reach for the handle below. It turns on its own before I can wrap my fingers around it. I feel my heart speed up.

Jennifer bursts inside, making me stumble back a few steps. She shuts the door as quickly as she opened it and lets out a long puff of air. "Finally. What took you so long? It's so cold out there."

I move past her and lock every bolt I have available to me. I then turn the deadbolt and face Jennifer with watery eyes. I practically dive into her arms and wrap them around her body. Without any explanation, I cry into my friend's chest as I bury my head down into the safety only she provides.

It takes me some time to calm down as I continue to cry into Jennifer's warm chest. She lifts my head up and gently back, possibly trying to stop me from crying or to inspect the number of tears I have splashed on her clothing.

"Sorry about that," I say with a sniff. I'm so pathetic. "I didn't mean to—"

"It's fine. And here, take this." She hands over a few tissues from her handbag.

"Thanks," I say. I grab the soft paper and apply it to my nose. Once I finish cleaning up, I stare into Jennifer's eyes with a weak smile.

"Why are you crying?" she asks.

My eyes go wide as I think about the man I saw in the distance and the phone call that I swore was from a crazed stalker. I've added these events to my list now. I also think about Layton and the list of debt he found. Did John owe a bunch of people an insane amount of money? "Come and sit down," I say.

We sit down again on the sofa. Jennifer is really geared up to know the truth. It's no doubt been eating her up inside to learn about everything that has been causing me to act like a lunatic.

I let out a heavy breath and decide I am going to tell her everything that's happened today. But first, I need to prepare myself mentally. "I have coffee and cocoa ready to go in the kitchen," I say, letting the thought out to help delay what needs to be said.

I sense a slight bit of annoyance in Jennifer's eyes. "Tell you what," she says, "I'll fix those up for us while you have a good think about things. Sound good?"

"Sounds good," I echo. I watch Jennifer go to the kitchen and flawlessly prepare the coffee and cocoa for us. I take the time to center my thoughts and my breathing. After a few minutes, she brings the hot beverages over and sets them down in front of us.

"I want to thank you for coming. I'll start by saying that I'm sorry for all of this. For everything."

"It's fine, Grace. Really. Just let it all out, and we'll call it even." I see her warm smile keen as ever to extract the truth.

"Okay," I say, welcoming the extra time I need to think. The next words out of my mouth are not ones I've ever wanted to say. "I've been seeing and hearing things."

Jennifer leans in closer to me. "Sorry?" Her brows twist in tight. "What do you mean?"

"Exactly as it sounds. I saw a man in the street staring at my house. And I mean really gazing in on my window where I stood and watched him. This was while you were still here earlier today. You came into my room and interrupted me. When I looked back outside, he was gone as if he just disappeared."

Jennifer lets out a confused groan. "That might not mean anything, Grace. Maybe he—"

"There's more. I also had several calls from an unknown number where I heard a man's voice grunting and chuckling on the other end. I thought someone was screwing with me, but it was just a telemarketer trying to sell me something. I imagined the voice. I dreamed up the man. I swear I'm starting to lose it."

Jennifer reached out a hand and gingerly placed it on my forearm. "Maybe it's just stress. Maybe there really was a man in the street who was lost. Maybe the telemarketer didn't realize he had called you at first. They do that sometimes."

"That's not all. I saw Layton today."

"You saw Layton? Like imagined him?"

"No, I invited him to come over and try to get me access into John's laptop so I could try and understand why John had taken out that expensive life insurance policy."

"So Layton actually came here?"

I nod.

Jennifer shakes her head. "Did he help you?"

"He did. We discovered that John had deleted all of his emails before his death and changed the password on his computer. We also found this." I pass Jennifer the list of names.

"What is this?"

"I don't know exactly. But I can only guess that it's a list of people John owed money to," I say.

Jennifer makes a face like she's calculating the figures in her head. "That's two hundred and fifty thousand dollars."

"In John's handwriting," I add. "I'd recognize it anywhere."

Jennifer's mouth hangs open for a moment until she stares up at me. "Wait, wait, what are you saying exactly?"

I let out a long breath. "I don't know. Maybe one of those names can help me try and understand what this all means. I know he had managed to pay for an expensive life insurance policy without me knowing about it from a secret bank account."

Jennifer stares at the list for far too long. She places it down on the coffee table as if the page is toxic.

"What is it?" I ask.

"You don't seriously want to look into this list, do you? How do you know if any of these names actually mean anything?"

I think about the business card. "One of them will. I have more information on Felix."

"The one with one hundred thousand? The biggest amount?"

I show her the business card and watch as she shakes her head. "What's the point of this?"

"Look on the back."

Jennifer flips the card over and almost falls backward. "Felix? Like on the list? Is this real?"

"Yes," I say. "I found this in John's study. He had to have known Felix. And I need to check him out."

"No, Grace. You don't. There's only one person you need to go to right now."

Don't say it.

"Doctor Sylvain."

CHAPTER 32

Silence fills the air. I avoid eye contact with Jennifer as we slide a few inches apart on the couch. I wasn't expecting her to instantly bring up seeing Doctor Sylvain once I told her everything.

Jennifer closes her eyes for a moment and focuses in on me. "I'm going to give Doctor Sylvain a call. You need to go see him right away."

I should have seen this coming a mile away. I was so desperate to unload my thoughts that I forgot what held me back from unloading in the first place. I can feel a layer of sweat glistening over my forehead. It begins to itch straight away. I'm losing my friend's confidence as she once again throws me on the doctor's mercy. Can I turn this around? "No, I need to go to that bar and see Felix," I blurt out.

"That idea is beyond a joke. It won't lead anywhere, Grace. You need help. You shouldn't be getting yourself all worked up over some list you found."

"What?" I say, standing up. I feel my breath flow in and out of my body as I attempt to calm myself down. I can't lose it just yet. Jennifer is supposed to be on my side no matter what. Why else would she keep coming here? Now she sounds like a therapist who doubts my every word. Why did I say a damn thing about any of this? I'm so stupid.

Jennifer edges closer to me with her hands extended out. "Grace, listen to me. You've been under a lot of stress. Why don't you sit down for a—"

"Why don't you believe me?" I shout, stomping a foot. I know I'm getting angry, but I can't help it.

"Grace, stop," Jennifer says as she grabs hold of my arms by the elbows.

I react to her touch and shove Jennifer back without thinking. She trips over the coffee table and twists sideways. She lands on the ground, narrowly avoiding a few dangerous objects.

My hands fly to my mouth. I rush down to her side. "Oh, Jenn, I'm so sorry. I didn't—"

"Don't," she says, one hand up to hold me back. "I'm fine. Just stay back."

"I didn't mean to," I whisper, backing up. "I didn't..." I let my voice trail off as I realize what I've done to my only friend in the world.

"Grace," Jennifer says.

I look down at her. Her eyes say it all.

"I'm calling Doctor Sylvain right now. I'm taking you in whether you like it or not."

※

I wait by the front door as Jennifer finishes on the phone. I want to ignore her demands to see Doctor Sylvain, but she is beyond serious about this. I've never seen her so certain about something in our entire friendship. If only she would listen to me and help me investigate the list John wrote.

Thoughts ping-pong in my head as I think about Layton and Hernandez. Who will Felix turn out to be? How does he know John beyond some crazy debt? He has to be someone that can help me; otherwise, I'll never understand why John took out that policy.

Jennifer clears her throat and redirects my attention. I need to win back her trust by complying with her demand that I see Doctor Sylvain. But doing so is a pain in itself. One I don't have time for. I don't know how I'll get through the session, especially if Jennifer has said anything to him over the phone about today. I couldn't bring myself to listen to her conversation when she called. All I can do is pray she has kept her input to him to a minimum.

"He can see you in the next hour. He has a gap in his schedule at the end of the day. We'll go there now and wait."

I nod, not wanting to argue. I don't want to upset Jennifer further than I already have. She walks up to me and opens the front door. I follow her out and lock up before I slowly walk down the path to her car. The silence is crippling. I feel like there are a thousand eyes on me, all staring from afar. A shiver runs down my spine, forcing me to hurry. Could there be someone out there watching me? When I reach the passenger side door, I fling it open and practically dive in.

"I'll wait with you at the session," Jennifer says. There's no happiness or concern in her voice. Her response is one of obligation rather than a pleasantry.

She drives us off in a hurry. She doesn't say another word to me about the session or the way I shoved her as we travel. I might as well have taken a taxi. The conversation would have been more stimulating.

"Jenn?" I say.

"Yes?"

"I'm sorry. I didn't mean to push—"

She holds up a palm to silence me. "Please. I'm not even close to being able to look you in the eye let alone hear what you have to say. I'm only taking you to see Doctor Sylvain because I honestly have no idea what you will do next if someone doesn't step in and help."

I keep my mouth shut despite the nagging sensation urging my brain to respond as the drive to Doctor Sylvain's office takes less time than I remember. Why couldn't he be farther away so I had time to think of a compelling argument to change Jennifer's mind?

Jennifer parks the car in the first available spot and kills the engine. She doesn't move from the driver's seat and stares straight ahead. I guess I will be going in on my own.

"I'll be waiting here for you."

"Thank you," I say, "for arranging this and for driving me. I really appreciate it."

She closes her eyes and squints away to my words as if they are laced with poison. She knows I don't want this. I shake my head and resist starting an argument as a thought hits me. "Jenn?"

"Yes?"

"What exactly did you tell Doctor Sylvain about today on the phone?"

A moment of silence fills the air between us as Jennifer fiddles with a setting on her dashboard. She continues to avoid eye contact with me like one glance will blind her.

"Jenn?" I press.

She snaps her head toward me and stares at me with a lowered brow. "I told him the truth: that you lashed out at me physically and that you are becoming more delusional with every moment that passes."

My mouth falls open. I try to respond, but nothing comes out.

"Best you go inside," she says.

"Okay," I whisper, defeated by my friend's cold words. I climb out of the car and slowly walk to the front door of Doctor Sylvain's surgery with my handbag by my side. Both lists sit inside it. When I reach the entrance, I grip the handle of the door and take a deep breath. I have no idea what I'm about to walk into.

CHAPTER 33

"Hello, Grace," Doctor Sylvain says to me once he reaches the waiting area of his surgery. I smile in return, already working on my weak defense. I'm sure he sees right through it.

I've been waiting for almost an hour to see him, not knowing how this session will go. I can't let the doctor mistrust me for more than a second. There's no questioning this man's ability to have me put into a mental ward for what he will assume are delusional thoughts and actions. Why did I tell Jenn any of this?

I got the overwhelming feeling that my friend was almost hoping that Doctor Sylvain would take one look at me and have me committed. Just like that, she'd never have to help me again. I'd be someone else's problem. I'd slowly become a distant memory of some crazy friend she once had to put up with.

I won't let that happen. I won't allow any of these people to persuade me that I need to be locked away. I know I've possibly been seeing and hearing things. I know I've been pushing myself forward through intense pressure when I'd be better off taking things slower and one day at a time. But I don't think the answer to my problems will come about by a forced stay in a mental hospital. I hope not.

Keeping focus, I move with purpose and don't drag my feet. I follow the doctor into his office and take my place, sitting up straight, precisely as I had on the last visit I made to this building. I have to appear as normal as possible. I drove myself here only a few days ago. This time Jennifer didn't feel confident enough in my mental health to allow me to operate a vehicle. I can only hope the doctor isn't aware of that fact.

Doctor Sylvain goes about the same routine as he did in our previous sessions. He checks over his notes at his corner desk before he takes a pen and notepad over to the chair opposite the one I am sitting in. The man's robotic-like demeanor is so mesmerizing to watch it's almost hypnotic. Is this part of his method? Is this how he got me talking?

Doctor Sylvain clears his throat as he sits down. He stares straight at me for a moment. "Grace. Why are we here?"

I take in a deep breath and let it out again. It's showtime. "Because Jennifer thinks I need the extra session."

Doctor Sylvain keeps his laser focus on me and doesn't let any doubt fall into my mind that he isn't in control of the conversation. "And why does she think that?"

It's a hard question to answer without having to talk about everything. The list of me seeing people who aren't real. The list of names and money. The insurance policy. What I did to Jenn. They are all tough pills to swallow on their own. Together they make me appear beyond stable, beyond help. So much so that it wouldn't take much to turn me around on the topic and confuse me. I am scared that Doctor Sylvain might do just that and make me doubt what I believe to be the truth.

"Well, Grace? Why would your closest friend contact me personally and express extreme concern that you are delusional and having extreme hallucinations?"

I grab the handbag I have stowed unconsciously by my side and place it on my lap. The lists each sit inside along with my cell. I debated whether bringing them along would serve me or make my situation worse. I see Doctor Sylvain staring at me, waiting for an answer.

"Because I hurt her."

"Yes, you hurt her, physically," Doctor Sylvain says to me. Jenn told him all about it. She must have said everything.

"Yes, I did. It was an accident, though. We'd already had a big fight that day, but I needed her. I managed to persuade her to come over again and talk to me, but things got out of hand. I snapped at her. I didn't mean to hurt her. I would never harm anyone let alone my best friend."

The doctor starts writing down notes one after the other. It frustrates me to see him scribbling away like this. He doesn't stop and continues to study me with an almost bored expression, like this kind of thing happens a lot.

"Have you told anyone about the hallucinations other than Jennifer?"

"No one," I say. The thought of John's friends and my family finding out about what I've seen forces my chest to tighten. My eyes dart about the room at the very thought of the conversations other people will need to have with them if I get committed. I start to breathe rapidly.

"It's okay, Grace. Take a moment to calm down."

"I'm fine. I haven't said anything to anyone other than the people who know."

"And why is that?"

"I don't know. I guess because it's embarrassing."

"Your friends and family will support you through whatever happens. Surely you can trust in that?"

I want to lie and say yes, but I almost feel confident that Doctor Sylvain is a human polygraph machine. "I can't be certain of anything, anymore. I can't say without a doubt that I can trust anyone."

"And why do you think that might be?"

I feel my head swivel away with a roll of my eyes. The doctor's questions are getting more and more annoying. I take a peek at the door and imagine running through it. "I just know they'll all think I'm a freak, so I have to forget about making them happy. I have to focus on my list of priorities instead."

"And what is on your list of priorities?"

Why did I use that word "list"? I should know by now that the doctor will scrutinize every word out of my mouth. He had his knowledge of the truth and would no doubt use it in his assessment. "You know, sorting out John's estate, moving forward with my life, trying to win Jennifer's trust back. The important things."

Doctor Sylvain nods. "And how is John's estate going? You are in line for a big payout. How do you feel about the money knowing it's only coming to you because John died?"

He wants to know my every thought. I can only try to give it to him. "I'm torn, if I'm honest. On the one hand, I need the money to secure my future. On the other, I'd give up any fortune to see John alive and well again. I keep thinking that once his estate is settled, everything will go back to normal, that things will be business as usual."

The doctor's eyes say a lot to me as he smiles and writes down one note after the other.

"What is it?" I ask.

Doctor Sylvain stops taking notes and stares straight at me. I feel my heart skip a beat. "You say that you hope things will go back to normal. How can that ever happen if John is dead?"

His question makes my eyes go wide. I grip the arm of the chair with my spare hand as my mouth falls open to answer.

Both of my hands shake as I reach for the box of tissues that sits on the coffee table between us. Doctor Sylvain jumps out of his chair and picks them up, bringing the box closer to me. I grab a handful of tissues and hold them to my face as I begin to sob in front of the doctor. I don't want to cry in front of him, but it happens whether I want it to or not.

"It's okay, Grace. Let it out."

I shake my head and focus my eyes on the carpet. "I know he's dead, okay? I know that John is never coming home."

"Good. Because I know you can beat this. I know you just need time to get through the pain."

"Okay," I whisper. "I can beat this."

We continue to talk for a while until we start to circle back around to the same questions. I make sure to answer them accurately as I had previously and don't point out any repetition in his approach. I know he is trying to test the waters, so to speak and catch me in a lie. I won't fail, though.

The session comes to a close without the doctor demanding I be put into a psychiatric hospital. As I walk out of Doctor Sylvain's office, the administrative assistant at the front desk asks if I need a reminder about my next session. I shake my head, knowing it's not far off at this stage. It almost seems pointless after today.

I move out the exit and head back to Jennifer's idling car. She has been running the engine to keep the heat flowing. I appreciate the effort whether it was for me or not, the second I open the passenger door and climb in.

"You're done?" she asks, doubts smeared across her face. "Just a normal session?"

"Yes, everything is fine," I say zeroing in on her gaze.

"And what about the hallucinations?"

"It's all fine. Can you please just take me home?"

"Are you serious? You drag me through some kind of crazy hell today and expect me to just forget it?"

"I don't expect you to do anything of the sort, Jenn. Please understand that I am sorry for everything, but I need you to drop the whole topic and get me back home. That's all I'm asking of you."

Jennifer cuts the engine, killing the comfortable heat that is keeping us warm. She faces the side of my head and stares. "I want to hear you say it."

"Sorry?" I ask.

"The thing you've refused to admit to me this entire time."

I stare at her some more. "What?"

"That you think John is alive."

I spin my head away from Jennifer's. I can't believe what I'm hearing. "I know he's dead. I saw him die, I heard his body get crushed by that pickup, and I felt him take his last breath." I can feel the sting of Jennifer's eyes burning a hole in my face without needing to look.

"You can rationalize this all you want, Grace. Your true feelings will come out whether you want them to or not."

I shake my head and lower myself down and away from Jennifer. She's right. I don't want her to be, but she is. These thoughts will come out of me one way or another, and there's nothing I can do to stop them. All I can do is try to rely on them less and less until they are a dull noise.

Jennifer starts the engine and gets us underway. I know that she can see through my lies. She knows that I still believe everything I had before I came to the session today. She doesn't need to say a word. I know today's visit and the allowance for me to continue back home unimpeded is a temporary one at best. From here on out, I have to keep everything to myself.

I'm on my own.

CHAPTER 34

Then

John was taking too long to back his car into our garage as I waited eagerly for him to come inside. I found myself pacing around the kitchen, anticipating the opening of the single door that led in and out of the garage. John's car was still running, its engine rumbling away in the limited space. He needed to hurry the hell up and get in here.

It seemed like a lifetime ago that I had said goodbye to him in the morning. I didn't know what emotion to access as I waited for him to kill the engine and come inside. I missed him, yet part of me was upset with his choices today.

Time seemed to slow down the longer I waited. What was taking him so long? Was he trying to hide his gift to me away in case I saw it before we went out to dinner? Again, I wish I could have had the courage to tell him I didn't care about getting a gift. There were more important things to worry about.

John's car finally quietened. The silence that settled made me stumble on the spot until I heard the sound of his door click open. A moment later, a thud reverberated throughout the house and collided with my chest. My heart pounded harder than it had all day as John silently made the trip from his car to the side door. Was I nervous?

The handle twisted. The door opened a touch to reveal John's face. His eyes darted left and right as he paused in the doorway. He was wearing the same clothing he'd had on this morning. If I didn't know any better, it would have appeared that he'd gone to work at the hospital. Why didn't he tell me he wanted a day off?

He continued to gaze around. Could he not see me?

"Hi, honey," I said, my brows raised.

The door opened the rest of the way as John stepped inside. He gave me a smile through a somewhat startled face. "Uh, hi, Grace."

"I didn't mean to scare you if you were trying to sneak something into the house," I said, rushing up to him. I instantly smelled a thick layer of cologne that had been recently applied. John had a bad habit of doing this.

"You got me," he said with a smile. "I thought I could get this in before you noticed."

My eyes doubled in size. "What did you get me?" I played at trying to see what the present was. It felt like the best way to break any tension that was in the air.

"Never you mind," John said. "I'll have to keep this in my pocket for now."

I scoffed. "No fair. I want it now." I didn't really, but I loved playing along with John. We needed to be friendly like this more often to each other.

He took a step toward me. I threw my arms around him and squeezed tight with closed eyes before he had a chance to do anything else. He held out his arms and placed them gingerly on my shoulders to pull me off him a little. "How was your day?" he asked.

My eyes shot open. "Long and boring. All I wanted was to spend time with you." I leaned up to his earlobe and whispered. "I missed you."

John lowered his head and smiled, his hands still gripping my shoulders. "I missed you more," he halfheartedly said. He glanced away and to the side for a moment as if he were trying to think of the right words to say. He seemed confused almost. I couldn't imagine he'd spent much time preparing anything decent to say to me. It wasn't his style to be cheesy and romantic.

"How was your day?" I asked to help things along. I realized one second too late that I shouldn't have asked about it. I knew John was uncomfortable lying to me.

"It was, uh, you know, busy," he said as he scratched at the back of his head.

"Busy, you say? That's good."

"Yeah, I guess. Kept me out of trouble."

I could see the lie on his face. Anyone could. I hoped he had kept out of trouble. "Is there anything that's bothering you?" I asked. I couldn't help the words from coming out.

"Nothing."

"Nothing? Sure seems like something is up."

John closed his eyes and shook his head. "Everything is fine. Sure, things haven't been easy for me lately."

"What do mean? Like at work? You haven't told me anything about it."

"You know how it is. You have a bad day that turns into a bad week. The next thing you know it's been a bad month."

I understood exactly what he meant, but I had never heard John speak about his job like this. Was this why he called in sick? He was usually too obsessed with the work to let any of it bother him. The last few months he had spent every waking moment studying for his residency. Perhaps it was all beginning to get to him. Was this why he didn't tell me about his day off? "I'm sure you'll get through it, honey," I said. "You just need a good night out to forget about it all."

He smiled out of the corner of his mouth the way he always did, but something seemed off about it that I couldn't quite place my finger on. What had happened?

"That sounds like a good idea to me," he said.

I took a moment to think about the last few months. John didn't seem to have behaved any different than his usual self. He'd go to work, come home, focus on his studies until it was late, and spend whatever little time he had left in his day falling asleep next to me on the couch or in bed. There was a distance between us.

I narrowed my brows at him with a slight smile. "I've got a good idea," I said.

"What's that?" he asked as he placed his work bag down on the island bench.

"Why don't I run you a hot bath? And better yet, why don't I join you?"

John scratched his head with a coy smile as if I'd suggested something that was against the rules. "Okay. Sounds amazing."

A moment of silence passed between us as we stared into each other's eyes. I hadn't seen him look at me that way in months. I shied away from him like we were a couple of awkward teenagers again. Where was this coming from? Whatever it was, we needed it.

I held out a hand and waited for him to take it. He grabbed hold of me, not too loose and not too tight. I led him down the corridor to our bedroom and into the bathroom. I threw my arms around him and felt his lips collide with mine in a hurry. He pressed his body into mine. We hadn't been together in so long a time we'd forgotten what it felt like to be caring toward one another.

Before I could make logical sense of what was happening or fight my urges, John was lifting me up with two strong arms and carrying me toward the bed. There was no time for a bath. He wanted me so badly that he couldn't wait until later. What had this day done to us?

I stopped thinking about my every problem. I stopped worrying about what John's issues were and focused on that moment.

I got out of my head. I was always so concerned with what was around the corner that I didn't know how to enjoy what was taking place. I felt tears run down my cheeks and past the smile on my face as John kissed my neck.

In that second, I was convinced that our marriage could survive anything, that nothing could stop us. It had to; otherwise, these last five years had been for nothing.

CHAPTER 35

Now

Jennifer doesn't take me inside when we get back to my home. She drops me off at the curb in the dark and leaves before I take two steps toward my front door. I shake my head at her car as it picks up speed down the street. I feel like a piece of trash thrown from her open window.

Nothing makes sense to me. Then again, nothing makes any sense to me lately. I feel so useless, like I'm trapped with no way out.

I walk up the path to the front door and fish out my keys from my handbag. The two lists brush against my knuckles, poking out as if I need reminding of their existence. I don't know why I keep the first list anymore. It's done little to keep me from feeling crazy. The second list is far more important, anyway. The hallucinations will never leave my brain at this point in time. I have no choice but to do what I can to push each one of them deep down and out of focus when I can. But no matter how hard I try to forget each moment, the hallucinations find a way to resurface.

I unlock the front door and move inside with a sigh. I have no idea what I will do for the rest of the evening. My best thought is to rest and have a decent dinner to attempt to put the session to the back of my mind. I can file the thought of Jennifer hating me to one side until my mind inevitably comes at me to strike when I am the most vulnerable

It isn't going to work, though. I can't shove the pain from my brain into the depths of my subconscious like I'm archiving a file. No matter how hard I try, I can't forget something so powerful as my best friend despising me.

I walk to the kitchen thinking about everything Jennifer and I had gone through over the years. We'd seen it all. Thick and thin. Nothing ever got in our way or threatened to end our friendship. How was it that John's death formed a rift between us so severe? It's a cruel aftermath.

I lean on the kitchen bench and try to focus on what I will fix myself for dinner. I'm not hungry. It's a labored effort to make the simplest of meals to eat. It shouldn't be such a challenge, but I can't get Jennifer out my mind. The more I try, the worse it gets.

I think back to how we first met in town when I initially moved here to be with John. John and I decided to head to one of the bars that had since been pulled down and turned into a supermarket. The place was a real dive to say the least, but it didn't stop us from throwing back shot after shot to celebrate moving in together. I never thought so at the time, but with a little bit of perspective, it was clear to me that we were both nervous about living together. John was knocking back the shots quicker than I could keep up—something he never normally did when we went out. The speed of our relationship had John unhinged that night to the point where he started a fight with some random guy he thought had bumped into me. I had to jump in between the middle of the two and stop John from getting his butt kicked by someone far more sober and more capable than him.

The other guy went to leave, possibly relieved he didn't need to defend himself when his girlfriend came back from the restroom. She asked what was happening and why everything had gone to hell in the brief time she was gone. Embarrassed, I explained the situation. I felt mortified, so I figured it was time to buy them both a drink. They deserved it.

Within an hour, things went from heated to Jennifer and I becoming instant friends, bonding over our stupid men. It was like we were always meant to be friends. We'd been close ever since that first day when she did what she could to make a terrible situation better. Now, she hates me and is on the verge of never speaking to me again. My memories do nothing but taunt me.

I sigh again and make myself a turkey sandwich, thinking of Jennifer at the café. I start to wonder if I'll ever head out to another bar again now that I am alone. I guess it doesn't matter in the grand scheme of things. My old life is over. I'm not going to be a mother. The thought sends a sharp pain to the pit of my stomach that makes me shudder for a moment with rage.

I fill up a glass of water and take it with me to my bedroom along with my sandwich. I settle everything on my bedside table, determined to spend the rest of the night in my room where I feel safe. It wasn't like I had anywhere to be or anyone to be with.

I brought my handbag up with me, so I could transfer the lists to my bedside table. I need to keep them close by, so I can keep track of anything that happens, and so I can keep my sanity levels in check. I think about the other paperwork I am yet to deal with: John's life insurance. Am I going to sign the document and finally put an end to keeping John alive in my heart? I have to. I just need to build up to the moment in any way I can with a bit of a distraction.

When I open the drawer of the bedside table, I see the insurance policy. I slide it out and slap it down on my bed. I decide it's finally time to read the damn thing and sign away John's life. I feel silly not having done this right away when the task was given to me. I've put too much stock into this thought and have to think about the future.

I get only a few pages into the document when I begin to nod off ever so slightly. I fight through the heavy sensation that is trying to overwhelm my eyelids and reread the same line five times. "Come on," I say, trying to stay awake. I know I'm going to fall asleep and there's little I can do about it.

The papers drop from my hand and slide to my bed as I drift off to sleep. I fall into a dream and don't even realize I'm asleep. Jennifer clouds my consciousness; her eyes glare at me and judge my every decision, past and present, as she approaches me from a distance.

"It was you," she says. "You killed John. You did it. He's dead because of you."

I try to fight back, to say that she is wrong, but my voice fails to work. I am weak. I try to scream, but nothing comes out. I am frail. I can't speak or utter a single word.

"It was all your fault, Grace. You killed your husband," Jennifer says. "You let that pickup run him down. You let him die."

Two headlights behind Jennifer blind me, drowning out her body in silhouette. I know there's no escape. I try to run sideways, but my feet are glued to the ground. I can't run from the oncoming vehicle. The headlights grow stronger and brighter. I hear the blaze of a horn trying to warn me, trying to bellow at me, but it's all too late.

The pickup rolls straight over me and snaps me wide awake in my bed. I gasp for air as a layer of sweat covers my body, head to toe. I crawl back up the bed and realize that I was dreaming.

After a brief moment of catching my breath, I pat down on the bed to find the insurance policy form that needs signing. I've had enough of reading the damn thing. It's time to just get it signed and sent off to Thomas Hart.

My hand finds more bed, prompting me to stand up and take a proper look. I lift the sheets and blankets up and check under the covers. My eyes take a moment to register, but I realize it's not there. I know that it was right here. In my frustration, I strip the bed in a hurry and throw everything back and away toward the door. Nothing but the empty bed greets me. I drop to my hands and knees and check under the bed, desperate.

There's nothing there, either. It's gone.

CHAPTER 36

I pace around my bedroom in a panic, clutching at my head like a mad person. How does a thick insurance policy document up and go missing? It's not exactly something that could be easily hidden. Plus, I only fell asleep for what felt like a minute, but according to the time, I was out for more than an hour.

"It has to be here. It has to," I say out loud to myself like a lunatic. Before I know it, I've pulled apart my bedroom and have checked every possible inch of the space, including between the mattress and behind my bed. There's just no way that the document is still in my room.

I wonder if I can ask Thomas for a reprint of the policy so I can get things underway as soon as possible. I'll have to wait until tomorrow to do so and fear any ramifications of losing such a sensitive document that may come about. Hopefully, Thomas won't be too annoyed.

I shake my head, still upset by its disappearance. A thick wad of paper doesn't just up and disappear like this. It has to be somewhere. I know it.

I decide I need to calm myself down and grab a drink of water from my bathroom. I keep a glass in there at all times and fill it to the brim with a shaky hand. I feel the liquid spill over my knuckles.

Was I even reading the contract when I fell asleep or was that a dream? I swear to God I had the thing in my hands and was trying to understand the complicated legal speak the contract outlined.

I catch sight of myself in the bathroom mirror and shake my head again. My hair is a frazzled mess in need of a wash like it was during my six weeks of near solitude, and my skin feels blotchy at best. I splash some water on my face and try to understand why I am dreaming about reading the contract in bed. Am I really that desperate to get it sorted?

I leave my messy bedroom behind to be dealt with later. I suddenly feel the urge to eat something, despite having just eaten a turkey sandwich an hour ago. As I walk along the corridor from my bedroom to the kitchen, a wave of fatigue washes over me. The small nap I had that ended in a nightmare wasn't sufficient enough to recharge my batteries. I can't seem to take good care of myself anymore. A good bite to eat will help me.

I head straight for the refrigerator and pull its door open. Jennifer has helped me to keep it well stocked with fresh ingredients over the last week. For once, I couldn't see its back wall so easily.

As I stand with the door open, attempting to work out a meal I can actually be bothered preparing for myself, I think back over the dark weeks I spent alone in my house. The loss of John was so sudden that I was in a state of shock for the most part. I wouldn't allow anyone to come to stay with me let alone visit. Jennifer was the only person I had any sort of contact with, but our interactions were limited at best. She tried her hardest to help me no matter how irritable or withdrawn I was. She didn't let my sour mood stop her from lending me a hand.

One day, halfway through my six weeks of misery, I had finally run out of clothing to wear that wasn't dirty and resorted to wearing John's shirts around the house. Everywhere I went, his scent followed, only serving to make me want to withdraw further away from the world. It felt almost like he was there with me, watching over my shoulder. I would reach a hand back as if he could comfort me from beyond the grave. I knew the danger of such thinking, but I didn't care. I didn't believe in ghosts or spirits, but it wouldn't have been hard for me to fall into that mindset if it meant I could hold John's hand one last time.

It was the single worst part of his death that I couldn't handle or process. One minute he was there. The next, he was gone. It didn't seem right or possible. He would never walk into our home again home from work. He would never tell me about his day or get something off his chest. He would never get to see me fall pregnant. He would never know what kind of mother I could have been.

The refrigerator beeps at me to hurry up and decide or close its door. The noise snaps me out of my thoughts and brings me back to the present. Has much changed? I'm still alone in a house built for a young family, pining over my dead husband. The only difference now is that Jennifer can't stand the sight of me. I need to fix that.

I finally decide to make another sandwich for dinner and pull out the necessary ingredients to put together a BLT. I only place down about half of what I need on the island bench when I feel the urge to have a bottle of wine with my dinner. I haven't had a drink since the night John died. I've avoided drinking anything of the sort up until now.

But now, I want to forget. I want a way to cope and manage. I've gone from coming out of the dark hole in the ground to worming my way back down it again. How long until I give in? How much fight do I have left?

I grab a glass from one of the high shelves and place it down on the island bench without looking. The bottle is going to go down with ease. No one can stop me.

From the corner of my eye, I catch sight of something on the far end of the bench I swear wasn't there a moment ago. I take a few steps toward the object as I hold my bottle of wine in one trembling hand. It can't be real what I'm looking at. Not unless I've completely lost it now. I'm doing everything I can to keep it together.

There, staring back at me is the thick insurance policy. I inch my way toward it and reach out my free hand. I turn over the cover page and feel the bottle of wine slip from my grasp. It hangs in space for a nanosecond before gravity claims the weight of the liquid. I don't even hear the sound of the glass breaking against the kitchen tiles.

All I can acknowledge is the signature I've scrawled and dated on the document meant for Thomas Hart.

CHAPTER 37

I check every page of the document that has a signature line. I even find initials on each page that show I have read and understood the lawyer's paperwork in full. It looks like my handwriting, too. I didn't read the majority of the document, yet it would appear that I have. I don't even know what it is that I am agreeing to at this point, but I'm too rattled to go back over the legal mess. I let the pages fold flat.

I have no memory of signing any of this or walking the paperwork out here. I was out of it for only an hour. Could I have sleepwalked in that time and brought everything down to the kitchen? Am I really that stressed? Why would I do that? I heard intense bouts of stress could make you do crazy things, but this seems ridiculous.

"What the hell is going on?" I hear myself ask. I back away from the document and try to contain my rapid breathing. I can't let it take control of me. If I do, I will have a panic attack for sure. It's been a long time coming. I slow down my lungs and try to take slower, more controlled breaths. Anxiety sends a shimmer throughout my core.

Never have I needed Jennifer here to help me so much in my life. But I won't be calling her anytime soon. How can I? I can't expect anything from her now. Not after the crap I've put my friend through.

I stumble back and away from the documents and the mess on the floor, unsure what I'm supposed to do. I wanted the forms signed, but not in this strange manner. I move around to the front of the island bench and grab the paperwork before I manage to spill anything over it. With it secure in my hands, I rush along the corridor and plant the papers firmly down on the desk in John's study, convinced I have finally cracked. I must have. Nothing else makes sense.

I head back to the kitchen and take some time to clean up the bottle of wine I never got to drink. It's far from my thoughts now, but its calming affects could help right now. Shards and fragments are scattered far and wide across the floor. It takes me almost ten minutes to sort out the glass and another five to clean up the wine, but somehow, I get it done.

After, I give up on the thought of dinner. I can't stand to be in this room any longer. Before I know it, I go to my room, remake the bed, unsure of anything else, unable to think straight. I sit up half the night, drifting in and out of consciousness as I try to decipher what's real and what is my mind playing tricks on me. How can a person ever tell the difference if both realities seem true? The insurance policy doesn't leave my brain, but I eventually ward off my terrifying thoughts and fall asleep.

※

In the morning, I am still faced with the reality that I have signed the life insurance documents with no memory of ever doing so. I don't know what to make of this. I decide to embrace my unconscious decision to sign the paperwork and get the thick pile out of my sight as soon as possible. It's all I can do.

With the policy signed, I don't waste another second and head for the study to load up the paperwork into my handbag. I'm semi relieved to see it hasn't moved from the study overnight.

I'm about to take a rushed trip to Portland to see Thomas Hart. I know it's short notice, but I'll get that lawyer to process the life insurance policy and speed things along. I feel like I have to get this process over with right now. The sooner, the better. If he tells me it's going to take a few weeks, I've thought of one piece of motivation that will get him moving.

I grab everything I need to take with me including some water and snacks. I went to bed without much dinner and didn't drink enough water as usual. My cell has a decent enough charge, and my car has plenty of fuel to get me to Portland and back in one piece. Nothing will stop me doing what needs to be done, short of lightning striking me down.

I reach the garage door and grip the handle. It seemed like only yesterday that John last came back through the entrance to our home and showed me how much he cared for our relationship. In that moment, I thought our union had been rekindled in full. If only we had stayed home that night. We could have talked about this debt together. Together we could have worked through whatever hell he had gotten himself into.

I close my eyes for a moment and take in a full breath, utilizing what little skills I have in my possession to calm my thoughts down and focus.

"You can do this," I say to myself. "You know you can." My eyes flash open, ready for anything. I give the world a nod and twist open the door handle. I step inside the garage to rush for my car. After fumbling with keys and my handbag, I pull the driver's door open and jump in behind the wheel. I start the engine after taking a deep gulp in and put the vehicle in drive. I hit the gas but realize almost too late that the garage door is closed. I slam the brakes on at the last moment and stop within a few inches of hitting the metal wall in front of me. My mind is too far ahead of my eyes. I want this done and dusted.

"Dammit," I yell. What am I doing? I need to focus and not be a complete moron for once. I'm just delivering documents to a lawyer. Nothing else. My fingers claw around the car looking for the button to open the garage door. I stab at the remote that John mounted near the dashboard for me. The engine kicks in. The door raises a moment later, blissfully unaware how close I came to slamming into it.

In a rush, I thump my foot on the accelerator and speed down the driveway. A second later, I feel the road clip the underbelly of my car. I don't care if I've scuffed and scratched my vehicle. All I care about now is getting this paperwork to Thomas Hart, something I should have done much sooner.

Before I know it, I'm heading out of town towards Portland. I use the time I have to call the lawyer's cell using the business card he gave me. I should have saved him as a contact, but the thought of doing so seemed all too much. I toss the card to the passenger seat the second his phone starts ringing.

"Come on, come on. Pick up." The call goes to voicemail. "No," I say as I am forced to listen to Thomas Hart go on about business hours and his office address. I am about to hang up and quit on this entire idea when I decide to leave him a quick message. The beep prompts me. "Mr. Hart, this is Grace Dalton. I need to see you right now. I have the documents signed and ready for you to process. I need this all to happen as soon as possible, so please call me back the second you get this."

I place my cell down on the passenger seat as a wave of regret follows. What am I thinking, driving out to Portland like a maniac? I shouldn't be doing this. I've had all this time to sign the paperwork, and now I want it handed in and processed immediately. Is there something wrong with me?

I contemplate taking the next exit, so I can turn this disaster of an idea around to head back home, but something refuses to let me stop and pushes me forward. I can't accept that Thomas is unavailable. If he can't make himself free down at his office, then I'll just have to show up at his home and get his attention. It wouldn't be hard for me to find out where he lives, right?

I continue down the highway, going over the speed limit. I slow down a little to avoid getting pulled over. I shouldn't be driving with so much emotion under my belt, but I've made my decision. I have to get this payout started, so I can move on with my life, so I can regain my sanity.

My cell rings out loud, coming through the speakers of my car via the handsfree connection. I hit the "answer" button the second I recognize it's Thomas Hart calling me back. My message must have gotten his attention.

"Mrs. Dalton, I hope you realize I can't see you without first making an appointment."

"I know, but I want to hand in the signed documents for John's estate. I need you to get the process started right away."

"It will have to wait until tomorrow morning, I'm afraid. I'm with another client."

I knew he'd say this. It's like we are following a damn script. But scripts can be changed. "I'll give you one percent of the estate on top of your fees if you fast track this thing and get the ball rolling today."

A quiet lull fills the air for what seems like an eternity. "One percent? Are you sure?"

"Positive." I can almost picture the grin on his face as I speak.

"You've got yourself a deal," Thomas says, clearing his throat. "I'll need to add an addendum to your file."

"Whatever you have to do is fine. Just get things going as soon as possible. Get the investigation started. I want this over with."

Thomas makes some sort of groan down the line like he's thinking about what I just said. "I'll see what I can do."

"What do you mean?" I ask. "If you want your generous bonus, I want a quick turnaround on this. No maybes."

"Why? What's changed?" he asks me. "Before you didn't seem like you were too keen to get this process started, now you want it done yesterday. I know you are running out of money, but surely that wouldn't have happened yet?"

"Please, Mr. Hart, just get the claim sorted as quickly as you can," I say.

He sighs heavily down the line. "Okay. I'll do everything I can today."

"I know you will. I'll meet you at your office in fifteen. Are you far away?"

"I'm in the city," he says.

Perfect. "Fifteen minutes then." I hang up the call on him like I'm a big CEO playing hardball in a corporate merger. Thomas must think I've suddenly grown a spine. In reality, I am merely trying to push through and survive whatever it is that is happening to me. I don't know how or why, but I feel like once I have enough money, I will have options to escape my world. I could sell the house and move away from town, away from this pain. Sure, I'd miss Jennifer and the life I've built in Sherbrook, but I have to move on from John and the problems he's left behind. Nothing else can save me.

I don't know if Jennifer will be upset if I leave town. I can only hope our friendship means something to her. I owe her so much. She doesn't deserve any of the hell I've placed upon her over the last few months. If I leave, we can still be friends. If she wants that. I certainly still want her in my life.

I reach the outskirts of Portland and breathe a sigh of relief. I feel like I'm actually achieving something today just by driving this far on my own. Would Doctor Sylvain be proud? I push on and into the city.

When I pull into the nearest space outside of Thomas Hart's office, I take a moment to catch my breath. I've been breathing so frantically the entire way, that I didn't realize what kind of stress I may have placed upon myself. I can't keep doing this.

I go to climb out and wait for Thomas by the front door of his office, but I stop myself short. My eyes zero in on it. I instantly notice a car pull into the far end of the street and park three hundred feet away. It's a dark blue beat-up sedan sitting on the opposite side of the road. I stare through my windshield and realize that no one is getting out of the car parked. Why?

I get the feeling I am being watched. Why hasn't anyone gotten out of that car yet? I wait as patiently as I can for someone to open a door and prove me wrong, to help me not feel crazy, but the sedan remains motionless. I decide to forget about it and continue on and out of my car. I can't let idle vehicles control me.

A tap on my shoulder almost sends me flying out of my skin, and I turn to see Thomas Hart standing behind me. He waves with a weak smile as I scowl at his sudden disruption.

"Mrs. Dalton? Are you coming inside?"

I nod as I look beyond my car to see his convertible parked behind me with the hard-top up. I didn't even hear him pull in. I was too distracted.

I gather my handbag and glance forward to the other car in the distance. It remains stationary, as does its occupant. I can only make out one person in the driver's seat. What are they doing?

"Come on, Mrs. Dalton. I've got a client to get back to. There's no time to waste if you want this done in a rush."

"I know," I mutter. I pull my gaze from the car. Thomas ushers me to hurry toward his building as if there are reporters all around desperate to get a photo of me. But this back street is mostly empty apart from us and the single car. There don't seem to be any pedestrians walking around like last time.

As I move, the beat-up sedan starts its engine. Before I'm about to reach the front door to Thomas Hart's office, the vehicle pulls into the street and drives slowly past the two of us. I can't help but stare like a stunned fish. The driver is wearing a dark, hooded sweatshirt and sunglasses and avoids eye contact with us. The figure stares at me for a brief moment too long.

"Let's head inside, Grace," Thomas says, grabbing my attention. But I don't know how I'll be able to get through this meeting with the number of thoughts going through my head.

CHAPTER 38

Then

John brought me a glass of water after we got dressed. I drank the whole thing in only a few gulps, completely drained of all my available energy. It had been a long time since John made love to me the way he had just moments ago. It was like our brief time apart made him appreciate me more. I never wanted to lose that feeling again.

"John," I said to him when he laid back down on our bed and gazed into my eyes. "Where have you been?"

"What do you mean?"

"I mean where have you been? I've missed this old John so much, I barely remember him."

He laughed and shook his head, his eyes still distant at the moment we just shared. "I'm here."

I smiled at him and leaned down toward his chest.

I felt a lungful of relief flow out of me, fearing he would say something else. "It's okay, though," I said as I grabbed his bicep. "We can start afresh."

He smiled at me with smooth lips. "We will," he said.

I pulled him in tight and wrapped my arms around his body. I melted into his warmth and felt loved. Had he come back to me? Finally, had John returned from the dark? The last few months made us feel more like roommates than husband and wife. But now it was time to forget the past and look forward to the future. Our future. I thought about the wooden pacifier and smiled. Instead of feeling nervous, I was excited.

"So," he said, clapping his hands. "We've got dinner reservations."

"We do," I said. "You still want to use them, right?" I asked with a lowered voice. I had no idea where we were at that moment; if dinner was asking too much. John had been out somewhere today on his own. But whatever it was he was working through, I had to keep him back on track the way he was now, even if it was only a simple meal in town with me.

"I wouldn't miss it for the world," he said. "Nothing could stop me from taking you out tonight."

I could not remove the smile from my face. I know I could have been upset with him for calling in sick and not telling me about it, but neither of us was perfect. We both had our flaws and made mistakes, both had chosen hurtful words at times and made the wrong choices.

We kissed again. His lips took me to another world from five years ago, one I thought I'd never find again. I felt my knees shake to the slight touch of his hand against my face. I gently pushed him back before we made love again. I couldn't resist him.

"I have to get ready," I said. I stood and stared at him with a coy smile. "But maybe later you should try that again."

He returned my cheeky expression as he leaned back in our bed and placed both hands behind his neck. His head sank into one of our soft pillows. "I'll be waiting for you."

"In those pants? I don't think so. Come on, buddy. You need to get dressed and make yourself look halfway decent if you want to get lucky again."

I playfully shoved his legs and walked across the bedroom, heading for our bathroom.

"I'll start getting ready soon. Just going to rest my eyes for a moment."

"Okay," I said. "Don't fall asleep, though. We're leaving in an hour or so." I smiled the whole way into the bathroom. My messy hair stuck out at me in the mirror and made me laugh. "John, you dog," I said. It was something I jokingly said to him once when we'd first made love. He thought it was one of the funniest things he'd ever heard, so I always mentioned it after. I couldn't remember the last time I'd said those words and meant them. It amazed me how in one moment we had managed to reconnect. We truly had been wasting our time together, letting atrophy claim our marriage.

I decided to take a shower after the long day I'd had. I had some doubts before about us going out to dinner given the way most of this day had been spent, but I pushed away any concern I had for John and allowed my happy mood to continue. I felt like nothing could sour things ever again. I didn't want his problems to get worse, whatever they were.

When I finished in the shower, I tiptoed my way to the door of the bathroom and called out to John. "Time to wake up," I said. I knew he'd be asleep. He always fell asleep after sex, without fail. He didn't respond, so I wrapped the towel around my chest tighter and stepped into our bedroom to help project my voice—but he wasn't there.

Before I said a word, I heard John talking from what sounded like his study. But to who? Was he on the phone? Had someone come to our house while I was in the shower? No; he was on his cell. I moved silently to the doorframe of our master until I could hear John talking with enough clarity to understand his words.

"Is everything all set for tonight?" I heard him say. There was a pause for a few moments before John spoke again. "Good. We'll see you then. Bye."

I felt my forehead crease as I wondered who he was talking to. "John?" I called out.

"Yeah, honey," he said to me, his tone a little startled.

"Who was that?" I said as I walked across the way before turning around the corner to his study. I saw him sitting at his unorganized desk with his cell in hand.

"Just checking on the reservation."

"Oh, okay." Of course.

"I just wanted to make sure we didn't miss out for any reason. This night is important. I don't want to see even the slightest thing go wrong."

I gave him my best reassuring smile. "It won't," I said as I entered his study and walked up to him. I placed an arm on his shoulder. "Everything is going to get better from here on in."

"Is that so?" he asked a second before he grabbed me and pulled me down to his lap. My towel barely stayed on. Before I knew it, he was kissing my neck again, drawing me down and over. I couldn't fight it for a few seconds and let him continue to work his magic until I tapped on him to stop.

"Down boy," I said, barely controlling my urges. "I need to get ready. And so do you. Come on. Move your butt."

"Yes, ma'am," he said. "I just want to check my emails real quick." He turned to his computer, which was open on the login screen.

I pushed up from him with a frown just as he caught hold of my towel without looking. He tried to unwrap me and get a good look like he'd never seen me naked before.

"John," I said. "Stop it. I have to get ready, you dog."

He stared at me with his smile for a second before bowing down in defeat. "I'm sorry. Go. Get ready. I'll be there in a second. I just need to find an email first."

"Look for it later," I said. "We need to get a move on."

"Five minutes and I'm done," he said, holding up a hand.

"Fine," I huffed. I didn't care. As long as we didn't miss dinner.

I didn't think to ask what email he was looking for on the computer that night. I was too high on my new outlook on life to think it meant anything. If only I had realized what he was doing in that room, on that machine, maybe things would have turned out so different.

CHAPTER 39

Now

"That should do it," Thomas says to me as I finish signing the amendment that will give him an extra one percent of John's estate on top of his fees. The man is going to make a little over ten thousand dollars for very little work, but the life insurance policy will be paid out a lot sooner with any luck. Thomas could have extorted me for a lot more if he realized how desperate I am.

"The investigation could be underway as early as tomorrow morning," he says.

"That's good," I reply, happy with the result. "Just want this all over with."

He didn't follow up as to why I was doing this or even care to warn me about the ramifications of trying to speed things along. He just happily took his extra share with confidence, blissfully unaware. Maybe that's how a man like him justifies their actions. It amazes me the control money holds over our lives.

The money makes me think about John. I can't help but imagine what we could have done with this kind of cash if he were still alive and we had a baby on the way. We could have been spending this time painting the spare room for the baby, arguing over which shade of yellow to use, deciding on which room at the hospital we'd try to snag for the birth, along with figuring out which doctor we'd request to deliver the baby. Happy problems.

Instead of such cheerfulness, I had to face a world without John. One where I constantly had no idea if what I was seeing was real or not. One where I was constantly questioning whether the man I married was good or up to something shady.

I think about the investigation I have just authorized to go ahead. Will the investigator find anything that could potentially see the claim denied, such as a large debt to a few unknown people? With the things I've discovered, there is a strong possibility everything will come crashing down, but in some ways I don't care. I just want this all over with however it goes.

I still don't know what John was trying to tell me when he died. Maybe the investigator will learn the truth and fill in the gaps.

My thoughts turn to the business card I discovered of the bar named Hernandez and especially to a person named Felix. Would I find any answers there? I shake my head at the very idea of approaching a stranger in such a way, especially one who John might have owed a hundred grand to.

"Have a good day, Grace," Thomas says to me as I head to my car. He rushes to his own and leaves as fast as he can. His tires squeal and make a small skid mark as he accelerates more quickly than is necessary. He really does have another client to get to. Time is money.

I start the engine of my car and stare around the filling street. After my cursory glance around, I determine that no beat-up sedans are lurking about, so I get underway. I don't dare look where I saw John that morning. As much as I want my brain to summon him up again, I can't have anything ruining my ability to drive.

I pull out into the road and stop mid-way. I can't help but stare at the spot where I almost got hit by a taxi after my first meeting with Thomas Hart. I still didn't understand how John was killed by a driver in our small town of Sherbrook while I was spared in the far busier streets of Portland.

It's frustrating, but I'll never forget that my husband is gone. That he will never come home to me the way he did on our anniversary. If I could relive those few hours, I would stay in that bubble until the end of time. I rub at my stomach and think of the baby that never got a chance to exist. Was I truly ready to be a mother then? Would I have managed to adapt and survive? Will I ever be willing to let another man into my life in such a way? I close my eyes and remember to breathe.

These are questions I can't answer and don't want to answer, so I hit the gas and get moving. I aim for home without thinking.

When I reach the edge of Sherbrook, I think about my next move. I glance at the business card for Hernandez and tap it against my steering wheel. I don't take the normal exit that brings me toward home. Instead, I head over to that bar.

I must be crazy, going out of my way to speak with a man I know nothing about, who John potentially owed a lot of money to. Does Felix work there? Is he a patron? I just need to find this man and ask him what he knows about John. I'll keep the debt out of the conversation.

I drive along a highway that people use to go straight through and past Sherbrook without stopping. I take a long, looping exit into an area known as The Plaza. It's primarily a hub surrounded by a parking lot for small businesses and franchises. I roll along The Plaza, taking in the various businesses that fill its spaces. Restaurants, fast food chains, a hair salon, a liquor store, and an insurance broker share some of the leased shop fronts, each with their own clashing façades. There doesn't seem to be any order to the types of businesses that are near one another. A gift shop sits right next to the large bar I am trying to find: Hernandez.

I pull into a spot out front. I have to be calm in my approach. I can't go into Hernandez with anything less than a relaxed demeanor. I have no idea who I'm about to talk to or what I'm about to find out. People could be unpredictable when it came to money they were owed.

I know this idea is crazy. I can hear Jennifer telling me to stop being stupid and go home in the back of my head. But I can't. I need to know the truth, whatever it may be. I won't be able to sleep again, otherwise.

Thick windows line the front of Hernandez, allowing me to see inside the relatively empty establishment. I'm surprised to see anyone inside the bar considering it's late on a Monday morning. It's now or never if I'm going to go in there and ask for a stranger named Felix.

What am I doing here? This is beyond senseless. What am I going to say to this man if I even find him? "Hi, I'm John's wife. I believe you know him possibly because he owed you a hell of a lot of money. I was hoping you could tell me all of his secrets. Oh, by the way, he died recently." It's not your typical conversation to have.

I sit in the parking space, trying to decide if I should go home or go inside the bar. I miss the days when the hardest choice I had was what to make for dinner. Those days are gone.

My eyes snap open as I make my decision.

CHAPTER 40

I open the driver's door to my car, as confident as I can be about the decision I've made and climb out. My legs carry me toward the entrance to Hernandez. I almost feel like I'm floating along with no control. In less than thirty seconds, I could be face to face with a man who knows why my husband took out a million-dollar life insurance policy. Better yet, he might be able to explain to me why John had a list with his name on it beside a staggering amount of money. Do I really want to know?

I pull open the glass door to Hernandez. When the door swings fully open, I step inside, around a couple of loud-mouthed individuals who have already had too much to drink. When I clear the pair of foul-smelling men, my eyes light upon a bartender who doesn't look too busy.

I stand in the middle of the bar and realize I stick out like a sore thumb. Once I get my head screwed on straight, I walk to the bar and take a seat at one of the stools. I don't know what else to do. I've never been to a bar on my own. Should I leave? I flick around some broken peanut shells on the counter and realize I'm lost in a world I know nothing about.

My old world no longer exists. One where I'd come to such a place with friends and have a good time. I wonder if I'll ever go back to my social circles, back to the hospital, back to the friendships, back to a relationship with a person I love. I think what it was once like to work so close to my husband. I was so fortunate.

I felt blessed for a time to be able to take a break in the hospital with John when we could. There was no more significant boost to my confidence as a registered nurse than to know that he was in the same building as me, caring for the same people. Just the thought of him being close by gave me the ability to go the extra mile with the patients that needed it. I doubt I'd ever find such confidence again. I'd be a liability to the hospital now.

"What can I get you, ma'am?" the bartender asks me.

"Oh," I say. "I hadn't thought that far ahead, sorry. Just some apple juice, please." I need the energy to get me through this disastrous idea.

"Is that all?" he asks with a narrowed brow.

Why is he staring at me? He's probably confused by my answer. "That will be all, thanks."

The bartender walks away to pour me a glass of apple juice. I think about all the bars John and I used to frequent when we were first dating. In that first year, we went around Portland, soaking up the nightlife wherever we could find it. We'd be out drinking and dancing until the early morning and then follow that up with some late-night serving of something greasy from a food truck. We wouldn't make it to bed until five in the morning and enjoyed every second of it. How did we manage?

As time wore on, we spent fewer nights out with friends at clubs and started going to restaurants instead. By the time we'd been married for four years, a night out was a rare thing that took too much brainpower to organize. I spent more time at home with John until even that was too much to manage. We then started to exist in our house as two separate people.

My drink arrives. I pay whatever it costs on my card without taking in the actual amount. The bartender could have charged me a hundred dollars; I would have paid for it. I'm too out of sorts to think straight. My mind keeps trying to distract me from the unavoidable need I've had to come in here and find a man named Felix. I don't blame it. This has to be my worst thought yet.

I take a peek around the bar, using my drink as some sort of cover. I sip the apple juice with a shaky hand. The few patrons all seem happy. Most are having a good time drinking the morning away. Only a few have angry faces over by the dart boards as they argue over a game.

I spin back around, not wanting to be so conspicuous to the world, and take another sip of my juice. It's sweet, though watered down a little by the overwhelming amount of ice the bartender scooped into the glass.

The bartender returns to me. "How is your drink, ma'am?"

"Fine, thanks," I say. I realize this man might be able to help me, so I lean forward. "Say, you don't happen to know anyone around here named Felix?"

"Are you serious?" the bartender asked with a raised brow. "Is that supposed to be some kind of joke?"

I don't understand his response in the slightest. "No, I'm just looking for a man named Felix," I reply.

The man stares at me for a moment until his eyes drift away. He turns and walks down the line to help someone else.

"What the hell?" I call out. Why did he walk off on me like that?

"Maybe I can be of help?" says a voice behind me.

I try to spin on the stool, almost knocking my drink over, and feel a dominant hand come down on my shoulder. I can't turn my body around enough to see the man holding a hand on me. I glance at the bartender to see him intentionally ignoring the situation like he knows what is about to happen. What have I gotten myself into?

"Don't turn around," the voice tells me.

"Okay," I say with a nod. It must be Felix, but I can't tell. I have no idea what he sounds like or looks like. He's just a name to me.

"What are you doing here, Mrs. Dalton? This is no place for a grieving widow."

How does he know who I am? "Who are you?" I ask.

"Who am I? You can't be serious," he says.

"I honestly don't know, but I need to talk about John."

The man chuckles. "You want to talk to me about John? That's rich."

"I do," I say with closed eyes.

I still can't see Felix's face. He stands over me in silence for far too long before he finally speaks. "I think it will be best if we head out the back to have this conversation in private."

In private? I nod as my lips quiver. I try to stay strong as this man overwhelms me with a feeling I can't quite shake.

"Let's go, Grace," the man says. I feel his grip twist me up and turn me around. I start to walk ahead of him, unsure where we are going. He releases his grasp on my shoulder. "Go straight through to the back."

"Okay," I say as I stare up toward a door in the distance that must lead to the back. Without looking, I could quickly run off from Felix or whoever this man is. I could run through the front door and climb into my car and never come back, but I want to know everything this man knows about John.

"Push through the door and head straight," he says as we pass the last lot of happy, clueless drinkers.

I feel his thick paw on me again as it guides me along and through. The strength his fingers alone possess frightens me. I head straight as ordered and am gently moved in through another door to a private office. I walk inside and turn to face the man.

The overweight person who I can only guess is Felix is staring at me in an expensive shell suit, his arms crossed. He takes a few steps forward and walks around the front of his desk, keeping his eyes on me the entire time. He takes a seat at his large office chair and offers me one of the visitor seats.

"Come on; sit down. I don't have all day."

I comply with shaky hands. The only thing that settles them is gripping the two armrests as I take a seat. My eyes slowly run up his meticulously neat desk to the two meaty hands of Felix as he interlaces them.

"Now, Mrs. Dalton, may I ask what the hell you are doing in my bar?"

CHAPTER 41

I stare at Felix Hernandez sitting behind a clean desk in the back room of his bar. There doesn't seem to be much here apart from some storage and Felix's office.

"Well?" Felix says. "Why are you here asking for me?"

I try to answer him, but I choke on my own words. I feel about three feet tall.

Felix leans forward on his desk. His chair creaks and moans under his weight. The guy looks to be in his sixties. He'd have to be about six feet five and at least three hundred pounds. The office is undersized for his frame, making the desk feel tiny. He lets out a sigh. "This is a waste of my time."

"No, it's not. You know why I'm here," I finally blurt out. I have to be strong and get my words out. I have to learn the truth.

"Is that so? Well then, let's pretend that I *don't* fully understand why you of all people would come to such an establishment as Hernandez. Please enlighten me."

"I'm here to talk about John."

The instance I say the word "John" Felix's eyes narrow in with a sneer from his lips. "What about him?"

I need to choose my words correctly, so I take my time. "I found a list he wrote with your name on it. Beside your name was a figure: one hundred thousand dollars. Did John owe you that much money?"

Felix nods. "Along with another hundred and fifty grand to some of my associates."

My heart thuds in my chest harder than it ever has with the confirmation that the list is a large collection of debt. My breathing quickens as I grasp at the desk in front of me. My eyes pop out wide. The room seems to close in on me as I try to understand what kind of debt it could be. Whatever it is, how could John owe so much? How could I have never known about this?

"Mrs. Dalton?" Felix asks.

His words manage to snap me out of an imminent panic attack. I push through it. "Why did he owe you and your friends so much money?"

"Gambling. Poker, mainly."

"Gambling? Like in back rooms? At this bar?" I'd never seen John so much as place a bet on a horse.

Felix laughs. "Not these days, sweetheart. It's all online. Less risk. We just loaned him the money. You see, my associates and I run a discreet service to allow someone such as your husband the ability to keep their habit away from the family credit cards and accounts. Once this person's tab gets out of hand and they ring up a sizeable debt, we step in and take something of theirs as payment, say the house they live in."

I stare at Felix in shock. This explained why John spent so much time on his laptop in his study. I'd often find him in there with a frustrated look on his face I assumed was related to his studies. Was he really in there losing money? I put aside that idea for a moment as reality sets in. "You were going to take our house?"

"It covered the debt plus a nice bit of interest. I told him he had one week to hand it over before things got out of hand. Of course, we never got to that point because John made his last mistake and got killed by some hit and run driver."

Hearing this man speak of John's death as an inconvenience gets at me the wrong way, but I have to bite my tongue and not get upset. This man is apparently a criminal. I have no idea what kind of criminal he is or what he is capable of. And now that I am here, the topic of compensation for John's debt will no doubt come up. Have I managed to walk myself into a spider's web? I can't say a word about the life insurance.

"So, Mrs. Dalton, I have to know: what are you doing here? You clearly didn't know about John's gambling habit."

"I suspected John owed you money from the list I found. That and a business card with your name on the back led me here. I guess now you are going to take my house."

Felix huffs out a bark of laughter. "Not at the moment. Consider yourself lucky. My associates wanted to come after you for what was owed to them. Fortunately for you, someone out there is holding me back for now, which in turn, holds them back."

I lower my head and try to process a million thoughts clouding my brain. Who is holding these people back? And what are they holding them back from exactly?

I try to understand how this all happened. What had John done to us? How could he have let this happen? I stare at Felix and realize he definitely has no idea about the life insurance policy I am about to claim. And why would he?

"I don't think you understand the gravity of the situation, Mrs. Dalton," Felix says. "Someone out there has asked me for a favor to hold back from taking your house from you for the moment. But let me tell you this: he is playing a dangerous game."

He? Who is this man? "I understand," I say. "What I don't understand is who and why. Are you holding your associates back?"

Felix holds up a palm and shakes his head at me. "Not me. There's someone out there who has been keeping the wolves from your door."

"Who?" I ask, having no idea. There can't be more to this. Haven't I already been through enough? What was John thinking? Gambling? With every game of poker he played, he threw away another piece of our future.

"You truly have no idea, do you? Didn't think so. Tell you what, I'll point you in the right direction."

"The right direction?"

"Yes. Take a look at John's past. Find a man named Elliot, and you'll work out just really who your husband was."

I can feel my forehead wrinkling so hard a headache is coming. Who the hell is Elliot? My mouth opens to ask one of many questions, but Felix holds up a hand to silence me.

"Time for you to go, Mrs. Dalton. I would suggest you never show your face around here again in case one of my associates decides to take matters into their own hands."

"Okay," I mutter, unsure what to make of Felix's indirect threat. I allow him to guide me back out to the bar and to the front door. Without another word, Felix ushers me through the exit and sends me on my way with one question on my mind:

Who is Elliot?

CHAPTER 42

Then

John offered to drive us to the restaurant. He always drove us everywhere we went, and I never complained. But for once, I should have been the one to offer. John was apparently at the end of a long day for reasons he wasn't ready to share with me and needed the break. It's funny how such an insignificant gesture could have changed our lives for the better. Like, if I had driven us to the restaurant, our car might have been parked in a different spot. John might not have walked into the street where a dangerous driver was lurking.

I stared at him from the passenger seat wishing I could have told him to come home earlier than he did to celebrate our anniversary. If I had a backbone, I could have been honest and said I called into work to surprise him and knew he had called in sick. Would he have been happy to come home to be with me? I shrugged. Maybe whatever it was he spent his day doing was something he needed more than his wife. I can only hope it was important.

We rolled through the center of town. "I can't wait to eat," I said, breaking the silence.

"Me either. I haven't eaten anything all day. I need to get some steak in me."

It was John's favorite food to order for dinner whenever we went out. I'd be shocked if he ever ordered anything else.

"Are you sure you're okay just eating in town? I could have taken you to Portland to somewhere a bit fancier."

"No, here is perfect. This is our special place. It's one of the first restaurants we ate at when we started to live together." I smiled at John, thinking about Sherbrook. It's where we lived. It's where our baby was going to grow up one day, as long I got the courage to give John his anniversary gift. My strength was in there somewhere, waiting to come out.

John returned my grin, but his smile faded after a short time as he refocused on the road. What was going on inside that head of his? What had stopped him from going into work? The more I thought about it, the more I knew it wasn't about buying me a gift.

We turned off the main street and into a road that ran alongside the single rail track that ran through the middle of the town. We drove past the small restaurant we had a booking at named Ethan's. The building wasn't much to look at from the outside, but within the simple façade existed a classically decorated Italian restaurant with a sophisticated menu and wine list. I couldn't pronounce half the items on either menu, but I loved any outing that took us to Ethan's. It was our special place.

"Damn, no spots out front," John muttered.

"There's one up ahead," I said, pointing out to a free parking spot roughly six car lengths away.

"I wanted one up front, though."

"It's fine, John. Take it before someone else does."

He huffed at me a little. "It'll have to do."

I stared at the side of his head with a frown. I didn't know what the big deal was. It was only a short walk away. It wasn't like we had to cross several streets to reach the restaurant. That was when I started to notice something was off with John. I couldn't explain it, but he seemed to be on edge the second we arrived with a crease across his brow. Was he feeling guilty for something? For taking the day off? Did he not want to spend the evening with me?

I tried to calm myself down. I stopped myself from thinking too much and tried to get back into the evening. We climbed out of the car and strolled toward the restaurant as a man in a pickup drove past at a speed that was clearly too fast for the area. I slowed my pace.

"Come on; let's go," John said. "Dinner is calling me."

I ignored the bad driver and turned to John. "You mean your steak is calling you."

John chuckled as we continued to walk to the restaurant. We arrived a short time later at the entrance. John opened the door for me.

"Reservation for Dalton," he said to the hostess once we cleared the front door.

A young girl in a tight black dress tapped in the name on her iPad and gave us a confirmation of the booking with a flash of her pearly whites. "Right this way, please," she said, grabbing two menus and a wine list in the process. She guided us to our intimate table for two and asked if we wanted to order any drinks. I ordered some house red while John glossed over the wine list like he knew what he was doing and ordered something he could hardly pronounce. It was eighteen dollars for a single glass of red wine that supposedly came from Italy. We usually went as high as five or six dollars a glass, picking wines we knew little about. My eyes almost bulged out of my head.

"What?" John asked. "We're celebrating. You have one, too. Forget the house wine." He changed the order before I said a word. The hostess smiled and left us to return to her post.

"We must be doing some serious celebrating for that price," I said once she'd left. Did John know I was going to give him the wooden pacifier? Is that why he took the day off? Was he not ready?

"It's from Italy," John said with a mock accent.

I refocused. "You'd hope so," I said. I didn't want to grind him about it, but at the same time, we couldn't afford to go crazy on the meal either. We were on a tight budget.

Our wine came out and was poured into two glasses. John took a swig and swirled it around and held it against the light as if he knew what he was doing. A smirk coated his face.

"Good year?" I asked, trying not to laugh. I had no idea if that's what you were supposed to ask someone when they drank wine that cost around seventy dollars per bottle.

"Oh, of course," he said. He took a big gulp of the glass, ingesting probably ten dollars' worth.

"So how's everything going at work?" I asked, not thinking straight. I felt all over the place with nerves.

"It's fine," he said with a flap of his hand to dismiss any further questions.

"What's wrong?"

"Nothing. I just don't want to talk about work. Not tonight."

"Okay, that's fine," I said as a dozen possibilities entered my mind at once. Was he going to quit or change departments? It might explain his recent behavior. But he was too far along in his residency to do such a thing. He just had to stick it out for a few more years. I wondered about today: how he hadn't shown up for his shift. How many times had he called in sick like this? I never saw his pay slips. My mouth opened to ask him, but I changed my mind at the last moment, not wanting to bring anything up about today. I couldn't ruin this night.

"What were you going to say?" he asked me.

My mouth betrayed me. "It was nothing. Don't stress."

An awkward silence broke out between us. It didn't take long for the night to shift in that direction. Maybe it wasn't a good idea to celebrate five years of marriage when we were having some problems.

"Are you ready to order?" a waiter asked us with both hands behind his back.

I stupidly hadn't looked at the menu yet, so I quickly opened it and rushed my eyes over my choices. I could remember a few of the dishes, so it wouldn't take me long. I looked up to John. "You order first, honey."

We ordered our meals one at a time and sat back after the waiter crept away.

John stood in a hurry and said he was off to the restroom. He couldn't get away from me quicker if he tried. When he came back, he settled down into his seat and let out a sigh.

It took some time, but we eventually started to enjoy each other's company. The longer the night wore on, the more the wine flowed, the better we were together. I began to remember what it could be like to be in a fun relationship. I reminded John not to have too many drinks as he was driving us home. I couldn't stand the thought of us having an accident so close to the house. He agreed to cut himself off after a couple of glasses.

By the time we were finished with our meals, John seemed to be like his old self, as if he had worked something out today that had been bothering him. If only I knew.

I wanted to ask him what problems he'd been facing, but I didn't want to spoil our evening that I so desired to have. If only I had done so. If only I dared to see the writing on the wall.

CHAPTER 43

Now

A wave of exhaustion comes over me as I leave Felix's bar around midday. I feel a sudden urge to get home and sleep before I pass out from the maelstrom of agony that has claimed me this Monday morning. The stress of rushing to Portland to meet with Thomas only to come back to town to see Felix is too much to bear. I need a good nap if I am going to be able to face the rest of the day. Pathetic.

"*Take a look at John's past. Find someone named Elliot, and you'll work out just really who your husband was.*" Felix's words follow alongside me in the car, echoing in my ears, leaving me feeling light-headed. I don't know who this Elliot person is and what he meant to John, but something tells me I have to find out sooner rather than later considering he is the one keeping Felix from taking my house.

I drive myself slowly home, not wanting to let this day consume me and cause an accident. It's hard not to let it all into my brain at once as I think about John's ridiculous gambling habit. How could he have racked up a quarter of a million dollars in debt without me ever knowing? How did he then afford to take out the life insurance policy? I feel like I didn't really know him as a person, like John had two lives. How can I say he was my husband when I didn't know about his other world?

I reach my house and click the garage door button. I stop just short of colliding with the metal wall as it rises up and folds itself away. I can barely function.

When I get inside, I settle into bed on autopilot despite it not being night-time. I let the weight of the day drag me down as I drift off to sleep in an instant. I have no idea what the next few days will have in store for me but they can't be good. If only I had Jennifer by my side to help me through this hell.

*

I wake up far too late in the afternoon. I've spent most of my rough sleep dreaming about John, Felix, Jennifer, and now some mysterious figure named Elliot. It's the last name that has me the most restless and on edge. Who is he and why did Felix feel the need to point me in his direction? Whatever reason he had must be important, so I pull my laptop from my bedside table into bed with me to do some much-needed research. After all, this man is the only one keeping the wolves from my door.

I get comfortable and lie back down to start a search online for John Dalton. I figure the name Elliot is too vague to do much with, so I first try to look into John's life and go from there. The usual things populate the top of my search results. I see John's Facebook page, his Instagram account, his LinkedIn profile, and a bunch of other hits that are too recent to be of use. I try to think of John's past and what it might be that Felix meant for me to look at. Only one thing stands out from everything else; the one topic John rarely spoke of.

"The group homes," I say out loud as the thought hits me. I start to frantically search with more refined strings of text, narrowing down my results. A few records come up with little effort. I find the Catholic group home register John belonged to. I scan through the list and run a word search on the name "Elliot." What I find forces my mouth to drop open. It can't be right.

I almost push the laptop away from myself as I read the two words over and over. They don't seem real or seem to fit together, but there they are for all to see.

"Elliot Dalton," I say out loud, needing to parse the words through my system. What does this mean? Are John and Elliot related? Are they brothers? I stare at the computer for far too long and realize I need to keep digging. With a full name to work with, I start to search for Elliot Dalton.

All of the usual social media sites give me no results. Either he doesn't use them, or he does so under a pseudonym; I refocus on the group home angle. As I dig deeper, I confirm that the two were indeed siblings who arrived at one of the homes at the same time, age unknown. It must have been when they were first abandoned. The confirmation that John's parents left him and his brother tugs at my heart, but any sympathy I feel for John is quickly extinguished when I think about the debt. I force myself to continue.

Apart from the group home, no other records exist online for Elliot Dalton. He doesn't have a web presence or so much as a photo of himself anywhere. It's like he lives off the grid. The group home records are nothing but text. I need to know more, but there is nothing else online. It's as if Elliot is some sort of ghost.

I roll out of bed and begin tugging at my head. What does this all mean? Why did Felix want me to know that John had a brother named Elliot? What did he have to do with any of this?

I think about John never telling me about having a brother. Why would he keep something like that from me? Did they have a falling out before we'd met? Or was he simply ashamed of any link to his past? Either way, it was another thing he was keeping from me. What else would I discover about John in this process?

Then it hits me. This Elliot person. I think about the strange things that have been happening to me ever since I came out of my six-week void. Seeing John in Portland, seeing John come online on Facebook, receiving the strange text message, spotting the man staring at my house from the corner, finding the signed forms. Was Elliot behind some of these things? I'd thought I was losing my mind, but all along it could have been him screwing with me. But why? What reason would John's brother, whom I've never met, have to make my life worse than it already is? And more importantly, why would he do so while also holding back Felix?

I hold both hands on my head to stop myself from screaming. I need to reach out to Elliot and speak with him before I lose my mind. If Felix thought he was important enough to mention, then I have to talk to him. There's no other option.

I rush across my bedroom and grab my handbag from my dresser. I rummage through the main pocket until I find the business card for Hernandez. I see Felix's name and number written on the back.

I need to call him.

I have to call him.

Right now.

CHAPTER 44

I dial the number written on the business card I found. It's a cell number that I assume belongs to him. If it doesn't, I don't know what I'll do short of driving back down to his bar again. I don't care about the dangers of angering his associates, as he told me; I have to reach out to Elliot, and Felix is the only person that can help me achieve that.

My call goes to Felix's voicemail. I let out a long sigh as I debate leaving him a message. I listen to his pre-recorded voice and wait a few moments for the beep. I pause for a second with hesitation. "Felix, it's Grace—Mrs. Dalton. I need to talk to you right away about Elliot. I promise this will be the last time I bother you, ever. Please call me back immediately on this number." I hang up knowing Felix will see my cell come up on his phone. All I can hope is that he calls me back soon.

※

Three hours tick by. Three long hours. I've done what I can to distract myself as I wait for Felix to call back. I pace around in circles in my bedroom like a mad person. Every minute or two, I take a peek out of the window, unsure what it is I'm even looking for. Am I expecting to see Elliot out there watching me? I don't even know what he looks like or what reason he would have to be watching me. With each glance outside, I see nothing but my empty street. The same cars are parked where they have been all afternoon. The same scene greets me each and every time.

As night falls and a dense fog begins to roll in, I see the usual commuters coming home from work. The mist makes it hard to see after some time. Maybe that's a good thing, though. The less I know, the better.

My cell buzzes on my mattress. I jump, stumbling on the spot as I pull myself together and answer my ringing phone. I pick up the device and see Felix's name come up on the display. Finally.

"How did you get this number?" Felix demands the second I pick up.

"I found it on a business card John had."

"Well, it's time you lost it. I'm hanging up."

"No, please don't go. I'll just be a minute."

A moment of silence meets my request, then, "You've got thirty seconds."

I try not to panic. "Okay, it's simple. I just need Elliot's number. That's all. I know you must have it."

A few seconds of silence answer me back. "Why should I give it to you?"

I close my eyes for a moment and collect my thoughts. I only have one shot at this. Don't screw it up. "Because you told me to look for someone named Elliot, that he would help explain my late husband's behavior. I did just that, and now I know Elliot and John were brothers. I have questions. Elliot has answers."

Felix sneers on the other end of the line. I don't need to see it. I can hear the parting of his lips. "Why do you think he'll tell them to you?"

"He has to. He's the one holding you back, right?"

Felix groans.

I clearly am pushing my luck. "You don't understand. He may be the only person who can help me." I can't say any more without having to tell Felix everything. There isn't enough time to tell him even a third of what's happened.

"Okay," Felix says. "You can have his number, but this is the last time you and I will ever speak. Got that?"

"I understand, and I promise you I'll delete your number and throw the card away."

"You'd better. I'm texting you Elliot's cell. If he asks, you got it from John."

"Okay, thank you for—"

Felix hangs up on me. I shake my head and hold up my cell in anticipation of his text message. I hope he wasn't lying to me. Ten seconds slowly tick by with nothing coming my way. Twenty seconds turn into thirty. Soon, it's been a full minute. What the hell? I'm about ready to freak out when my cell buzzes with a new text. It's Felix with Elliot's number as promised.

"Thank you," I blurt out loud despite the fact Felix can't hear me. I save Elliot's number to my cell. I then delete Felix from my contacts list but keep the Hernandez business card just in case I ever need to call him again, despite my promise.

Overwhelmed with my small victory, I take a moment to sit down on the edge of my mattress and remember to breathe. It's the start of the night, and I have Elliot's number ready to use. Do I call him straight away? I need a moment to think first.

"Okay," I say to center myself. I think about everything I know to be true. I know that John is dead. I saw him die. I know that over the past week odd things have been happening that have left me questioning my very sanity. Now, I've learned that John had a severe gambling debt that I am off the hook for because of his brother Elliot—a man I never knew existed.

It's a lot of chaos to handle at once. It's no wonder Jennifer thinks I'm a lost cause and has given up on me. Even if I sat her down and told her everything from start to finish, she wouldn't believe me. I'd sound even worse than before. I'd just get hauled off to the doctor's office for the last time and be committed to the nearest psychiatric hospital soon after.

I can't let that happen. Not after coming this close to knowing the truth. It would burn me up inside forever. I knew something was wrong the day John died, but I was too caught up in my own world to see more than two feet in front of me. John was a gambler and not just one with a small problem; he was an addict. Maybe worse. To have reached the point where he owed Felix and his friends so much money they had no choice but to come and take our house away was pure insanity. How was he going to explain that to me? Did he expect to be forgiven for ruining everything we worked toward? He knew I'd leave him if I found out.

On top of all that, there is still the matter of the million-dollar payout I have coming my way. Will the investigator find out about John's gambling and stop the claim? Felix's discreet gambling services may be put to the test without him ever realizing it. And finally, what happens if I get the money and Felix finds out about it? Would he do more than take my house?

I force myself to stop and head to my bathroom to take a long shower. I need time to switch off and try to calm down my brain so I can get some sleep before I make the call.

As soon as I gather the courage needed to call Elliot, I will be asking him to meet with me.

CHAPTER 45

I don't really sleep through the night. I go between a half slumber and conscious thought about what might happen when I call Elliot. I still have too many unanswered, damning questions rattling around in my noisy head. Sleep will evade me until I get a response for at least some of them.

The only time I fall asleep results in a nightmare I'd rather not think about, but I can't stop it coming into my head. I was out to dinner with John, reliving that moment over and again when he realized he was about to die. Those two seconds before the pickup slammed into his body were the longest of my life. At no other point in my existence have I been weaker or as powerless. I feel heavy and useless. All I can do is watch and let it happen on a loop until I pull my mind out of that dream.

When morning comes, I drag myself from my sweat-soaked bed and pull on some clean clothing. I feel like death on two legs as I scuff my feet along the carpet. John always hated when I did this. He isn't here to tell me what to do, though.

I try to eat some breakfast in the kitchen, but the task is near impossible. My appetite is nonexistent at this point. How can I possibly think about food at a time like this? It seems pointless.

I toy with my cell for a moment, spinning it around on the counter as I stare into space, attempting to avoid what needs doing. I stop playing with the device and take a deep breath. I bring up Elliot's number on my list of contacts and stare at the name. I still don't understand how John had a brother that he never told me about. He let me believe he was an only child to parents who didn't want him. Why wouldn't he want me to know about his family? Was he ashamed? Did Elliot beat him up?

I reach out my finger to tap the call button for Elliot's contact, but I hesitate and pull it back. My arms tremble as I hold my cell in my hands. My thumb hovers over the call button. Will he answer if I call? Will he panic if I call? I still don't know if this is a good idea or not, but I have to think that Felix told me about Elliot for a reason. He could have taken everything from me to square away John's debt, but his relationship with Elliot stopped that from happening. I have no idea why Elliot would do such a thing or how he had such influence over Felix. I need to find out.

I tap the button and listen as the call connects and begins to ring. I count each tone as it rolls down the line. One, two, three, four. He doesn't pick up. Five, six, seven, eight. Should I give up? Nine, ten.

"Hello, Grace," a voice says. It sounds strikingly familiar.

"Uh, hello, Elliot," I say with a weak mutter.

"So, I suppose you have a few questions for me?" he asks.

"I do, yes," I reply.

"Well, you'll have to save them for now. There's no way I'm doing this over the phone. It's going to have to be face to face."

He wants to meet? Why?

"Grace?" he asks. "Are you going to meet with me?"

I pace around my kitchen with my mouth agape. His voice is getting to me. He sounds so much like John, only deeper. "I, uh—"

"Come on, now. Don't be scared. I know you've got questions. I won't bite."

"Fine. Let's meet," I blurt out. What other options do I have left?

"That's better. Now I've got a few things to take care of first, but I think I could see you later tonight. I'll text you when and where."

"Tonight? Okay," I say, accepting.

"Good. Oh, and it goes without saying, but come alone. This is between you and me, and we have a lot to discuss, especially the life insurance money you're about to receive. Do you understand?"

"Wait," I say. "What is that supposed to mean? I thought you were helping keep Felix away?"

"I am, Grace. You see, Felix and I go way back. As a personal favor, he has agreed to keep his people on hold from taking your house as I've promised him that he will be paid cash instead. Say cash from a nice life insurance policy. But don't worry, we'll work this all out soon."

I don't know what to say. Elliot is threatening me in a similar way to Felix, just to take the million dollars for himself once he pays off John's debt. How could he have even known it existed or that John or I would get a big payout if one of us died? Did Elliot make John take out the life insurance policy? Or did he apply for it in John's name, pretending to be him when he met with Thomas Hart?

My head begins to hurt.

Then I start to think about all of the strange things that have been happening to me over the past week and realize something.

"Is it you? Have you been screwing with me, making me think I'm losing my mind?"

Silence. It's all Elliot gives me. It's far more damaging than him admitting to anything.

"Elliot? Please. I need to know if it's been you all along. Have you been watching me? Was that you on John's Facebook? Did you come into my house and forge those forms?"

"Enough. We either have an understanding, or we don't. What's it going to be, Grace?"

My mouth opens wide to argue, but I stop myself from making things worse. "We have an understanding. I'll meet with you alone."

"Good. Now don't bother trying to call me again on this number. As soon as you hang up, I'm destroying it. I'll text you from a new number with instructions when I'm ready."

"Okay," I say, defeated.

"Goodbye, Grace. I'll see you tonight."

"Wait. Your voice. You sound just like John, only a little different."

I can hear the grin in his voice. "Well, of course, I do, Grace. We are twins after all."

The line goes dead. The arm that is holding my cell falls away. I shake my head and cover my mouth with my spare hand. Elliot's confession changes everything. I realize in a flash that I wasn't losing my mind with stress over the last week.

It wasn't John who was watching me from the grave sending me off the deep end; it was his twin brother Elliot all along.

CHAPTER 46

Then

We finished dinner with some dessert. We had ordered two cannolis and sat in silence while we ate, enjoying the food and each other's company.

"That was delicious," I said as I pushed my plate and fork away, satisfied.

John let out a contented breath. "I'm sure I'll be paying for that one," he said as he slapped his stomach. He had barely an ounce of fat on his lean figure. He also enjoyed his gym sessions too much to gain weight.

I, on the other hand, didn't have the perfect body and never would. I wasn't overweight, but I was comfortable in my own skin. I enjoyed chocolate and wine too much to be a perfect angel.

John stared at the flake-covered plate before him and toyed with his fork. He was deep in thought again. It was the third time I'd caught him like this throughout the night. One minute he was happy and chatting, the next he was lost inside his head. It had to be related to today. What was going on in that head of his?

"Everything okay?" I asked.

His eyes took a moment to snap up to mine. "I'm fine, just thinking about the first time I ever ate a cannoli."

"When was that?" I asked, wondering why he was thinking about such a thing.

"Back in the group home. The main one."

The group home? I had to tread carefully. He refused to talk about it most days.

"Did you have it for a dessert one time in the home?"

"God, no," he said with a chuckle. "They would never give us something that held any flavor. We didn't have desserts the way a normal family would. It was three small meals per day on a rotating schedule you could set your watch to."

"Then how did you have a cannoli?"

John smiled. "There was this kid in the group home. He and I were close and always got into trouble. Thick as thieves, we were, for the longest time. One night, we broke into the office of the pastor who ran the home while he was asleep. He was such an asshole, this guy. He really had it in for my friend and me. We were always the ones who got the blame when things went wrong." John shook his head as he stared off into space.

"What happened?" I asked.

He glanced at me in surprise and continued his story. "Well, we broke into his office, knowing he had some cannolis in there all wrapped up and ready to be eaten by him the next day. The bastard would never give us anything as delicious, but he didn't mind devouring the damn things in front of us."

"So you ate them all?"

"Every last flake of pastry," John said with a smile. "You'd swear they never existed."

"Wow. How much trouble did you get into?" I asked.

He smiled inwardly. "Enough so we'd never try to steal from him again. At least that's what he thought. We just got better at not getting caught."

"So you were quite the criminal back then," I said with raised brows.

John's smile faded into a flat line. "They were some crazy days. I know that much."

I could see him slipping back to that dark time of his life. I needed to pull him out of it before the night was ruined. "Look at you now, though. You're a smart, handsome man who's on his way to becoming a successful physician in a busy hospital. Also, you are married to one awesome nurse, I might add." The wooden pacifier sat in my coat pocket, begging to come out. Was it a good time to put such a thing on my husband? I held back.

He smiled at me, but I could see the expression was almost forced. "Come on," he said. "Let's get going." He leaned forward to stand.

I reached out a hand. "Wait, John," I said. I still needed to find the courage to give him my gift. "I'm trying to compliment you here."

He slumped back down. "Why?"

"Because you're a good man who has achieved a lot considering your upbringing."

He snorted at me. "I'm not a good man, Grace. Sure, I might have made something of myself now, but I did things when I was younger, things I can't atone for, things I can't stand to think about."

Where was this coming from? John had never told me this much about his past or that he'd done bad things. What had got him thinking about his life all of a sudden?

"You're not that person now, are you? You need to remember who you've become and not what you were."

He waved a hand at me and turned partially away. "Some things shouldn't be forgotten."

A silence formed around us despite the restaurant still being busy. I fiddled with my hands a moment. What could I say to make things right? "Like are you happy?"

"You know I am. What makes you think I'm not?"

"I know you. But I also know when something is bothering you, and you don't want to talk about it. Well, maybe it's time to start talking about things."

John shook his head and ran a hand through his hair. He went to say something to me but paused to look at his watch.

"What is it? You can tell me," I said.

"It's nothing. Anyway, we better get going."

"Why? We've got nowhere to be."

He huffed at me. "I want to go home. It's been a long day."

I crossed my arms. "What about presents? We haven't given them to each other yet."

His brow furrowed ever so slightly. He dropped down to a small bag I knew was sitting beside him at the table. He fished something out and handed over a wrapped box to me.

I didn't want him to give this to me. I needed an excuse to bring out my gift to him. Still, I had to accept, so I unwrapped John's present with care to see a gold watch with a light gray leather band inside a box with a transparent lid. "It's beautiful," I said.

"The time doesn't work, but I'll have it repaired for you."

"Thank you," I said as I looked up at him with a smile. He knew this was the exact kind of watch I liked. I placed the gift down and felt into my coat pocket for John's.

"Your turn," I said.

"I don't want anything. I don't deserve it."

"You do. You deserve more than you believe, okay? You are a good man. And if something is bothering you, I want to know about it."

The restaurant went silent. The only bit of noise came from the generic background music and John's heavy breath. I let my gift to him stay where it was for now. I couldn't have this moment ruined. We were already on the cusp of spoiling everything.

"Okay," he said with a shrug.

I could feel my eyes darting all over the features of his face as I tried to analyze his response. What I found, right there, tattooed across his forehead was not what I wanted to see: he was too tired to argue. He didn't care about us anymore. We would fall back into our rut the second we went home. I couldn't let that happen. Not again.

In the past, he'd never been too tired for a heated discussion. It was the way we communicated some days. We'd come close to yelling and shouting about anything and everything. We'd argue down to the sharpest points of nothing, neither one of us conceding no matter how pathetic our stance, until we broke down and stormed off to the bedroom to have sex. It kept us alive.

"What's going on today? I've never seen you like this before." I asked. "After everything we've been through, I thought you cared about me."

"Grace, I do care, it's just..."

"Don't bother." I turned away from him and stormed off. I glanced over my shoulder to see the waiter bringing John the check. Had the manager given the order to push us out the door as soon as possible?

I continued to the exit. What was the point of this whole dinner? There was no way in hell I was going to pay for that meal. Just as I was about to leave the restaurant, I stopped. I turned around and stomped back to John. He needed to hear me.

"I don't understand you. One minute we are about to patch things up and move forward, the next you are off in your own world ready to ruin everything we've worked on."

John's frown dropped into a smile, but it wasn't a happy one. Was he taunting me? Was this a joke to him?

I didn't let him say another word and left the restaurant. The entire night was nothing but a mistake.

CHAPTER 47

Now

I drop my cell down on the kitchen counter. I don't know where to turn to or what to do with the knowledge I now have in my possession. Elliot is John's twin brother. They were at the group home together according to the data I found. So why did John keep Elliot a secret?

I try not to let the storm of thoughts in my head overwhelm me as I think about all of the things Elliot has been doing to make me feel I'm insane. I thought I was hallucinating, especially when I saw John. Instead, I was staring at his twin.

Why did he do it?

Up until now, I didn't know he existed. But he knew me. What had I done to warrant this kind of response? Did he blame me for what happened to John? I fought day and night not to feel responsible for my husband's death. Could Elliot be out to settle the score?

A shudder runs down my spine as I go into a panic. I'm struggling to breathe and my heart rate is spiraling out of control. I'm all alone in this house with no one to help me.

I think about my house and try to fathom why Elliot would stop Felix and his men from taking my home from me while simultaneously screwing with my head. It didn't make sense. But I don't have time for sense.

What if Elliot were to come for me right now? How long would it take someone to find me? Everyone at work isn't expecting my presence back for a long time, my best friend hates me, and I'm not scheduled to see Doctor Sylvain for another day. Would he bother to check up on me if I didn't go to my appointment? It wouldn't seem that odd for me to skip a session at the moment.

A thought throws me: Elliot might not be on his way, but what if he could see me? Was he watching me? Did he have hidden cameras placed around my house? How else did he get in here and move the insurance policy around and sign it? The violation of my privacy makes me want to hurl. My home is no longer a safe sanctuary.

My cell lets off a ding in the distance, notifying me that someone has sent me a text. It can't be Elliot already, can it? If so, he's not wasting any more time with threatening notes. He's got me exactly where he wants me, whatever that is.

I drop my feet to the ground and stand. I slowly move toward my cell. At this point, I'd be happy to throw the damn thing out the window and cut myself off from the world. But it wouldn't stop the dark forces at play. It wouldn't make everything all better or bring back my dead husband, but at least it would mean that Elliot couldn't talk to me.

When I reach my cell, I see a message on the lock screen from Jennifer. It's brief, and only says, "We need to talk." My heart skips a beat.

I scoop up the device with both hands and call her. I know I can't tell her what's happening or say if I'm in any danger, but I just need to hear her voice, even if it's only for a moment.

"Grace?" Jenn says after three rings.

"Jenn, please don't hang up."

"I won't. Is everything alright? You sound funny."

"I'm fine," I lie as best I can. "Everything is fine. How are you?" I can hear the crazy in my voice as I repeat myself. I can't help it, though. I'm being threatened by my dead husband's twin brother and am powerless to do a thing to stop it.

"Grace, you don't sound fine at all. Do you need to go see Doctor Sylvain?"

The damn doctor again. "No, I'm okay. I just had a bad night, is all. Didn't sleep much."

"Are you sure? Is there something you want to tell me?"

Her words sting. I have no idea if Elliot can hear this conversation or if he is watching me in general. Either way, I can't risk telling Jennifer, can I? I already told her a different version of what I thought was happening. Lucky for her I was wrong. She can stay out of my terrible life if that's what she wants.

"Well? Grace?"

"It's all good. Everything is okay. I'm just a little bit lonely, is all."

"Lonely, huh?" I hear her sigh heavily over the phone. "Would you like some company?"

"No, you're at work. It's fine."

Jennifer forces her words out. "I've got the next three hours spare before I have to go in. Why don't you meet me at the café? We can talk some more there, okay?"

"Uh, yeah, sure," I say, agreeing with her. I don't know how to say no. Should I say no?

"I'll be there in twenty minutes. Is that enough time for you?"

"Plenty," I lie. Why do I keep doing it? Especially to my friend, the one that is still there for me even when she clearly doesn't like me anymore. I can tell she is merely checking up on me. This isn't a social conversation.

"See you soon, Grace," she says.

I hang up the phone without saying goodbye. I can't bring myself to say the word in case it is indeed the last time we speak.

※

I get ready in a hurry and jump into my car. I glance in the mirror and sigh at the poor job I did of getting myself ready. I didn't have time to do things right.

I make sure to open the garage door before driving out. At least I have some of my wits about me. I can't say the rest of my brain is making much sense.

I drive into town and notice every car that travels near or behind me. Is Elliot following from a distance? Is he keeping tabs on my every move, making sure that I don't drive to the police station instead of the café? I don't even know what I'd tell the cops if I went and saw them. They'd think I was nuts like everyone else.

The longer I drive, the worse I get. As soon as I think I've spotted Elliot in one of the cars, the person overtakes me and morphs into an impatient soccer mum on her way to drop off her kids.

Worse still, if I do spot Elliot, would it be like seeing John again alive and in the flesh? They were twins after all. When I thought I saw John in Portland, it was simply Elliot wearing clothing that covered part of his face. At that distance, it was no surprise he was able to fool me. I think about Elliot's voice on the phone. It was essentially a deeper version of John's with a few other slight differences.

I arrive on the street before the café and see the spot John was run down. Why was Elliot treating me like I was the one behind the wheel of the blue pickup that night? No one had loved John more than I did when it happened.

I bring myself back to the present before I start to see it all happen again. I can't lose my focus now. Not while my friend is close by.

Jennifer's car is parked up ahead by the café. I get my head back in the game and drive. After parking a few lengths away, I rush to the restaurant and find Jennifer already inside waiting for me.

She looks up from a booth by the far wall and gives me a polite smile. It fades in less than a second, taking away all hope I might have had left that she still cared about me other than simple guilt. Her stiff arms are crossed over the table. She lifts her shoulders up as I get closer and pulls her hands to her sides. "Hi, Grace."

"Hi," I say as I sit down in the busy café.

Jennifer takes in a deep breath and tries to put on her tender face, the one I've seen her use on me a few times this week when I've been too much to handle. I wish I wasn't such a burden.

"Thanks for coming," I say. "You have no idea how much it means to me to know that you still care."

"Of course I still care about you, Grace. I always will, no matter what. But I can't continue to be your friend if you refuse to get help. We shouldn't be meeting here when you're in the middle of a crisis. You should be seeing Doctor Sylvain instead."

I close my eyes for a second to compose myself. When I open them back up, I lean forward in my seat and place a hand on the table, palm down. "He can't help me, Jenn. He never could. I'm only just realizing that now. And it sucks, I know, but you have to trust me and listen when I say this: no one can help me, not even you."

Any politeness Jennifer had managed to project drops away in a flash as she sits up straight as an arrow. I'm about to get it. "Listen to yourself," she says keeping her voice level not to upset the rest of the café. "You have no idea what you're saying. You think you're above all of your problems, that they don't exist. Well, I've got news for you, Grace: they do exist."

I remain silent, pushing down my every desire to respond to Jennifer's misguided words. She has no idea. I have to screw up and twist my face away from her as I do everything in my power to not shout out about John's debts or the fact that he has a twin brother who is out to get me.

Jennifer slumps back down and places a hand on her forehead. "Maybe this was a mistake. Me coming here thinking I could help you."

"It wasn't," I say, almost at a whisper. "Because you're right. I do have problems, ones I can't ignore. Ones that aren't going away anytime soon. But what you don't understand is that they aren't just difficulties I've created for myself. Things are happening that I can't tell you about no matter how much I want to."

Jennifer's eyes go wider than before as her lips curl into a sneer. She doesn't have to say a word for me to know she doesn't believe me. She opens her mouth to speak, but nothing comes out. As if giving in, she throws up both of her palms for a moment and shakes her head.

"It's okay. You don't have to believe me," I say. "It's probably better this way." I lower my head, feeling the defeat take over.

Jenifer responds by pinching the bridge of her nose with her thumb and index finger as she leans heavily on her elbow with closed eyes. She sits up straight again and looks me in the eye. "I'm going to the bathroom. I would hope you have come to your senses by the time I get back and can tell me the truth."

I don't respond and watch her push herself up and away from the booth. I hear her mutter things under her breath. I've done a number on her. So much so, I'm surprised she hasn't left.

While Jennifer disappears into the bathroom, I take it upon myself to check and see if Elliot is outside the café, watching me. I creep my way to the front of the building, pretending to be looking at the quirky ornaments that line the walls. He's driving me insane with paranoia. What does he want from me?

I glance out the door and try to see if any cars are rolling slowly by, or if there is a man in a black hooded sweatshirt watching me. The street appears normal with only minimal local traffic. If he's out there, I can't see him.

I head back to the booth before Jennifer sees me being suspicious by the front door. When I sit down and slide back into position, I feel my handbag vibrate. I unzip the bag in a flash and rip out my cell. When I hold up the device to my face, I can see that someone has sent me a text. It's from an unknown number, but I know it has to be Elliot. I don't want to read it, knowing that it will be him telling me where and when to meet. I put my phone down by my side as Jennifer emerges from the bathroom. She mustn't see this text.

She walks back to the booth in a more measured fashion than before. She sits down and keeps her shoulders up. The visit to the restroom has given her a second wind to be able to face me. Am I that bad?

"Should we order some food?" I ask.

"Why not?" she says with a huff.

I smile at her, giving my friend the most positive face my fragile mind can manage.

Jennifer reciprocates. "Should we get the usual?"

I smile at the thought and go to answer, but my cell buzzes again. I feel it vibrate into my leg. "Sure," I reply half distracted.

While Jennifer calls over a waitress, I give my phone the attention it so sorely desires. I open the notification and see two texts from Elliot. I read them in order.

Tell your friend you have to leave.
I'm not messing around.

CHAPTER 48

I reread the texts Elliot sent me as my brain tries to come up with a solution to leave the café without giving Jennifer a reason to follow. What do I say? I look in her direction to see her about to interact with a waitress to order our food.

"Actually, I'm not hungry," I say.

She turns to face me. "You need to eat."

"True, but I just had a big breakfast. I don't think I could stomach anything else. I might throw up."

Jennifer dismisses the waitress and stares into my eyes, scrutinizing every muscle in my face for a lie. I try to look away from her, but I can't. She knows me too well.

"How about a drink then? Something light?"

"That would be nice, but I think I should head back home. I'm not feeling the best."

"Okay. I'll take you home. I can get a friend to come to pick up your car and drop it off later."

"No, that's okay," I say as I wriggle out of the booth with my cell and handbag. "I'll be fine."

Jennifer's anger spreads across her face as she narrows her brow. "Are you really leaving to avoid facing the truth? I can't believe this. Why do I bother?"

"I'm not avoiding anything. I need to go, okay?"

She shakes her head at me with closed eyes. When she opens them, I can see the rage in my friend that has been brewing since I buried John. "You're unbelievable. I don't know why I was worried about you and came running here today or why I felt guilty. I knew this would happen. You are beyond help."

"Jenn, you don't understand. I—"

"No, forget it. I'm not listening to your delusions anymore. This friendship is over. If you value your life and your future, you will see Doctor Sylvain. I'm going to tell him what's happened here today and leave the rest up to you. I'm done. I'm out."

I stumble back as Jennifer brushes through and storms out the door of the café. She doesn't stop to look back or pause in her step. There's no regret. Her decision is final. I pushed her to the limit.

I fall back into the booth knowing I have done what Elliot wanted me to do while simultaneously and permanently ruining the last friendship I have left. My mouth drops open as my gaze floats about the café and lands somewhere near the floor. Now what?

"Happy?" I ask Elliot out loud as if he can hear me. I know he is out there watching me.

My cell buzzes in my hand. I look down at it to see another text from Elliot.

Keep her away. Time to head home.

The message is quick and to the point. I don't bother to write back. He knows where I am and that he has total control.

※

I go home and try to get some rest.

The hours tick away in slow motion. I check my cell a few dozen times but find no more messages from Elliot, so I try to think about anything else.

I can't concentrate or distract myself no matter what I do. I fail to sleep, to clean, to cook some lunch, or to read the news. I am a wreck.

I find myself pacing around the house in random patterns like a lunatic as I wait for Elliot to text me where we are going to meet. I hold my cell as I walk from one end of the living room to the other. Each time I pass the middle of the space, I glance at the clock on the wall and see the time not moving. I don't know why, but I want it to be night again. I feel like Elliot won't want to meet once the sun goes down and that I'll be safe until morning. The thought makes no sense, but I need something to keep me going. Anything.

Finally, my phone vibrates. The sudden burst of energy makes me almost drop the damn thing. I flip the cell over, expecting to see a text from Elliot with instructions on what to do next, but instead, I realize it's ringing. Thomas Hart is trying to call me. What does he want?

With a shaky hand, I hit "answer" and put the rectangle to my face. "Yes?"

"Grace, it's Thomas Hart. How are you going?"

"Not the best question to ask me right now. Trust me."

"Fair enough. Listen I thought I'd call you to let you know the investigation has been completed. Everything is clear for you to receive the money."

My mouth drops open. "Already?"

"Yes."

"How did the investigation finish so quickly?"

"That's a question best answered in person."

"Tell me," I beg. "Please."

"Okay, fine. I'll tell you, but you don't repeat this to anyone else."

"I won't. I promise." My heart is still racing at maximum speed. I hold one hand against my head, clutching it for dear life.

"Let's just say I took it upon myself to handpick the investigator. One who doesn't do a thorough job and is willing to sign off on a claim for a small fee."

"I understand," I say, catching his drift. "What about the money?"

"It's already been received at my end. Had it all fast-tracked as requested."

My eyes almost bulge out of my head as I pace past the entry corridor. Thomas really wants his one percent.

"I'm just going through and deducting John's debt and my fees. You'll have the money in your account within twenty-four hours. Most likely less."

The phone falls away from my face. This can't be real. This can't have happened this quickly, but it has. Thomas has done his corrupt part to bypass the investigation to guarantee me the money. I can start my life over and move on, but I have other problems to deal with first.

"Mrs. Dalton? Grace? Are you there?" Thomas asks down the line.

"I'm here." Barely.

"Excellent. So, I imagine you are nothing but pleased with this result. I didn't think I could pull it off, but I did it."

He sounds like a school kid who got out of detention. "Thank you," I say, my voice flat and lifeless.

"You are welcome, Mrs. Dalton. And let me say that you have been the most wonderful—"

I hang up on him. He got his pound of flesh from me. There's no need for him to lie and tell me how I'm a special client.

I place my cell on the kitchen counter. I feel myself floating away from the device as I think about Elliot doing all of this just to get John's money. He tried to send me off the deep end, so I'd sign the insurance forms and get the money into my account. Now, he's going to steal it.

Why else would he want to meet? Why else has he been screwing with me? He knew about the life insurance policy from the get go and that I'd have to sign the documents to get the investigation underway. He probably knows Thomas Hart just called me to say I'm about to come into a huge sum of money.

"This can't be happening," I tell myself. "It's just a nightmare. It's not real." My words fail to change a thing as I try and work out how long it will take Elliot to contact me now that the money has been approved. He must have someone watching the case ready to alert him the second they can. I can't escape his reach.

I think about leaving, about fleeing the state in my car. If I went now and never looked back, would Elliot find me? Would he know exactly where to start the search? I can't rule out that he doesn't have the capability to track me. Plus, I don't exactly want to be hunted down like prey, but at the same time, I don't feel much like being led to the slaughter.

The next two hours are ten times more agonizing than the last. I check my account, again and again, to see if the money has made its way in there somehow. Instead, I always find the tiny number that is my savings account. It's not enough to leave with, but the rest would come in over the next day. I could definitely start over with close to nine hundred thousand dollars to my name. I guess, deep down, I'm too afraid to run.

More time passes until I realize it's almost gone dark. The kitchen counter buzzes. I rush over to my cell and drop my eyes down to see that Elliot has sent me his instructions.

It's all happening faster than I can fathom.

On jerky legs, I pick up the phone and read the message.

10.00 p.m.
Southmoon Chemical. Building 8.
Come alone.

With my history of texts disappearing off my phone, I write the address down. Reality hits home. One that has been building since I exchanged the first words with Elliot. My eyes dance around my house, seeking out a solution. I have to decide right now if I'm going to run or face Elliot.

Do I leave town, or face the man who wants to take all of John's life insurance money?

CHAPTER 49

I had no idea there was a chemical distribution company on the edge of town and that the site would be so big. I could have happily lived out the rest of my days never stepping foot in such a place. There are twelve buildings at the address, according to the map I found online, and Elliot is waiting for me in number eight.

I'm not planning on going. The decision came to me quicker than I thought it would. If ever there's been such an obvious trap to walk into, this has to be it. I'm not going to let this man take everything from me. Instead, I'm going to rush off to the police station just before ten, armed with the knowledge of Elliot's location. I'll tell them some story to get an army of police officers out there in a hurry and have him arrested. Once I know he's in cuffs I can clear up my story and show them the threatening texts he's sent me. It's a little extreme, but I'm sure the police will be happy to arrest him.

Suddenly, the worst thought so far occurs to me. John was murdered by Elliot. All this time I thought some reckless driver had struck John down by mistake and driven off from the scene, incapable of dealing with the reality of what they had done. The truth is far worse. Elliot was behind the wheel of that pickup, driving like a maniac on purpose. He ran his brother down like a wild animal, all because he needed John dead to get the million-dollar payout.

I sit on the sofa, staring at the walls of my home as I wait to leave. I wish John were still alive. He was always better at handling a crisis than me. I wonder to myself for the hundredth time why

Elliot's existence was kept from me. Was it because John knew he was bad news? Did Elliot's association with Felix and his people have something to do with it? John did run up a huge amount of debt. Was John trying to protect me from his world of criminals? No one kept him safe that night on the street. Instead, the town watched him get run down like a deer caught in headlights. Was he trying to warn me about Elliot in his last dying seconds? Had he worked out who ran him down?

The time to leave creeps up on me and arrives. I take in a deep breath and gather my keys, my cell, and my handbag. Every bit of limited evidence I have is in my handbag. I've also sent the texts on to my email account as a backup. It's not much to go on, but if I can get Elliot arrested first, I'll have a chance of pulling this idea off.

I hop into my car and adjust the mirror slightly. My reflection stares back at me, leaving me unimpressed. Either the bags under my eyes are starting to get worse or this entire stress-filled week is breaking my soul. I suspect a combination of the two is to blame and start the engine.

I wait for the garage door to rise, painfully slow. Once there is enough room for me to go, I accelerate like hell out and down the drive. I need to floor it to the police station if I want half a chance of succeeding. I couldn't leave any earlier in case Elliot saw me flee the house. This way, I know where he is and can quickly drive over to the police department.

I rush through the suburbanized streets of our mini-estate, which is bordered by trees and agriculture. The entire town is composed of this clashing mix until you reach the commercial districts.

When I hit the main road toward the town center, I'll be faced with two options: one that veers off towards the City of Sherbrook Police Department, and one that will take me out to Southmoon Chemical. There's no chance in hell I'm going to Southmoon.

As I take the main turnoff towards the police station, my cell rings. The call comes through the dashboard of my car. I check the display first to see who would be calling me at this hour. All I can see is the word "Unknown." A sinking feeling stabs at me. I hit "answer."

"What are you doing, Grace?" Elliot says through my speakers. His voice echoes. How did he know?

"I'm driving out to meet you," I lie.

"Is that so?"

"Yes. I'll be there very soon."

"Oh, I don't know about that. It might be a little hard when you're driving in the wrong direction." I pull my car over as fast as I can. The loose rocks on the side of the road flick and crack into the body of my sedan as my brakes shudder me to a stop.

"What did you say?" I grip the steering wheel with both hands as a wave of dust flows over the car. I can feel my knuckles turning white. My breathing rapidly changes to short, uncontrolled breaths.

"That you'll be late to our little meeting because you are heading to the police department instead."

"No," I let out. He figured out my plan. He must know exactly where I am. Is he tracking my car? Is there a piece of software on my phone? The cabin of the vehicle begins to close in tight around me. What have I done?

"How stupid do you think I am?" he asks.

"I just took a wrong turn, is all. I'm nervous." I hear the lies flowing through my voice.

Elliot laughs louder than I expect him to. His voice fills my car as if he is sitting in the back seat. "Don't lie to me. It's too late for games. Now turn around and drive to Southmoon Chemical, right now!"

My hand moves to shift the car into drive, but I freeze. "Wait. Why should I?"

"Excuse me?"

"I said, why should I? Why should I walk into your trap?" It takes all of my courage to answer him in such a way.

Elliot doesn't respond. Have I stunned him? Have I found a hole in his plan?

"I thought you might say that. Fortunately, I came prepared. Grab your cell out of your bag. It's time we chatted face to face."

I shook my head and mouth a "what?" as I try to understand what he is on about. How much worse could this hell get? Needing to know what Elliot has in mind, I lean over to my handbag and rummage through it to find my cell. I see a message come up on the display that the caller is trying to turn the call into a video chat. With a hesitant finger, I tap accept.

"Hello, Grace," Elliot says. His face is on screen in a darkened room, almost filling my phone. It takes me a moment to adjust to the image of John's twin. They look so alike apart from Elliot having a shaved head.

I can tell he is calling me from somewhere industrial like a chemical distribution plant and that he's inside a building. He is wearing the same black hooded sweatshirt I saw him wear when he stared at my house from the street. I knew I wasn't losing my mind. Elliot was quietly watching me, making sure I did my part to get the money. Part of me wishes he had just been a hallucination. What I didn't understand was how he planned on taking that money from me.

"What the hell do you want?" I ask him.

"You know what I want. The question is, are you going to give it to me?"

I feel my throat tighten as I think about John dead in the street after Elliot ran him down. He knew I'd get the payout as soon as John died, so he called him on his cell and tricked him into standing in the road only to run him down. "Screw you. I'm not giving you a damn cent."

"Now, Grace, is that any way to speak to me? I've been perfectly polite this entire conversation. I think it's time I got your attention."

Elliot disappears from view as he gets up and walks to the left. The phone stays level. I have no idea what he is up to, and it makes me want to scream.

"Elliot? What are you doing? Where did you go?" My eyes go wide as I try to take in as much as I can. I start to look around and outside of my car as if he could be hiding nearby. But I know he can't be.

A figure comes back into view, grabbing my attention. It's not Elliot. My hands fly to my mouth as I suppress a scream. I try to speak, but nothing comes out as I stare at the person Elliot has tied up with a hood over their head. This can't be real.

"Now," Elliot says, "have I got your attention?"

CHAPTER 50

Then

I stormed out of the restaurant and down the street. I couldn't believe John's BS. More importantly, I couldn't believe I fell for it. Why did I even want to come out tonight? We had slapped a weak Band-Aid over our relationship and thought it would stem the bleeding. But the main artery had been severed the moment John lied to me about not going to work. I thought I could justify it all in my head, that I could reconcile it as John needing time to buy me a gift and be by himself. But now I'd had enough. No amount of faked passion could repair that.

I was barely keeping myself together as I thought about the present I had for John in my coat pocket. I didn't know if I even wanted to give it to him now.

The many thoughts rattling around in my head stopped me at the next park bench I could find in the street. I clutched at the handrail and lowered my shaking body onto the hard seat. Tears rolled down my eyes as I tried to avoid the gaze of other people in the street as they happily left their restaurants of choice. Was I overreacting?

None of them stopped to see if I was okay, not that I wanted them to. I needed to be alone to try and process what would happen next and what choice I would make in the heat of the moment. I honestly didn't know.

A set of feet came up to my lowered gaze. "I'm fine," I said, dismissing the passerby.

"No you're not," John said from above. He leaned down and gently grabbed my chin. He lifted my eyes up to his and smiled. "I'm sorry, Grace. For everything."

I shook my head at him as I maintained my stare. It was dark out on the street, but I could still make out his face. "You apologizing is not going to fix anything. We're broken. Both of us."

"No, we're not. Not yet. We can still turn this around. We have to."

"Who says we do?"

John holds my gaze, never letting his eye contact falter. Maybe I was being stupid. "Come on," he said. "Let's go. Why don't we grab a cup of coffee and head home? We're both tired. We've both had long days. How about we give each other a fresh start, like you said."

As much as I wanted to continue to argue, I knew John was right. Even though I didn't know if our relationship would survive, we had to try. Plus, a caffeine hit would give me the boost I needed. "Okay," I said, giving in. I felt embarrassed after a few moments. Why did I have to lose my cool like that?

John guided me across the street to a coffee truck. He ordered for us while I stood back. I thought more as we waited. There was still anger and bitterness between us, but a calm understanding was keeping things on course. Maybe we could go home and talk things through. Maybe there was hope for us. I loved John so much, no matter how much he hurt me, or I hurt him. Could this fire be the thing that keeps us going?

At any moment, a barista was going to shout out my name for me to collect my coffee. The clock was ticking down the last few minutes of John's life. There was nothing I could do to stop the inevitable.

John was on a path that would only lead to his death. There were no other options or choices to be made. Death awaited him.

CHAPTER 51

Now

I drive straight to Southmoon Chemical without stopping for anything. Realizing a second too late, I plow right through a stop sign and come close to clipping another car. The screaming horn barely registers in my mind. I'm going over the speed limit along a single-lane road that heads to the edge of town. The turnoff to the chemical distributor comes out of nowhere. I slap my foot hard on the brake pedal and narrowly avoid missing the turn.

When the wheels of my car roll into the work site, they are met with gravel and stone. I slow right down to a crawl to prevent the car from spinning out of control. I take a moment to calm myself. I shouldn't be heading into this so aggressively.

The place is empty. Not a single car is in the staff parking lot. Only a few company trucks are here, empty and lined up, ready for work when the sun comes up. I try my best to navigate the scarcely lit factory buildings to get an idea of where building eight might be.

The map I briefly studied seems almost useless now. It wasn't a detailed, to-scale map but more of a general information diagram that I didn't pay enough attention to. I was too nervous to think straight before I left.

I thought my plan with the police was foolproof. Little did I realize how many steps ahead of me Elliot was. He had been the entire time, from the moment he ran down John to the second he stared at me from across the street in Portland. He knew about John's debt and the life insurance policy. He also knew that I would get the money and also be facing Felix and his people. I figure the only reason Elliot kept Felix and his men away from me was to keep me from going to the police. Without me, there is no million-dollar payout.

I find building ten. It's easy to spot since there is an enormous "10" painted in the top right-hand corner of the metal paneling that makes up the structure. But I bring the car to a stop, needing to seek out building nine or eleven so I can work out which direction to drive in.

I see building nine and head toward it, driving along the edge of the site by an overhead loading bay where the trucks must line up to be filled with whatever hazardous chemicals the drivers are paid to haul. I can't even imagine how stressful that job must be. I have enough of my own troubles to feel for anyone else.

An image burns into my mind, one I've done everything I can to avoid seeing. I thought I could use the distraction of finding building eight to get it out of my head, but I can't. Elliot has Jennifer in his possession like an attack dog with a chew toy in its mouth. I couldn't see her face behind the hood, but I know it's her. I could see her hair sticking out the bottom. Elliot tried to warn me to do what he said, but I didn't listen. He knew exactly how to get me here while at the same time making me understand how this entire situation was all my fault.

I round the corner once I clear the loading bay and see building eight staring at me. It's the only one with every exterior light on. The other buildings almost appear dark by comparison.

Elliot has made this building a beacon for me to find in the dark. He is luring me in like a moth to a flame. It's working. His plans are all falling into place. He knows I can't turn around now and run.

I park my car right next to the only open doors to the building and get out in a hurry. As far as I can see, there are no security cameras in the area and few to no tire tracks on the roads. Elliot picked his building well. So much so that none of this seems real. How can it be? I feel like I've slipped down the rabbit hole to Wonderland. It's the only possible explanation for this insanity.

I climb a short set of stairs, sweeping my gaze left and right as I go, to the open double doors of building eight. When I take a peek inside, all I find is darkness. Every exterior light to building eight is on, but within its walls is a black void waiting to swallow me whole. I can't go in there. It will be my end.

I creep up to the edge of the double doors and feel my every sense heighten in response. I can hear the echoes of my movements, I can see shadows dancing within, I can smell the crudeness of the decay and neglect inside, I can feel the rusting metal of the handrail, and I can taste a fear brewing in me.

"Hello, Grace," a voice speaks into my ear from behind.

I spin around to half see a figure standing right behind me. But before I can make heads or tails of anything, two quick arms wrap around me. They pin my limbs tight against my body and throw me to the ground. The arms slide up to my head and neck and yank me sideways into a painful hold.

"What are you—"

My useless words are stunned in their tracks as a syringe is shoved hard into my throat, and its contents pumped into my blood a moment later.

The arms let go of me, allowing me to roll over. The figure stands over my body, the powerful beam of a floodlight above hiding his face in shadow.

All I can see in my fading moments is Elliot's sneer taking full pleasure of my pathetic attempts to fight him off. I begin to fade.

Without a single word said between us, we both know he has won.

CHAPTER 52

I come to, rolling my head around to find myself in a half-lit room. I have a pounding headache, and I try to lift my hands, but a pair of chains stop their movement dead. "What the...?" It takes me a few seconds, but I remember what brought me to this moment.

My eyes fill with panic as I try to take in my surroundings. Where am I? My head flicks left and right, up and down to discover what appears to be a storage room made from corrugated metal. I feel the cold biting at me from the dark.

"Help," I call out. My throat hurts from Elliot's attack. "Please, somebody help me." I stop shouting and listen for an answer. I'm met with silence. I continue to panic and yell until I remember the other person Elliot has tied up: Jennifer. Where is she? "Jenn!" I yell as dread floods my body. "Where are you?"

A door I hadn't noticed before opens in front of me. Elliot strolls through wearing his black hooded sweatshirt, now with a black leather jacket open over the top. The hood sits out over his shaved head.

"Hello, Grace," he says to me again in his low voice. It still confuses me seeing John's twin with a different voice.

"Why are we here?" I call out to him.

"The money, of course," he says. He reaches into his pocket and pulls out my cell. The screen is locked. He rushes over to me and grabs my right hand. He forces my thumb to unlock the phone. Next, he navigates to a banking app that I regularly use to pay bills and shift money around. He uses my thumb again to gain access to my bank records by bypassing the fingerprint security. My eyes run up and down the rows of accounts and see that the money hasn't come in yet.

I breathe a sigh of relief. I know in my heart that Elliot will kill me the second he gets his money. He already took out John.

"It's not in there. But it will be very soon."

With the knowledge that my time may be near, I go on the offensive. "What do you need me for then? You've got my cell. You can just take what you want as soon as it goes in there, right?"

"Not quite. Unfortunately, large sums of money can't just be gifted away without drawing the attention of the authorities, so I'm going to need you to talk to someone on the phone and authorize a transfer to a little offshore bank account I've got set up."

"Offshore bank account?" What the hell?

"You heard me. It's as simple as that. You just have to play along and say the right words."

"And what if I don't do that? I'd rather die than give you that money."

Elliot raises his eyebrows. "So forgetful, Grace. I thought you were better than that." Elliot turns away from me and heads out the open door. I hear the sound of wheels squeaking and see Elliot walk back in with Jennifer tied up to an office chair. How could I forget? The drugs must have messed with me a little.

He has wrapped a thick hood over her slumped head. I can just make out strands of her hair poking out the bottom. For some reason, he has dressed her in coveralls that hold the Southmoon Chemical logo on them.

"No," I say. "Don't do this."

"I won't have to if you play along nicely and give me my goddamn money." Elliot produces a knife from the pocket of his leather jacket. He holds it against the hood and presses in against Jennifer's neck.

"No, please. Don't do that. You know I'll do what you say. Please just—"

"Of course you'll do what I say, Grace. We both know how weak and pathetic you are."

I lower my head and shrug. I can feel tears filling my eyes. "You're right; I am weak and pathetic. This is all my fault. None of this would have happened if it wasn't for me. I understand that now." The last six weeks flash through my head. I know I'm the one that allowed Elliot to take this opportunity. I recognize the danger I've created for my friend.

I glance up at Elliot. "But this is just between you and me. No one else needs to suffer." I stare at the hood and feel my heart pick up its pace. I stare back at Elliot with a furrowed brow. "Why do you even care about her? This is just a payday for you. It can still be that if you let it."

Elliot smiles at me, his eyes narrowed in. He grabs the chair and wheels it as close to me as he can. What is he doing now? He leans down by my ear and speaks. "You think this is just about the money? Honey, this is so much bigger than you realize."

Elliot stands up straight and grabs hold of the hood. He yanks it hard and clean off Jennifer's head. But it's not Jennifer's unconscious body that's less than a foot from my face. It's Layton's. His long hair was sticking out the bottom.

Elliot strolls back and around with his hands out wide. "Here he is, Grace."

My eyes flick from Layton's broken face to Elliot's sneer as I try to understand why he has kidnapped Layton and brought him here to make me transfer the life insurance payment. My eyes close as my brain does what it can to process the night that has befallen me. I have no choice but to think about everything that has happened in my life over the last six months.

My pupils go wide, throwing my lids open as I realize what has happened and why Layton has been served up in front of me all bloody and bruised. How did I not see this?

I stare at the psycho before me brandishing the knife and see cuts and bruises on his knuckles. I now understand in my heart the truth that has been in front of me all along.

I ask the one question that will throw my world upside down. "John, is that you?"

CHAPTER 53

John stares at me with his head held high. "You finally worked it out, didn't you, honey?" His voice is no longer forced deep and is back to its normal tone.

My mouth tries to form words, but instead, it jitters and quakes mere utterances. "How? You?"

"What's the matter, Grace? Don't you know when you're staring at your own husband?"

"But, I—"

"Wow, listen to you. You can't speak. You don't know what the hell is going on, do you? But I think you have some clue."

I force my eyes shut and then back open, trying to make him go away. This can't be John. It can't be.

He moves in close to me. "That's not going to get rid of me, Grace. I'm as real as they come. I'm not some hallucination dreamed up by your shrink."

I keep my focus on him as best as I can while the world around me spins. "I don't understand. I watched you die. You're dead."

"Am I? Or did you watch someone else die that night instead?"

"Elliot?"

"Yeah. Elliot. My stupid twin brother. That piece of trash was the one you cried over, the one you've pined for. Not me."

I let the thought run through my head as I try to understand. "You faked your death using your twin brother?"

"It was a simple plan, really. Convince Elliot to take you out to dinner in my place while I run him down in the street. I knew you'd tell the authorities what they needed to hear. Boom; I'm dead."

My mouth falls open. "This was all so you could steal the life insurance payment the second it came into my account."

"Bingo," John says, his voice bitter.

"Why? It's more than you need to pay off your pathetic gambling debts."

"You know why."

I let more tears flow down my face. I try to look away from my husband, but he won't let me. "Did he know? Did Elliot know anything?" I asked.

John sneered at me. "The moron was in the dark. He thought he was doing me a favor. I told him to take you out for dinner and to keep you busy no matter what. We switched in the bathroom at the restaurant. I told him what to say and how to keep you happy."

I think about the sex I had with John. He had this planned the whole time and still thought he could screw me one last time. I stare up at John and don't hold back. "You killed your brother. You murdered him in cold blood."

"He had it coming."

I shake my head as I try to understand what that is supposed to mean. What happened between them that would push John to such extremes?

"So where were we? Ah, yes. I asked Elliot to keep you busy for our anniversary. If he did that, I said I'd owe him one. He knew I was in debt and needed help, so he didn't question me. He fell for my lies and walked straight into my trap. It was perfect."

My mind is swimming with the insanity before me. How could John be like this? How could he be so cruel and psychotic? I stare at Layton's closed eyes and get my answer.

"Did you really think I wouldn't have found out about you two?" John asks me. "How stupid do you think I am?"

"It was a mistake. It happened once." I think about Layton and the one night he came to see me at my home a month before John set up Elliot. We'd had too much wine together. We'd danced to the same song for too long. We were both in relationships on the edge of collapse. All of my efforts to hide the truth were for nothing. I face John and bare my teeth. "You were distant. You didn't care about me anymore. He did." I pointed to Layton.

"And that gives you the right to sleep around with some loser, does it?"

"No, but—"

"No, Grace. There's no excuse. Nothing can fix what you did."

My head falls slack and drops low as a shame overtakes me. This is all my fault. All of it. I cheated on John. I never meant to, but it happened. As soon as it did, I realized what John and I had. I thought after that slip up, I could fix things, make us the perfect couple. But it was too late. I should have broken things off with him when I knew we were done, but instead, I thought having a baby would change our lives.

I stare at the ground, deep in a spiral of guilt until I remember I'm not the only one who had secrets.

"You can't judge me," I said. "You owe Felix and his people a quarter of a million dollars. You killed your brother just to pay them back."

John stares at me with an intensity I'd never seen from him before. "And who do you think introduced me to Felix? Who do you think got me hooked on poker in the first place?"

I close my eyes for a moment as John pieces it all together for me. "Elliot," I say.

"That's right."

I let my eyes wander away as I try to will this nightmare into oblivion. A chuckle from John raises my head slightly.

"Oh, would you look at that," he says. "The money has just come into your account."

CHAPTER 54

John taps away at my cell, arranging the funds through some third-party clearinghouse that will allow for one significant transfer to go through once I give authorization. He looks like he has practiced this a few times.

I stare at the man I once shared a life with and try to understand how he could be so cruel. It can't be him I'm seeing. "Why would you do this? Why would you plan to murder us over an affair?"

"Because, honey," he says with a burn of sarcasm, "you betrayed me. You took our marriage and treated it like garbage. Did our vows mean nothing to you?"

"We were drifting apart. You barely saw me as your wife. We were almost nothing by that point, and you know it. And besides, you betrayed me too with your insane gambling."

"Yes, but I remained faithful nonetheless. And by keeping it a secret, I spared you from that world."

"You think you did me a favor by not telling me you had a gambling debt of a quarter million dollars?"

"I did. Your fragile mind couldn't handle such a thing. You were too busy screwing this idiot."

"I made one mistake. How many times did you gamble? How many times did you lose? And look at you: you're a murderer. You killed your brother."

"You killed him," John roars. "The second you betrayed me."

"I killed him? You can't be serious. What about your debt? Is that my fault too?"

John laughs. "No, but I knew Felix and Elliot went back a long way. Felix would listen to Elliot. I needed them to keep back from you until you finally got around to signing that damn insurance policy. And wouldn't you know it, Elliot stepped in after poor old John died and told Felix to leave the debt be for a few months."

My mouth is stuck open as I realize what he really means. "You went to Felix as Elliot so you could control the money as it came to me."

"Of course I did. Felix would do anything for Elliot. Hell, he'd even die for the man. It was embarrassing."

"Elliot wasn't embarrassing," I yelled. "You were. You had a gambling problem you could barely contain."

"Don't judge me, Grace. You don't know the pain I've suffered. You don't know what went on at those group homes. You think you can rely on your own flesh and blood in those places, but it was survival of the fittest."

I shake my head. "I could have helped you. I could have been there to help fight through it."

"Is that right? Is that what Grace the saint would have done, huh? Well, honey, let me tell you something: you don't know what you are talking about. Not one bit."

I shake my head at him. "It's simple from where I'm standing. You're a killer. One who murders his family to make a few dollars." I see John's nostrils flare out wide ready to unleash hell upon me. I don't know why I'm egging him on, but I am.

John shouts out loud as he paces around the room. He still needs me alive until the money is transferred. "Don't you say another word. I'm going to get this money and start a new life away from you."

I shake my head, knowing John will kill me the second he no longer needs me. I blink rapidly and stare at Layton. He shouldn't be here. It's not his fault that my husband is insane. My mind drifts back to my conversation with Felix. He thinks John is Elliot. There must be something I can do with that.

"Now stop trying to get inside my head and do as you are told. If you don't, then I'll cut Layton up, piece by piece." He hands me a script and a cheap looking cell. It must be a burner phone. "Follow the instructions. Do not screw this up or let the operator know what is happening. If you do anything I don't like, Layton loses an eye. Just transfer the money to the account specified."

I don't answer him at all. I don't even read the notes. I just stare out into the distance. If I do this, if I let John take the money, I'm dead. Not only that, Layton will suffer a slow death. He was far from perfect, getting involved with a married woman when he had a girlfriend of his own the night we slept together, but he doesn't deserve any of this.

"Hurry up. These transfers take up to twenty-four hours to complete."

"Twenty-four hours? Are you planning on keeping us here for that long?"

"Building eight is out of operation. No one uses it or even goes near the damn thing. We can take as long as we need. But, if I'm honest, I want this sorted out as soon as possible. I don't know how much longer Felix can keep his associates off Elliot's back. Word around town is they are getting closer to losing their patience."

I take a moment to absorb what John just told me. "No," I say.

"No? What do you mean 'no'?"

"I won't do it. You can sort things out with Felix for all I care. I'm not letting you take the money just to kill Layton and me."

John grabs Layton by the back of his neck and holds the knife to his eye. "Do you think I'm messing around here? I will cut this piece of crap into a thousand little chunks of meat if you don't do what the hell I tell you to do."

My eyes don't leave John's for a single moment. I'm running out of time and options. One idea comes to me. It's a long shot, but I have to try. "He was better than you," I say.

"What?" John asks. The knife slips away from Layton's eye.

"Layton. He knew how to please a woman. I never realized what I was missing."

"Bullshit." John leans in close. "If you think I'm going to fall for your lies, you are severely mistaken. I am in control here, not you. Do you think I haven't thought of everything? Who do you think sent you those chocolates that got you up and moving around?"

"I know you did everything, freak. I know you were trying to send me off the deep end."

John holds up a palm. "Enough chat. It's time to make a call. I've been patient for about as long as I can be, but if you don't dial that number and follow those instructions, I'm going to take one of his eyes. I'm not playing."

John lifts Layton's head up and holds the knife to within an inch of his eye. I can see with absolute clarity that he is dangerous.

Layton stirs and blinks awake a few times. The sudden movement causes John to release his kidnap victim. "What the hell?"

A glint of something shiny grabs my attention behind John. I swear someone is lurking behind him in the shadows at the very moment Layton drifts back into unconsciousness. I can't help but stare out into the darkness of the empty building John has commandeered.

"What are you looking at out there?" he asks while Layton tries to make sense of the world around him.

"Nothing," I say back. It's beyond obvious that I have spotted a person in the building. John holds the knife out wide as the shadows dance around. He takes a step toward the intruder.

I panic. I don't want another person to fall into John's clutches and have to pay the ultimate price because of my failings, so I say the first thing that enters my brain. "John. I'm pregnant."

My lie turns John around long enough for a lead pipe to fly out from the dark and collide with his skull. The blow strikes the back of his head so hard that he falls to the ground in a heap.

Jennifer emerges from the dark and takes a follow-up swing at John, hitting him in the back.

He doesn't move.

Jennifer rushes in and sees the scene before her. Her mouth flies open at the sight of Layton and me. She doesn't take long to gather herself and start undoing the chains that are holding me down.

I look up to Jennifer. I can't even speak. I get out a whisper. "Thank you."

CHAPTER 55

Jennifer frees Layton after me. I climb out of the chair and welcome the flow of blood back into my hands while Jennifer holds Layton up. He is half awake, but still out of it.

"How did you find me?" I ask.

She smiles and suppresses a nervous laugh. "I was worried about you and couldn't sleep, so I came around to your house. You left the garage door and the interior door open. I could tell that you'd left in a hurry and that something was up. I found the note you wrote with the address of this place and time. I didn't know what to make of the note, but I knew I had to act fast. I figured something was off, so I drove here as soon as I could. I had no idea this is what I'd find."

I stare down at John. "Neither did I. How much did you hear?"

"Enough to know that your husband is still alive and is insane. What the hell is going on?"

"It's a long story. I'll tell you later," I say.

"Good point. We better go," she says. "Layton needs to get to the hospital right now." He tries to speak, but he can't seem to open his mouth.

Jennifer glances at John's motionless body on the concrete floor. "And what about him? I suppose we should call the police."

I think about that for a moment and come up with a more elegant solution. "No, leave him to me."

⁂

We walk out of building eight holding Layton up as we head to Jennifer's car. We place him in the back seat and call for an ambulance to pick him up a few miles from the site. It's the best we can offer him.

Before we left the room John had us in, I chained my husband to a pipe and put the same hood he used on Layton over his head. I moved back to my car and leaned down to Jennifer.

"Thank you so much," I said. "I owe you my life."

"It's okay. Just do what you need to do and get home safe. I'll make sure Layton gets to a hospital."

I nod. "I don't deserve you, Jenn."

"That's not true. I should have believed you when you said you weren't nuts. Maybe then you would have told me the truth."

"It's okay. You came through for me. I knew you would, but it's time we all moved on. Now, get out of here and save Layton. I've got one last thing to do."

I wave Jennifer off and stumble over to my car. My head is pounding from whatever it was that John injected me with. I climb inside and take a moment to breathe. My eyes fall closed as I feel a sense of relief wash over me. When I open my eyes, I grab my retrieved cell and one other item from my handbag. John had kept my things close by and had dropped my phone when Jennifer clocked him in the head. The screen is a little damaged but still functional. Reading from a saved business card, I make one phone call. It's all I need to make things right.

"Hello, Felix. This is Grace Dalton."

"What the hell do you want now?"

I smile as I hear the big man breathing. "I just thought you'd like to know where John has been hiding from you."

"John? What the hell do you mean?"

I explain everything to Felix. The big man's rage almost breaks through my cell.

"I'll send you the address."

I talk for a few minutes with Felix and promise him the money John owed him and his associates plus fifty thousand dollars in exchange for a favor. The only catch is they won't be receiving the funds for at least a day. Felix catches my drift and promises to clean up the problem at hand.

I start the engine to my car and shift it into gear. I drive away from Southmoon Chemical to begin my life again without John.

I wasn't the perfect wife. I have to live with the mistake I made for the rest of my days. But despite the pain it caused John, I sure as hell never let my emotions drive me to the murder of an innocent man.

I don't need John. I never needed anybody, and I am ready to face whatever comes next.

A NOTE FROM ALEX

Thank you for reading *Tell Me No Lies*. If you loved this book and want to keep up to date with all my latest releases, then just sign up using the link below. Your email address will never be shared, and you can unsubscribe at any time.

www.bookouture.com/alex-sinclair

I hope you got an emotional kick out of this book. It was a lot of fun to write, and I enjoyed the challenges that came along with each moment. If you liked *Tell Me No Lies*, I would love it if you wrote me a review. Your feedback is highly welcomed, and your words would help other readers to discover my work.

I also love to hear from my readers – you can get in touch with me on my Facebook page, through Twitter, Goodreads or my website.

Thanks,
Alex Sinclair

ASinclairAuthor

ASinclairAuthor

alexsinclairwrites.com

ACKNOWLEDGEMENTS

As always, a huge thank you goes out to the amazing and awe-inspiring team at Bookouture. *Tell Me No Lies* received the same love and attention to detail as any other book I've written for Bookouture thanks to commissioning editor, Abigail Fenton. Her ability to keep the story on the right path always motivates me to work harder and harder with each and every project.

A big thank you goes out to my wife for her loving support on this book. Without her, I would not have been able to achieve even half of what I have during my time as an author. And of course, a big thank you to my young daughter for just being herself and making me want to be a better person.

Thank you, as always, to the authors at Bookouture. Even though I am across the globe from most of these talented people, they still make me feel like one of the family.

And finally, the biggest thank you goes out to the readers who allow this all to be possible.

www.ingramcontent.com/pod-product-compliance
Lightning Source LLC
LaVergne TN
LVHW011806060526
838200LV00053B/3680